BRITISH BULLD

A Scott Dalton thriller

To Jenny,

By

Paul R Starling

I am, by default, editor of my own work
so I apologise for the spelling defects
which are my own imperfections, and
until I get myself an agent, publisher
and editor, these mishaps will continue.
Thank you, reader, for putting up with
these mistakes and I hope they do not
deter from your enjoyment.

This book is dedicated to my loyal
readers, without whom, these words
would be for my eyes only.

PROLOGUE

British Secret Agent Phil Starline hauled himself over the edge of the sheer cliff-face, his muscles taut, hands burning from the exertion of the two-hundred foot climb. Not an insignificant effort. Phil's face was ruddy and glistening with sweat. He rolled onto the rocky promontory which permits entry into what he anticipated will be a secret entrance to a cavern base via a naturally formed exhaust-port for the dormant ViaAltai volcano. Phil lay still, breathing heavily to control himself for what comes next. He slips off the gloves. A smile which could almost be arrogant formed on his mouth. Phil Starline has come further than others predicted he would. The naysayers laughed because however skilled the Secret Agent undeniably was, this climb alone was daunting even to the most experienced mountaineer.

Yet there he was.

The facility hidden within this long dormant volcano amidst the Mongolian Altai range of mountains belonged to criminal mastermind Joseph Tucamkari, whose reign of terror was set to be curtailed on the very same day if Phil Starline had any influence over forthcoming events.

The cavern wends it's gloomy way into a void of utter blackness so Phil flicked over a miniature toggle switch on his glasses, allowing him to see beyond the spectrum of normal human vision, tinged with a green unnatural hue. He made a mental note to thank the Armoury Chief upon his return to England. These same glasses have served to defuse the glare of the sunshine during his climb, they could high-light crevices in the mountain while he ascended, and then they were able to aid his walk into pitch darkness without much fear.

All the same, Phil Starline proceeded with extreme caution along the middle of the cavern, his experience giving him an instinctive

3

sixth sense. There was barely enough height for a tall man like him and, with awareness that despite the apparent lack of life and supposed inaccessibility of this entrance, there would likely be a variety of early-warning alarm systems in place along the route. Kicking up a stone might activate a sound detection device, while it is inevitable there would be motion sensors.

Walking onward the only sound was Phil's feint breathing. His mind was cleared of everything except his objective, which he must achieve without setting off a motion sensor. A tiny pinpoint of red light punctuating the green hue signalled the first of said devices barely three metres in front of him. Upon closer, but not too close, inspection, Phil noticed a micro-microphone also set in the wall, not concealed well enough to avoid detection by a professional. One or both would alert the occupants of the facility, and Joseph Tucamkari's henchmen, to his presence, and that just wouldn't do.

The British agent stooped down carefully, trying to will even his clothing to be silent, until he was kneeling on the ground before he took out a suitable gadget from the box of tricks in his belt-buckle, which successfully nullified both sensors left and right. Phil made this task look simple, like a walk in the park, but not everyone can possess his superior set of skills. This was just one of many reasons why his crotchety chief, Sir Miles Booth-Royd, the Head of MI6, entrusted him with this assignment of utmost importance to the protection of Great Britain. In fact, he was sent on all the best assignment's because Phil was that well-known stereotype; better than the best of the best.

Continuing onward, the tunnel ahead gradually unfolded into a twilight grey with a thinly veiled grille at it's end, and Britain's finest agent slowed his pace, successfully stepping over further light-sensors and deactivating the microphones as he went like a master surgeon.

Everything his informant told him last night about the monumental sized cavern is as Phil envisioned when he looked through the grille, and the agent said a silent thank you to the man who had since been secreted to a British safe-house somewhere in the world other than here. From Phil's advantage point the array of arc-lights illuminating the cavern was positively dazzling, so much so that the almost futuristic glasses he sported adjust themselves automatically for daylight. What the British agent could see in the depths far below him was quite breathtaking to behold, not to mention difficult to take in and process. Hard to comprehend that the lair belonged to an despotic criminal secretly concocting who knows what kind of mayhem for the rest of the civilised world, and not merely a high-tech research facility. There were five gleaming clear Perspex biospheres featuring research laboratories containing varieties of fauna visible. Also present were glass-roofed living accommodations, a central complex which must be the command module, a spaghetti lattice of yellow walkways, sentry gantries and even a miniaturised monorail system which presumably connected to a main entrance located somewhere, probably many miles away.

It was challenging even for an agent of Phil's experience to tear his eyes away from this sight and think about the assignment, which was to destroy this place and Joseph Tucamkari along with it. Pity, really, to lose such a stunningly modern setup.

The man of the moment was clearly visible in his green tracksuit amidst the scurrying white-clad laboratory workers and black-clad security guards. Joseph Tucamkari was vertically challenged, an uncharismatic, nondescript human being who one might assume to be nothing more than a Supermarket manager. Only this managers power had utterly gone to his head. Only thing was, this man's sights are set terrifyingly further than as a puppet on a string for others. Joseph

5

Tucamkari was the foremost criminal mastermind on the planet - at least until the next one came along! But in reality this man had a woman of uncanny strength alongside him; his wife, Claudinalli. She was tall, dark-haired, powerful, domineering and the complete opposite to her husband. Yet, very much like her husband, she stood apart distinctively from the lackeys around them in her flowing gown, more suited to a Royal engagement, rather than a hollowed-out secret base.

Starline watched objectively from afar, his frown deepening when he considered the death and destruction this deadly duo have caused in their domain over the past decade, costing lives of countless civilians, and some of his own lesser co-workers who were unable to outwit the mastermind and their organisation.

But not today.

No way, no how, was Phil letting them get away.

The British secret agent tested the sturdiness of the grille, pushing and pulling to discover if there would be any play in the metal or the wall around it, but it resisted all attempts to be moved by even the slightest millimetre. So, Phil slipped the black rucksack from his shoulders and surreptitiously removed the contents. First of all he squeezed the product from a tube, running plastique around the grille, assuring himself the explosives would have a devastating enough force to dislodge the otherwise reluctant opposition.

Next he set up the mini-missile launcher and catapult before setting twin timers within one second of each other.

Once activated, Phil Starline moved away slowly, without looking back, so it was obviously his own fault when-

"That's far enough."

A voice in dark from somewhere slightly behind him, and to his left, said firmly.

By now the British agent's glasses have adjusted to compensate for the darkness and he could see two figures clad in black, only the whites of their eyes visible. They aimed powerful pistols at him, the red targeting laser on each accurately aiming directly for his heart. Clearly they meant business, but so did he! Phil already counted down in his head, knowing there were only ten seconds remaining before the first explosive, the plastique around the grille, ignites. Within two-seconds he had appraised his two would-be assailants, their build, stances, and comfort with the guns, judging distance from him, the walls, and the explosion.

Phil is, after all, the best of British!

A bulbous flash of light bursts, illuminating the rocky tunnel blindingly, and a precision crack of plastique temporarily deafened the trio of men in its presence.

Phil Starline opened his eyes after the flash without delay, his glasses switching modes instantaneously and without trouble, which gave him a great advantage over the two gun-wielding killers.

One second after the first explosion a low-bass thump rumbled through the ground and pumped out a gaseous plume of smoke and light as a succession of six missiles were hurled into the huge cavern at different speeds and distances, to ensure an evenly spread attack on the devil's research facility.

The British agent who had caused this did not watch his own handiwork. Instead he pounced on the first gunman, stabbing him viciously through the heart while grabbing the man's weapon and using the finger on the trigger to squeeze it and shoot his companion. Both the men dropped to the floor of the tunnel the same moment the six explosions boomed and echoed in the cavern, each setting off their own further explosions as gas and other flammable items ignited with a satisfying finality.

Glass shattered, plastic splintered, and people screamed and died from within the cavern. Phil Starline could not see too much because the smoke billowed upward and flames licked out their fiery tendrils searching for oxygen, but he could see his quarry, Joseph Tucamkari, very much dead on the ground along with many if his minions.

Without further ado British Secret Agent Phil Starline ran back from whence he came with the completion of another successful mission under his belt, thinking, as he departed, of the spoils which awaited him in the bed of his hotel suite upon his return. Motivation accomplished.

ONE

Connecting North Lincolnshire and the East Riding of Yorkshire by spanning 4,626ft across the Humber estuary between Burton-upon-Humber and Hessle, the Humber suspension bridge was the longest of its type in the world at a total length of 7,280ft when opened to traffic on 24th June 1981 - in 1998 Japan's Akashi Kaikyo Bridge topped the record span by a distance of, almost, a further 2,000ft. The Humber Bridge has four lanes for motor traffic with a walkway/cycle route on either side, and is a Toll bridge on its northern end, costing £1.50 for cars, but the Prime Minister of Great Britain has certain privileges, one being a special free pass, which he would soon enjoy after 8:00am on a mild late-September morning were it not for an extremely professional series of events, months in the planning, mere minutes in execution, far reaching with aftereffects.

One hours remains.

Unyielding grey clouds hang unresolved in the sky and there is not so much as a breeze to buffet the huge structure, which dies allow for several degrees of movement before being closed.

This is a day when the weather seems undecided what it shall do, one where it is most definitely advisable for anyone on foot to be fully prepared for rain or sunshine, such is the scatter-logical forecast.

Prime Minister Alfred McCann need not worry. He is comfortable in his air conditioned car.

McCann has a lot on his mind this morning - what is new, you might ask, because the man in charge of England and it's principalities will by nature of the job inevitably have lots of things on his mind, as well as multiple tasks on the agenda. So much has been done already in the relatively short time he has held this office, with so much to continue and so much more to implement. But after yesterday's catastrophic events in Oxford which wrenched at the core of his very family McCann's emotions are understandably all over the place.

Last night he consulted numerous advisors including his best friend and associate, Giuliano Badalamenti, upon how best to forge ahead after yesterday. Should he cancel today's trip to York Minster? And they all presented individual balanced approaches toward the next step he should wisely take, while others were not too balanced, yet in his present turmoil his knee-jerk reaction is to strike hard at these anarchic monsters who have created havoc in England and for he and his family, personally.

But power must be wielded with care.

He sighs, absent-mindedly admiring the 500ft-high towers visible yet two miles distant, standing majestically astride the Humber estuary which itself is yet to come into view except for during the earlier flight, before they made landing at Humberside Airport in the private jet he his privileged enough to use, from the relatively small but very convenient London Airport.

Traffic has been very kind to him today - another PM privilege, he thinks wryly? - and the journey from No.10 has gone without incident, the ride comfortable, the flight without turbulence, so much so that Alfred McCann has sifted through the variety of documents which his secretary placed in the briefcase before his arrival at "the office", along with the two newspapers he likes to read every morning, and the one he doesn't particularly care for but is popular amongst the population of England. He likes to know what the propaganda says people think. Inevitably the Oxford attack dominates with the erroneous headlines declaring terrorists to be responsible. The Downing Street spin-doctors have indeed worked their magic once more, as they have done numerous time's in the past to cover-up the real reasons behind such incidents. Making terrorists the scape-goats

10

appeases the Prime Minister's few detractors while taking their eyes off those real perpetrators: anarchic civilian rebel rousers.

McCann mentally shakes his head disbelievingly: how can the people in his own country be so violent in their actions against his policies? Has he and Generation You not brought a renewed spirit to the land? Have they not brought about unity in England which has not been felt for decades? Not to mention the ever increasing prosperity of her citizens with the improved monetary system and single-market trade agreements with nations hindered during their entrapment by the European Union! Are the people really so ungrateful?

Look at this headline from the more radical London Eye Express: Government Security Promise? With a question mark! Yes, the transition to total protection and security in the country is taking longer than McCann expected, and definitely longer than his Parliament promised, but what do these unsanctioned tabloid's really expect?

They say Rome wasn't built in a day and so be it.

Many reforms happened instantly, within days and weeks of him being voted into office, so he has set quite a high precedent to begin with.

Hindered by ones own success.

These people forget such things when situations suit. Situations like the new one. Opposition parties conveniently forget the past which, more often than not, they were responsible for. What about the Manchester riots, the Grenfell false promises, the ISIS radicalism? Only those people directly affected remember, not the people in their ivory towers blinkered from the reality of the people. The common people. Elitism and privilege are things of the past. The Royal family no longer wield assumed power, earning their own way now, the many houses now accessible to the public. Do the tabloid's point out these positive changes? These popular successes? If they do its with reluctant admission. Maybe McCann should clamp down upon such vitriolic fear-mongering publications, but if he does that, if he strangles all means of free-speech, then he shall be looked upon as nothing more than a dictator running a a Totalitarian country.

Wheels glide with reassuring heft on the road surface as the car sweeps along the final wide bend leading immediately onto the Humber bridge, jogging McCann from out of his angry reverie, taken by surprise at how far they have travelled while he was enjoying his impatient musings.

There are a trio of Governmental cars in their convoy, each having made it's journey to a convenient hotel a mile outside Humberside Airport the previous day, the British Security Service drivers checking and double-checking their vehicles in the morning for any unscrupulous tampering.

Excessive security or wise precaution?

McCann doesn't usually like to travel too conspicuously, another policy, be more like the people, but after yesterday the Security Service wouldn't sanction this preplanned trip without the proper protection. As if an armoured vehicle with all the latest counter-measures and a skilled driver isn't already enough, two back-up's assist.

"How's the family, Mike?" Alfred McCann asks his driver, realising his own quite uncharacteristic rudeness for not having spoken to this man, except for the customary greeting when the Prime Minister boarded. Mike has served him for twelves months and McCann was too caught up in his own thoughts, his own work, reading and rumination to invoke common courtesy.

"Never better, sir." Mike replies, smiling with mixed sympathetically at his bosses plight, no sign of irritation at the bosses distance, and not venturing to ask how the Prime Minister is because anyone can see from the vaguely haunted expression on the man's face that he is suffering.

McCann nods, watching idly as they sweep across the macadam toward the white pylons and supporting structures and mindbogglingly long and thick suspension cables.

"Quiet morning, sir." Mike states.

At first the Prime Minister is going to reply that he wishes it truly were quiet until he realises Mike is talking about the traffic on the southbound carriageways of the Humber Bridge, which is usually rammed at this time of the morning. On this occasion it is much more sporadic. Thinning appreciably as they drive further along the curvature. If McCann had been properly observing he would also notice a drop in their speed from the imposed fifty mile per hour limit, while a glance back would reveal something more sinister is afoot. But instead the PM wonders if the country is perhaps in hiding, scared to travel for fear of being caught up in another damn act of terrorism. But thats just another cynical thought clouding his already stormy mind.

The reduced flow is owed to a control during his journey.

Abruptly the Government car in front slews across the right-lane and crashes into the central reservation, the huge barriers easily absorbing the bow to the structure. Despite minimal damage to the non-standard reinforced body and chassis of the car it has been rendered immobile.

Both lanes are blocked.

Mike applies the brake until they have come to a standstill twenty feet from the incapacitated vehicle.

McCann's curiosity is now peeked so he turns in his seat to witness what is going on behind: the men in the rear Government car have stopped fifty-feet back, a van has edged them into the Humber-side barrier, the occupants of the van standing on the roadway brandishing machine-pistols with a Furniture Van completely blocking the carriageway and preventing anyone from following them.

"We're being hijacked!" McCann shouts, trying not to panic but it isn't easy to be calm in a situation like this, not that he has experienced it before, only in training exercises, but this is definitely the real thing. Just the sort of inconvenience he needs!

"I'm sorry, sir." Mike says flatly.

Confusion is soon broken by McCann's abrupt realisation that his driver is unnaturally calm, as if this occurrence wasn't wholly unexpected, and judging from his unapologetic expression, this is not going to end quickly or easily.

TWO

Despite history providing proof to those who might be interested that corruption in perfectly capable of ensnaring even the highest power in the land, toppling foreign Governments, subverting the faith through blinkered religion, and besetting global corporations with financial ruin, Scott Dalton cannot quite believe the thoughts he is entertaining about the culpability of his own Government. And he officially works for their Security Service. Right now. Scott is working for them, right now! A position given him by the very man in charge, the enlightened Prime Minister himself, Alfred McCann This is the man who Scott's very own boss, the Chief of the Joint Security Services, answers to. This is the man who is in charge of Great Britain and her dwindling, once mighty, colonies. And Scott was truly nervous that if he had refused the job his life would be placed in danger. Belief is beggared!

Fifty-Five hours remain.

Alfred McCann and Generation You has wrested our country, Scott Dalton's country, from the ruination of the European Union. They are returning England to a patriotic, free country where her citizens are proud to live and work for the common cause - or so we are led to believe. Is it truly conceivable such an ancient and cherished institution as our Government could be functioning under the grasp of an insidious overseer? Are we pawns to some power-crazed unknown King or Queen or worse? Such a possibility surely beggars belief even to the most ardent conspiracy theorist. Could Prime Minister Alfred McCann really be a puppet ruled by the dictatorship from some remote organisation?

And does it stop with England?

Yet the contradicting optimistic realist in Scott Dalton's social makeup gathered this distinct impression from the ruler of the land

15

when he first met him, eight weeks ago. And absurd irrational nightmares have been plaguing him every night since, while his waking hours are filled with the workload of his job. His career.

Can such a diabolical thing be conceivable?

In other countries, indubitably. Those plagued by war and religion and greed. But not England. There has been so much good which has come from this new Government and their defiant strategy. The entire populace is behind the young Prime Minister one-hundred percent. Except for a few radicals whose acts of terrorism have resulted in the death-penalty being reinstated. Yet even this extreme punishment was greeted with enthusiasm from the majority population when a countywide vote took place. A further display of citizenry unification which has seen many other popular changes made within the constitution. The population vote in their droves. Excitedly. Like nothing before. The public now justifiably feel included in decisions made for their own country. Populist, maybe, but this system is working.

A cold spray cast on the wind from the North Sea dashes Scott Dalton across the face like a gentle slap back into reality from his wildly speculative daydreaming. A reminder him of the purpose of his covert journey from Bergen, Norway, to the land of Scotland. Scott shudders. The black silhouette of land ahead of the fishing boot seems to roll with the waves upon the dark grey and green-hued horizon, the skies a velvet cloth dotted with stars.

This is probably the purist vision by which Scott has taken in the Earth, naturally lit, vast, and epic.

At two in the morning.

Splendiferous!

The anti-seasickness tablets given him by the Security Service's deputy medical officer are working their magic, for which

Scott says a silent thank you, eternally grateful, because the fishing vessel isn't the largest of its kind his team could've provided for this journey, nor is it the most sturdy. Thanks, guys! So the going has been rough. Perhaps they are trying to tell him something. Those people in charge, the one's dictating his path right now, commanding his fate. Or has the same organisation really been directing his entire course in life always, as it has everyone? Scott reminds himself that he isn't being cynical, just realistic. He is not a cynic by nature. In a time-honoured tradition to reaching enlightenment it has taken him years to free his mind just enough to see what lies beneath the cracked surface. It has taken many deaths to force these new doubts upon him. And maybe it has taken the shock to loosen the chains.

The scope of this expanse of water is spectacular while humbling - a cliche observation, but nonetheless true. Consider that humankind is but a small speck on this vast sea, and yet Scott's own thoughts are able to engulf it all, consuming him, threatening to swallow the very fabric of his reality. Nature in it's entirety and he and this vessel are there but for the grace.

Shattering events have unravelled in a comparatively short time it is little wonder Scott is feeling melancholic.

His best friend was murdered by a double-agent within the British Secret Service. And that agent herself might have been manipulated by the very powers who he, Scott, now works for. Thomas C. Match. Such a bright spark of character in a dim world of espionage. A beacon of light to Scott. Gone.

A puppet, perhaps? Two puppets. More.

Or was the double-agent being strung along by an outside source? Her life on taut strings.

Scott's old chief has been ingloriously murdered, which he shouldn't feel too upset about because the ungrateful old man hadn't shown an ounce of gratitude for Scott saving his life not two years earlier.

Plus there was Se-ri Solitaire. A woman of staggering beauty - a case of him hitting three categories above his weight - but who he believed actually cared for him, deluded as that belief was, and she double-crossed him and she too wound up dead. Lovely woman. Amazing how she manipulated him so completely, so utterly.

Maybe a wiser man would return whence he came, to the desk job and it's quiet safety.

No harsh environments.

No car chases.

No bullets.

Minimal physical stress.

Yet here he is, Scott Dalton, beginning an assignment which is technically his very first for the British Security Service, formerly MI6 - although this will not be his first foray into espionage, intrigue and action. This covert operation upon which he is embarking would seem superfluous if every new measure the Government had introduced had been successful, but certain sympathetic factions in Great Britain see the expulsion of illegal immigrants as a breach of decent basic human rights - the archaic official Human Rights Act has been abolished by Prime Minister McCann in favour of something more radical, something bordering on a Police State philosophy, brought about because of the detestable acts of terrorism being perpetrated with apparent ease in England and across the face of the globe. Subsequently McCann lost many foreign supporters, such as the US who are facing numerous challenges themselves, but equally he has gathered favourable support from many other countries.

Thusly, Scott Dalton is travelling under false papers in order to enter Scotland with the credentials of a deported sympathiser, in the hopes he can infiltrate the group of terrorists sending people into England and prevent more mayhem. The morally dubious folk he is to become acquainted with are expecting him - or his aka-alike! - with a rendezvous set up for later, and an event tipped to begin straight away. It's a gamble for his Government and for himself.

The reason he needs to enter Scotland covertly is because the country has split politically from England. Scotland unwisely chose to remain in the EU after England's hard and fast exit under Generation You, while the Central European Government allied themselves with Scotland, encouraging the move for independence. Inevitably the split has caused anger, distrust and prejudices to rear their ugly heads, seeing the beginnings of construction of a border similar to the Mexican Wall of the America's.

When Scott was given this assignment and sent immediately to Norway for briefing he wondered if in fact his own people were able to tap into his thoughts and extract his doubts about them, because it at first seemed one big coincidence that he of all people should be sent on this type of job, fraught with danger and exposure as it is. Yet, having his past success explained to him and recalling what the Prime Minister had told him, Scott concluded that his status as a trained Government nobody would indeed suit this operation perfectly. Since his proactive part several weeks past in thwarting a homeland terrorist lynchpin and a major network operating globally, and in the UK, his identity has been wiped clean and he has been brought into Prime Minister McCann's new Anti-Terror task-force. This is a vitally significant job he has been given, one of the greatest compliments too, to be entrusted with this task when previously shunned by his own country - or so the propaganda went! They have sweetened the deal: a new apartment, substantial pay package, amongst other platitudes. Scott found it very difficult not to be fully enthralled by all this capitalist hoopla which would be the envy of many a weak mind, but thanks to his inauspicious upbringing, and his grip on the reality of values, he hasn't been utterly sucked into this world of nonchalant egotism.

But without hard facts on Generation You and its Prime Minster his speculations would seem like words of a madman.

And is it right? Or is he mad?

Are his musings unfounded?

Can there truly be such an immense web of lies spinning beneath their propaganda?

Scott is quite helpless to untangle it all so best leave it alone and go with the flow until the opportune moment presents itself, if it ever presents itself. If it exists. Which is why he chose to accept the Prime Minister's offer of this job role in the first place. Where best to conduct his operations if not from the very heart of the corruption? Nobody else knows of the doubts Scott has, after all, because there is no longer anyone alive close to him to share his suspicions with, or confer with. Some secrets can only be suppressed for a finite amount of time before someone unearths them. Scott must hope he finds their secrets before they discover his. If they exist.

Scott holds onto the boat railing for dear life, or grim death, as the white water churns and bucks beneath its hull, the lovely sky doing nothing to allay the feelings of oppression. He knows first hand how fickle fate can be and says a silent prayer for his departed friend, CIA agent Thomas C. Match, while willing their imminent arrival at the welcoming land of Scotland so he might assuage the fear of drowning.

This should be a terrifically exciting adventure, for Scott Dalton has finally achieved what was, only a few years back, nothing more than a pipe-dream. Yet as he grips the railing of the fishing boat tighter, cold despite the thick gloves he wears, he cannot help but smile ironically at the good fortune and glory he has attained. He isn't just thinking outside the box now, no, Scott Dalton is living well outside the box.

THREE

Although working somewhere recently targeted as a small part of a significantly larger act of terrorism, not to mention the other chain of murderous events in the immediate locality, isn't perhaps the best place to try and blend in if one wishes to escape a very dubious past which is worlds away from supermarket trolley pushing, this is exactly what Ashley Barber has successfully achieved.

Barbs, as he is affectionately called by his colleagues, has been in the employ of TAMS Supermarket in New Wroxton, Norfolk, England for the past five years, while leading a quiet rural life in what was once a peaceful village barely registering on most maps. His existence has been led these past few years deliberately as an anonymous nobody, a bystander in the comings and goings of local life or, in other words, nothing more than an extra on life's grand stage. Yes. Acting is a good analogy. Barbs is performing a new role in his life, acting the part of a nobody!

Forty-nine hours remain.

Barbs was fortunate enough to be on holiday when the recent chemical attack took place at the TAMS store but he, like his colleagues, felt the loss of innocent life. Is he a hypocrite?

Many of his work colleagues perished in the attack, the store and village itself the centre of attention, are still coming to terms with what transpired that morning, soon to become overshadowed by global events that very same week. In all his fifty-seven years since birth and the considerable extremely violet experiences he has witnessed, Barb's was nonetheless genuinely shaken, like millions of others, with the carnage the world suffered on that fateful day which altered history and simultaneously realigned the global future. Two-dozen were killed in the New Wroxton store; hundreds of thousands suffering similar fates across the entire world the very next day. TAMS stores were closed for a month after this barbaric act of killing, such was the shock that was felt through its very foundations. But reopen they eventually did - although the investigation is ongoing. The general public, it's customers, need their food and drink.

On this particular September morning, at eight o'clock, Barb's is getting ready for his next routine shift. His next performance as the friendly, easy-going, trolley-man - or should that be trolley-person?

Barbs lives in a flat on Field Views which has no view of any fields these days because property developers greedy for ready cash, and without a care for the world, have long ago built more houses on the original field! His flat is conservatively furnished without any indication of his past except for a single photograph of his wife and children, back home in America, anonymous under the witness protection program, where they are safe from any of his old enemies. The picture itself is concealed, hidden from view until he and he alone desires to remember. An extra precaution. In fact Barb's too has disappeared from any grid where he might be touched, and his old life plays like a movie in his mind with even his real name fading from memory, but he cannot be too careful. Particularly now. The investigation into the chemical attack is unearthing other local details hidden.

Barb's has wondered for sometime now if he is actually suffering from the onset of a degenerative brain disease or if, in fact, he is repressing these memories of his past, deliberately locking them away to quash the nightmares. He knows with certainty that he deserves both the disease and nightmares for the things he has witnessed firsthand without acting, and those killings done by himself.

The autumnal air outside his front door feels damp and fresh from last night's rain. Is this the first sign that their lovely long hot summer months are finally reaching their end?

Barb's grins to himself wistfully, feeling his chest tighten slightly.

Rumination's of an old man!

He regulates his breathing as the Doctor ordered following his scare a few months back. How long ago he cannot recall exactly, and its definitely something he should sooner forget. Another sign that his body is ageing? The Doctor told barbs to slow down his life as a precautionary measure. Precautionary, what does that mean? Slow down seems ludicrous. Barb's has slowed it down merely by being in Norfolk! Yet he reduced his working hours at TAMS by a few hours as advised by the doctor. He could retire now, living quite comfortably, but he doesn't want to. Why should he? Who wants to sit around growing old? Better to run at it full-throttle, or as near as possible. The Doctor told him many things, such as he must start watching his cholesterol, cut out red meat, stop drinking wine. Sod that! What's the point in living if a person cannot have a few pleasures? So what if his next heart-attack is fatal? Bring it on! Steak and wine and the odd cigar!

When he passes by the door to Field Views No. 15 Barb's casually glances up at the unadorned first-floor windows, feeling no real sorrow for the occupants, long since gone. The young man living there worked at TAMS on the checkouts, but during a tumultuous series of events which Barb's hasn't entirely untangled despite reading much about them, Nathan Browne was shot dead by a police officer in the local churchyard. His fiancé, jilted and cheated on, left the maisonette many weeks ago and the property has been unoccupied since.

Barbs shakes his head at the sorry state of affairs. Trivialities of the weak.

Barbs greets the neighbours who he strolls by with his customary cordial friendliness because they are also customers of TAMS too, while taking the relatively short walk through the High Street to work. His friendly act perfected now. It took time to learn. It was difficult to realign his character.

New Wroxton is quaint, quiet, comparatively isolated from busy city- or town-life elsewhere, situated as it is in an area of Norfolk where the place suits the more sedentary pace, which is why the village is popular with retiring couples or those seeking peace. A few younger families do reside here, of course, because there are indeed desirable new properties on the village outskirts, but there is really very little on offer to teenagers or young people so they tend to venture to the nearest town, which is North Walsham, or drive to Norwich or Great Yarmouth for greater entertainment.

While walking he wonders what today will bring.

Life as a trolley pusher may seem fairly dull and routine to most people, requiring little skill or brain power, yet there is always something new, some unique customer interaction, even if this life isn't as unpredictable as his last. But trollies and baskets are an essential ingredient to a happy shopping trip.

The inquisitive novelty about the terrorist attack has worn off in the collective, and Barb's is now asked fewer questions from the curious, while a the post-summer/pre-Christmas calmness has settled upon the store. It is a time for the store to reorganise, assess and prepare. It's a time where the clocks tick along with little ado, much as Barb's likes, but someone is watching him intent upon reversing the clock, affecting the stable existence he is making for himself here in New Wroxton, turning forced mundanity on its head. Barb's is being watched by someone from his past who he never in his wildest nightmares expected to encounter again.

FOUR

It is quite easy to ignore the chilly September wind blowing in from an easterly direction when the view across Paltournay Harbour is so splendiferous in scope. Scott Dalton wonder why he has never visited Scotland before now. Grey clouds have blown inland and the vista is clear light blue with the horizon spotted with gas platforms and tankers. Scott wonders how the small fishing boat he arrived upon avoided them all in the darkness, recalling a few twinkling lights but none close up.

Undoubtedly Scott is like many citizens of Great Britain in that he hasn't ventured the entire length and breadth of their island nation, which has obviously been his loss. Sometimes a person really doesn't know what delightfully diverse scenery is on their very own doorstep.

Forty-eight hours remain.

Paltournay is tiny village with a population of just under five-thousand. It is nestled at the foothills of the National Park of the same name upon the shifting eastern coastline of Scotland, not more than forty miles north from Aberdeen. It is quite the little tourist attraction because of it's many ancient and traditional cobblestone-walled buildings, deliberately unkempt countryside and the proliferation of olde world Scottish customs and practices. Many of it's population can trace their regional ancestry line back hundreds of years.   Not quite Deliverance.

The fortified concrete and steel harbour where with its protected horseshoe bay, overlooks the great expanse of the North Sea between Scotland and Norway, which might seem uninspiring to some in it's bleak roiling grey, but Scott Dalton has travelled across the heaving unpredictable mass of water so has gained a significant appreciation of it.

Scott is standing in front of the Bed and Breakfast accommodation which his people at the Joint Security Services pre-booked for him under his cover credentials, and has been used in the past so the owners ask no questions of their English visitor. Scott's eyes water. The wind is cold. He sucks in deeply the clean, unpolluted air. Owing to the strained relationship between England and Scotland, and the very nature of his task, utmost secrecy is paramount. The B&B overlooks the stone and cobbled houses bravely nestled beside the harbour wall. Scott can only imagine what the residents of these homes must suffer during harsh winters in this part of the country, unless these homes are used during the more temperate months of the year.   Maybe he is right.

Perhaps these are mostly holiday homes.

Certainly the wide exposure of sea makes a man feel insignificant amidst its backdrop, and this morning the weather is fair but cold so its possible to see quite a distance.

Ships and offshore platforms appear like miniatures on the horizon.

Behind Scott's accommodation the hill rises steeply, imposingly. He has researched in a locally published brochure that it is a beloved National Park consisting of woodland broken by moorland, offering a picturesque walk among the rocks and hedges, stretching for miles into the very Highland's themselves.

With a delicious fried breakfast and coffee settling in his stomach, Scott walks up the hill westward, between the old buildings. On the streets left-side, facing northwards, a women's boutique has a large bright and garish display, the clothing inappropriate for the current weather, maybe a change is due. A unisex hairdressers, a barber snipping a weathered old residents thinning grey hair. Next door is a bakery, which Scott should've detected first by scent alone. South-facing motel, The Harbour Reach, is discretely adorned with a modest sign while next door is the only pub in the village, The Prancing Pony, it's facial taking up the entire middle block of buildings, offering food, drink and occasional evening entertainment.

A few people pass by. Locals and visitors.

Scott nods amiably. He doesn't wish to appear unfriendly, just aloof and disinterested. He is suspicious of everyone because he has yet to develop the sixth sense which other agents have when it comes to detecting unscrupulous customers. And here, everyone looks suspicious! He is due to make contact with someone in the organisation tonight. But it pays to be safe. Be seen. And observe.

And be observed by a watcher behind a net curtain in a first-floor window of The Harbour Reach. A corner room, so its occupant can watch three points of interest: Main Street, the harbour and the village through-road. The only points of interest, really, because she isn't interested in sight-seeing. Just watching.

The observer smiles ruefully to herself. She recognises the face of an outsider. They tend to stick out like a sore thumb in this small village.

Today there shall inevitably be many new faces. Tomorrow, Friday, and the weekend at the farm not more than a mile away, there is the annual festival. Music, games, beer.

But she isn't interested in any of those things. The observers job is more important. The observers job is to do exactly what she is doing: observe. And Scott Dalton is a new face worth watching.

There are four other guests staying at the family run B&B: a pair of newlyweds and two men on a walking holiday. None of these are

Government employees as far as Scott is aware and only the landlord has an inkling of what his presence here might signify.

The quaint stone-dashed house sits with a road on three of it's sides with access gained to the carpark between the building and rear garden, which is of a fair size and well maintained, colourful in the summer, but only a sun-trap during the summer, Scott assesses.

Undoubtedly its owners are well paid by the English Government behind the backs of the Scottish Government who, if they discovered the nature of this hideaway, they would probably raze it to the ground given the recent animosity between the neighbouring countries.

While Prime Minister Alfred McCann and Generation You are popular in his home country many of the policies instigated by them have proven unpopular in Scotland, whose own governing body subsequently severed ties with England in a power struggle which has created a virtual Hadrian's Wall between the old allies. There have been violent clashes since quelled by popular majority - although there will always be dissidents in any struggle for power. And so Scotland has slipped into its own independence after many years of unity with England, although they remain allied with the European Union. Generation You has accepted this choice gracefully, although reluctantly, acknowledging their neighbours decision even if they themselves are doubtful its survivability as a workable motion. Europe has too many disparate cultures to unify successfully, just look to history for proof: the Roman Empire and Nazi Germany both tried forcibly to unite Europe and failed spectacularly.

So today Scott Dalton is unequivocally a foreigner here. An outsider who must be careful to ruffle the right feathers! Not the law. He works for England. The Prime Minister. The man with the weight of the country on his shoulders. Should he feel sorry for Alfred McCann? The leader who outwardly extolls the virtues and freedoms of his people while surreptitiously alienating England from the rest of the world? Are things truly as bad as that?

Scott strolls nonchalantly along the old cobble pathway at the front of the B&B late in the afternoon, having discretely learned nothing about no one all day! He turns left into familiar Main Street and straight on to The Prancing Pony. He is hungry and thirsty and this is the rendezvous location. Scott opens the door after taking a deep breath to focus his mind on what he is here for. Remembering his task. He needs to blend in. At the moment he feels windswept, dishevelled, and in need of sustenance, so blending in should be no problem!

Meet the right people. Be amiable, but not too amiable. Pretend to get drunk. Basically, do not look like a policeman!

Tartans, greens, browns and traditional hues of Scottish colour greet Scott when he pushes open the inner glass door into the main drinking area of The Prancing Pony Public House, taking in the sturdy oaken bar running along the entire back wall, adorned with horse-shoes, rustic plaques and humorously quotable billings. To the left is seating with open booths and four-top tables and chairs, while to the right and through swing-doors is the restaurant seating.

Behind the bar are a variety of bottles and glasses and other paraphernalia one might find in any pub in any nation across planet Earth.

The barman smiles at him broadly while the patrons present glance in his general direction briefly, sizing him up as just another reveller arriving for the local festival taking place on a privately owned farm-building a mile-and-a-half from the outskirts of Paltournay village.

At least they do not regard him with suspicion! Yet. Nobody strikes him as a likely or unlikely candidate for a smuggling ring! The assorted patrons sit at dark well-warn tables on equally used dark chairs, and are a diverse mixture of ages and sexes and its surprisingly busy for such a small village. Scott wryly speculates that perhaps the entire population has turned up for dinner, along with a few other visitors such as himself.

The vibe is one of indifference to his presence.

A good start.

The air is heavy with smoke from cigarettes and cigars, like pub's should be but no longer are in England because of the self-righteous, self-proclaimed Heath and Safety lobbyists. This atmosphere of tobacco and alcohol is a whimsical breath of fresh air, so to speak.

"A fine evening to ye, sir." The barman says in a deeply rich Scottish burr which one has to carefully listen to otherwise the words might get mixed in a jumble of vowels to those unfamiliar.

"And you." Scott replies with a fractured smile that doesn't reach his eyes, keeping up his act.

"What can I get ye?"

"A pint of Paltournay, please."

"As ye wish, sir."

"May I get a meal?"

"Aye, sir. Go straight into the restaurant. My wife will see to ye. I'll bring your drink through."

"That's very kind, thank you."

Scott ate a delicious homemade steak and ale pie, made with suet pastry, washed down with the local brew, and thoroughly enjoyed both. The hostess was friendly, politely and provided him with everything he could wish for, so after settling the restaurant tab he left a fiver tip, before returning to the bar which was at the same capacity as three-quarters of an hour previously. Scott ordered another drink, this time a double-measure of single malt whiskey, meat and without ice.

While the barman tends the order Scott's fluctuating sixth sense detects curiosity from the young woman sat on a barstool next to where he stands, whom he deliberately seizes upon to be his first attempt at ingratiating himself with these people, and he turns to face her with what he anticipates will come across as cool detachment.

"No sense ruining a good drink by watering it down." Scott says to her. "My name is Scott. May I buy you a drink? I'm new around these parts." He adds with knowing humour because his strong English accent is a bit of a giveaway.

"I could've sworn ye were local!" Her accent isn't quite so strong as that of the barman, with perhaps mixed heritage detectable in the depths of the womanly tone, and she sizes Scott up in the way women do when deciding if a conversation is warranted. "I'm okay." She tells him, picking up her glass which is half-full - or half-empty, depending on the mood! "My name is Rose."

Scott wishes he could say something witty, perhaps a pithy off-the-cuff remark about roses and thorns, but he doesn't wish to sound corny, or too forward for that matter. Instead, when his drink of golden whiskey arrives, they chink their glasses amicably together.

A good beginning.

"What brings ye here?" Rose asks casually. "The festival?"

"Not exactly. Although I might give it a cursory visit. Is it worth it?"

"Aye. It is. Good music."

"Do you play or sing?"

"Neither. What about you?"

"I can do both badly."

Rose politely laughs. "So what are ye for then, if not the music?"

"Well, frankly, I'm looking for work."

"Really! No jobs back in England any more?"

"Several." Scott replies disdainfully, sipping his whiskey. "Wow, this is good stuff." He nods respectfully to the barman. "Yes, there are jobs in England but not for- Well, lets just say the job I am looking for doesn't fit in with good old Alfred McCann's regime."

Its a gambit which Scott must take. By being so open with his purpose, even if he exposes himself to being found out by someone from the Scottish Secret Police, is a risk. But he detects in Rose that he hasn't really anything much to fear because there is no police-vibe surrounding her. And there does exist such a phenomena.

This assignment is of the utmost importance if England is to use successful preventative measure to reduce insurgence and terrorism. At least that is according to his own Chief and the Prime Minister of Great Britain, but to Scott it seems like Fascist action to wipe out those who oppose some of the changes the Generation You political party have installed. He himself agrees that senseless acts of violence should be squashed, but at what price? Terrorists are being paid huge sums of money to carry out these atrocities in England right now. There is no idealism or religious belief behind them. These are acts where a third party are paying to instigate terror with an unscrupulous, unassigned purpose. These acts are being blamed for the unrest in England, with local media covering up by using Propaganda with a positive spin, making the Government look like the heroes and the victims.

"And what is that job?" Rose asks matter-of-factly.

"Oh, I don't know." Scott shrugs. "Its just- all these changes which our wonderful leader is bringing forth in merry old England, they are- I don't know. Is he hiding something? Reinstating St. George's Day as a national holiday, bringing back National Service, ploughing millions into the police force and NHS. Well, maybe its just me, but it all seems too good to be true."

The barman nods his agreement.

Rose too nods, thoughtfully, trying to size him up while finishing off her drink swiftly and ordering another. While doing so, Scott is able to scrutinise her with greater clarity - or the alcohol is taking effect. Her red hair hangs around her neck and ears with a sense of casual pride apart from the unruly carefree fringe which she is constantly brushing aside. Her face is free from make-up, fresh and rosy, no doubt apt. She is a little over five-feet tall, compact in brown ankle-boots, blue jeans and a figure-hugging beige sports bra, a bad weather appropriate coat slung over the stool, and no jewellery. Scott can tell from her eyes she is in her mid-twenties and has had an indifferent upbringing. There is fire deep within her green hues and a powerful personality waiting to burst forth at any minute. What is it? What drives her? She is a complicated person, but not the one he seeks. What secrets are beneath the facade? He realises he had better not overstep the mark with her because she could match him in not only words, but most probably deeds. Hopefully by ingratiating himself with her, he can spark the interest of his intended employer.

"Sounds like you need that drink." Rose says sympathetically.

"Well- That's enough about me." Scott says. "You live here, in Paltournay?"

"That's right. And I work in Aberdeen."

"Ship building?"

"That's right."

"I can imagine you high up on a crane."

"I'm afraid of heights."

"What do you do then?"

"I'm a steeplejack."

34

Scott raises a well-practised eyebrow, trying to enhance the act with a mixture of early drunkenness and nonchalance, but smiling despite himself - she is funny.

As the duo standing at the bar continue talking about everything and nothing a watcher in the corner of the pub, alone, drinking unhurriedly, a local sitting in the shadows, is eavesdropping with interest to what is being talked about.

FIVE

Ashley Barber's workday that morning had begun like any other for the general supermarket trolley pusher, tidying up after the nighttime shift. These are routines which he carried out like usual. Clocking in; greeting colleagues; banter with customers. All definitely in a days work. He even had time to help the fruit and veg department put out the morning delivery of bananas. These were things which might not appeal to everyone, but Barb's enjoys the simple pleasure of routine, blanking his mind, getting to the point where there are no troubles in his or any world.

Bliss!

Hence the day for Barb's went by much like any other and it would have been relatively uneventful except for something undefinable which was gnawing at the back of his mind, a sensation that all was not as it should have been in his world. His first thought was to modulate his breathing and check his pulse, both yielding no solution because it's an unsettling feeling, not like having a heart attack, more like a forgotten chore. During his shift he ran over everything in his mind that he has done in the morning to try nudging his memory, but to no avail. Barb's wondered too if there was anything about the day's date which might cause his niggling consternation but once again nothing instantly sprang to mind at that time. Unbidden he saw in his mind's eye the faces of his wife and children, his old boss, and faces of others who have crossed his path.

That's it!

Barb's thought, stopping abruptly in his tracks.

He had looked around the carpark as if expecting to see the familiar yet curiously new, somehow altered, face from this morning while he had walked through New Wroxton High Street. Someone sitting inside the Blossoming Cherry Cafe. Yes, the face was altered somehow. Not identical. A doppelgänger, perhaps? A good doppelgänger because the other one, the one who is surely long since dead, was the evil one! And her hair was a different colour to the woman Barb's once knew as Claudinalli Tucamkari, Joseph's wife, but it was definitely her. She was the one who had been true backbone of their evil empire. But it couldn't have been Claudinalli. She must be long gone from this earth by now, destroyed in the destruction of her lair along with her husband.

Thirty-nine hours remain.

Barb's sits in his favourite reclining armchair which is next to his drinks side-board and main lounge window, basking in the milky sunshine, its glare making him squint because opposite him is an alive and apparently quite well Claudinalli Tucamkari.

She and a yo7nger woman who he has never laid eyes on before were waiting outside his flat when he got home just before six o'clock that evening from work, which included a brief stop at the pub for a swift half-pint. The young woman has a familial similarity to Claudinalli, specifically in the structure of her cheek bones. Similar enough to be a daughter, perhaps.

Barb's reflects that Claudinalli is still a formidable woman to behold; tall, athletic and attractive in a severe way, almost catwalk model pouting coquettish. She must by now be in her early fifties but could pass for twenty-years younger, irrespective of the white scar of plastic surgery around her left cheekbone and puckered skin tracing from it to her gnarled ear.

They are both five years older. She and Barbs. Her husband long dead. His wife far away.

Time and life is catching up on both of them.

Naturally enough he is fearful that she has discovered the truth of his treachery against her organisation, because however good the protection the US Government has offered him and his family, where there's a will, there's always a way of extracting information from officials. Equally, though, he knows without doubt his family are safe and he himself must die sooner or later, so Barb's resigns himself to the fact it may be the former.

"Don't you want to know how I tracked you here?" Claudinalli asks, her voice now a rasping whine, unfamiliar, throat damaged because of the explosion that fateful night in the volcano facility in Mongolia.

Five years ago? Still hard to believe. Where have the years gone?

"What's the point?" Barb's tells her bluntly. "You're here now."

"And so are you,"

"At your service."

"Are you?"

"I never resigned."

"Not officially."

"Unofficially?"

"My late husband's organisation was open to interpretation of employment."

"Then is it too late to resign now?"

Claudinalli sighs in a fashion which might be considered disappointment. Barb's wonders if his nonchalant indifference to his fate has thrown her off-balance somehow. What was she expecting, an open-armed greeting of warmth at this reunion? Although he is intrigued by her presence to a certain degree. Barbs wouldn't mind the knowledge of how she found him, before she kills him. And what's the other woman all about? With her thigh-length black boots, skimpy skirt exposing her no-knickers unshaven bravado, a tank top which is under-worn and pointless facial fake-up galore? Is she the daughter?

"Make yourself useful, love." Barb's tells the young woman, not caring if he sounds chauvinistic in front of these pair of feminist flaunting women. "Fetch us a drink from the kitchen."

Curiously, the woman doesn't bristle at his direct request, merely unfolding her legs.

"There's a couple of beers in the fridge." Barb's says, silently asking Claudinalli if she would like a drink too.

"Thank you, Dee." She tells the younger woman as she disappears into the kitchen.

There is little doubt in Barb's mind that these two aren't here purely on a social call, but what can he possibly do here in New Wroxton which might be of benefit to her? Unless they are coming to punish him. But what's the point in that?

"What can I do for you?" Barb's asks.

"You always were to the point." Claudinalli responds.

"Where's the point in wasting time?"

"I thought some exposition might be required."

"Maybe later."

"Would that still be exposition."

"Who cares?"

"Okay." She says simply, resigned to the fact that he doesn't seem surprised or interested in her reappearance. "I am calling up a favour."

"I didn't know I was in arrears." He replies.

Claudinalli laughs coarsely, and when doing so the burn scar on her face wrinkles an angry red. He is surprised that with all the funds which must surely still be at her disposal and all her past vanity that she hasn't completely eradicated the scar, particularly when one considers the marvels which modern plastic surgery can perform these days. Maybe she is wearing it like a badge, Barb's muses. A symbol of the struggle she has endured since the downfall of her Empire and death of her husband. He wonders what she has been doing in the interim. Barb's also admits to himself that he is intrigued by the plans she has for him, to repay a favour. Maybe she is reformed and wants to do good in this world as repayment for all those past atrocities? And maybe not.

"You don't owe anything, really." Claudinalli tells him, resignation in her voice, unless she is faking it. "You deserted Joseph's new vision for the world to preserve your own life. I can understand that, and I won't hold it against you. There are not many of us left. But that was five years ago and I am here to ask for your help one more time."

Dee returns from the kitchen with a trio of cold beers, which she hands out. Barb's cracks his open, downs a little, and wonders how angry she would be if he suggested food next.

"Then you must be desperate." Barb's tells her. "And look around. I live in a small village in nowhere! What can I do from here?"

"This isolation is perfect."

"It offers peace and quiet, I'll give you that, but you aren't exactly the epitome of peace and quiet."

"True. But neither were you. Once."

"Now I'm dying. Weak heart. I'm no use to you." He looks from woman to woman like a wise old sage imparting knowledge to the younger generation. "If you want to see your vision, Joseph's vision, realised, then all you need do is turn on a television. Society is collapsing by itself without being pushed. They need no help! There ain't no need for some megalomaniacal plan to topple Government's these days, the Government's are capable of destroying it all themselves."

"You used to be a doer, not a thinker." Claudinalli states.

Barb's nods in resounding agreement because it's very true indeed, he did apply brawn before brains even though he has always possessed both. In the past he brought the opposite of peace and quiet.

"I've had plenty of time on my hands." Barb's tells her truthfully. "I live a quiet life, a peaceful life, amongst a peaceful community. Not to escape from my old life, but- because my time is past. This is a young man's game nowadays, so- I'm enjoying retirement."

"You look content."

"By content you mean overweight."

"By content I mean bored."

"I admit I miss those times, when I was a fit young buck causing mayhem, but-" He lets the sentence hang, shrugging his shoulders.

Claudinalli studies his face, scrutinising him. Barb's reflects that she too, in days gone by, would not have tolerated his laid-back attitude toward her demands, her presence, or her personality. Things have certainly changed. There once was a time when resistance to her will was a futile act. She and Joseph would severely punish the insubordinate who failed them. Maybe she is now acting. Maybe she knows of his duplicity and is simply toying with him. Yet, deep down, Barb's can see this woman has reached a point in her own life where she is acknowledging the possibility that she has become irrelevant in the world. Is there a place for people like him and her in this new changing world, where super-villains are spoofed?

"Tell me," Barb's says, "what you are planning. Perhaps I can help, for old time's sake."

"Revenge." Claudinalli states bluntly.

41

Slowly nodding, Barb's says: "Revenge is a dish best served with an ice-cold beer."

Dee laughs at this, uncouthly choking on, spitting out and dribbling her own beer down her chin. Barb's wonders why such a childish woman would draw Claudinalli's attention, unless- yes! Definitely. Could it be there is really is family resemblance? Could this Dee person be a Tucamkari offspring? Upon closer scrutiny she does have her Mum's stature and bone-structure, along with her Father's eyes and nose. Good grief, Barb's thinks, talk about keeping business in the family! And how about teaching the child a bit of dress sense!?

"I want the people who betrayed my husband." Claudinalli states bluntly.

Ashley Barber searches her face for any hint that this woman is targeting him with this statement of intent, but he cannot detect any inference that she knows of his own complicity in exposing the Tucamkari organisation to authorities. His family is safe, and he must cling to this belief.

"The British Government." Claudinalli says. "They sent their best agent after me and I want revenge. I know this new power, these new, corrupt officials had no direct involvement in the work of their predecessors, but they are equally guilty of delivering their self-righteous capitalist proclamations to those who do not desire it. You know best what we, my husband and I, were striving to achieve. We wanted to give balance back to those states who have felt oppressed by the US and UN and others. These people whose businesses peddle their way of life like it's the right way need to be removed from society if we are all to regain own identity. Corporations make people compliant sheep, unable to question and think freely for themselves. I intend to send a message to these people, my final act, as a reminder that people are as mad as hell and they aren't going to stand any more of this subjugation."

Finishing off his beer, feeling the false sense of confidence no matter what that alcohol can bring to a person's psyche, Barb's considers his options. This morning he was happy enough to continue in this life of normalcy, carry on with the routine existence until he drops down dead pushing a trolley. But in retrospect whats really is the point? Why exist with actually living? His body might be deteriorating yet his mind is as active as it used to be and who's to say that without a bit of exercise he cannot perform the feats of yesteryear? We all know that we shall inevitably die some day, so why spend time forlornly considering the what-if's? Why should there ever be a dull moment?

"Okay." Barb's says eventually. "You can't stay here, I have just enough room for myself. There's a hotel not far away, get a room there." To Dee: "I presume you're the daughter?"

Dee nods, smiling proudly, and from this general reaction and her demeanour he detects a hint of mental impairment.

"I shall help you both," Barb's says, "as much as I can, but in return, I want nothing to disrupt this life I here unless I choose to disrupt it myself."

"Agreed."

This mad-woman jumps up from her chair in delighted glee, extending her hand after clapping them both in an almost childlike gesture, and they seal the deal with a shake.

"But first we gotta have food, 'cause I still got a young-man's appetite."

SIX

In The Prancing Pony Public House Scott Dalton is sat opposite a man who has introduced himself with a just-for-show smile and an equally false name: Bob. This fifty-year old Glaswegian who looks nothing like a Bob wastes no time by telling Scott that if he proves trustworthy then he shall learn his true name soon enough. This would seem to be Scott's contact. The man whom his Service has set him upon. The first in a chain of people he is undoubtedly going to have to go through before getting to someone important.

Thirty-six hours remain.

Bob smells of smoke from the chain of cheap cigarettes he has been endlessly chuffing away at in the corner of the pub while surreptitiously eavesdropping upon Scott's conversation with Rose - among the numerous revoked laws is the ridiculous one made banning public smoking!

The English undercover agent would pigeonhole this man called Bob more as a man called Jock or Scotty, because his chewy accent is so heavily Scottish he can probably trace his history right the way back to Robert the Bruce. Scott has to strain his hearing that little bit extra to not lose his way in the tumble of worlds chewed out by this man. Adding to the stereotype Bob sports a kilt below his heavy woollen knitted jumper, even though trousers are warn disrespectfully beneath the more traditional ware. His ruddy face is etched with outdoorsman character, and his generously grey-flecked auburn hair and beard is unkempt, masculine, as are his penetrating brown eyes which possess a thoughtfulness infused with danger.

It now seems the young woman Rose was exceptionally adept at playing the British agent at his own game and he only hopes she hasn't rumbled his true intentions. Scott irritably admits to himself he wasn't aware the conversation was being overheard by a third party, with some chagrin. Rose and Scott had drank and conversed as naturally as any newly introduced couple of any decree might, talking about life, the weather, existence and the state of the World, finally ending with Rose quite abruptly, and to Scott's surprise, telling him that the man who he is now talking to, Bob, would like to introduce himself.

Which he has just gone and done.

Yes, Scott had dropped a few pointers into the conversation but none too blatant. Or so he thought. Rose was the go-between.

Without questioning the knowledge of what he and Rose had been talking about reaching Bob's ear, Scott had obediently taken his drink to sit at the corner table, while Rose subsequently departed The Prancing Pony with nary a backwards glance.

"I've checked your credentials." Bob says, his strong accent forcing Scott to continue to strain to understand. "And ye seem to be genuine." Bob shows Scott the mini-tablet in his hand by way of explanation. "Judging by what ye were saying to the wee lassie, ye are searching for work?"

Scott takes a moment to weigh things up by taking a sip from his fourth Whiskey-double, grateful for the alcohol-nullifying drug which the Service provided him with, otherwise right now his head would be swimming. Rose had him fooled. Could Bob be doing the same? Whoever Bob works for are well informed and prompt to dig up buried information. They can get the fake information on him planted by Scott's very own people without effort. Is this a good or bad sign? Could Bob he working for the Scottish Secret Police? There is everything in this man Bob's appearance and speech which tells Scott that he doesn't work for the authorities but everything about Rose seemed quite innocuous, too, and yet she led him to this man. All of which proves that Scott must keep his guard up, alcohol or not. Maybe being drunk would've improved his judgement and perception! If the Scottish authorities nab him then all this tomfoolery could be for nought. But if he doesn't take a chance, he may not get another. Tonight was to be the night he is to make contact, he has made contact. So what is there to lose, really, except for his life?

"I met a man called Joe in Norway." Scott says, noticing Bob's reaction to be one of recognition at this name. "He was my starting point when I got out of England. But you probably know that." Scott nods to the conspicuous tablet, which Bob slips into his pocket. "I told him what I want to do. I said I want to make a difference. You heard what I said to Rose. Probably through that thing. The wonders of modern technology, hey? I've had enough. I'm as mad as hell about the direction my country is taking and Joe told me this is a good place to come to do something about it. A starting point. He also said I would be contacted by one of his people when I arrived. I figure you, or Rose, are one of those people?"

Emotionlessly, Bob regards Scott's face and considers his words, while Scott muses once more over the human facets which we each possess, because although Scott is well aware we are all constructed differently, he considers it to be a pity some are unable to evoke emotions. But who is Scott to judge? This man Bob is obviously hiding behind a professionally inscrutable mask. Bob's life has clearly been hard fought, something which only recently Scott has become acquainted within his own life. Maybe Bob didn't have the strong family upbringing which Scott enjoyed, perhaps there have been ever present and consistent friendship disappointments, a fractured psychology? There could be countless reasons why Bob is a guarded person, and some might he due to his chosen profession. Scott decides this man does not work for the authorities, and believes he has chosen wisely. It can be no coincidence Rose interrogated him before placing him into Bob's hands. And it was an interrogation.

The moments tick by, during which time Scott has finished the last drops of the divine Whiskey, feeling at last the effects of the alcohol itself upon his innards, warming, entering his blood stream as such substance naturally should, the inhibiting drug having lasted little real time but served its purpose.

Bob rises slowly in his wooden chair, the frame creaking as it releases his weight from upon it.

"Come with me." Bob says.

Scott resists the urge to fist-pump the air: success feels good.

Outside and it is a chill wind that whistles up High Street from the exposed harbour end, with Scott following the surprisingly fleet-footed older man down the cobbled road, across the relatively smooth surface of the main through-road and down ancient steps to the lower, historically significant harbour. Scott is curiously finding it a real challenge to keep up with Bob. This man is fit belying his age. The pace aids circulation and keeps the body warm, an essential act right now.

The night isn't too old! The hour has barely passed ten o'clock and clouds have rolled down upon Paltournay. From the Highlands and across the sea. They temporarily block out the stars and are creating a milky moon, which casts it's eerie pallor despite the abounding darkness. Creepy, in a horror film kind of way. One can easily imagine wraiths amongst the shadows. Or blood-sucking vampires lurking around a hidden corner. This is prime Jack Asher territory.

While walking Scott mulls further over the conversations of the evening, wondering how much of what was scripted for him by the Government actually mirrors his own thoughts. Which they must, because the words wouldn't come naturally, they would've been stilted, surely? Noticeable as phoney. Lots of what he said made sense, despite the fact it was created solely for the purpose of ingratiating himself with the people who his Government want him to expose to their authority. Is it also possible his own people want him to get caught? Have they fed him to the wolves because they fear he knows too much? But why the elaborate set-up if they suspect his loyalty? Stupid. Are they testing that loyalty? No. But they could just as easily have shot him and dumped him at sea, no-one would be any the wiser. Ludicrous. What about Bob? He seems like a salty sea dog whose best years are behind him, a true patriot of Scotland. A Glaswegian monarch. Bob would be the perfect candidate to be supporting subversion in England, so why have the Scottish authorities not already done something about it? He sticks out like a sore thumb. Scottish Government have made it clear that they do not want any such subversive activities taking place in their country. They have already handed several insurgents over to Alfred McCann's Security Service as an example to others, and this is despite falling out with Generation You and regaining their own independence.

Then there is Rose.

Rose. A rare young woman whose professionalism at her task is unquestionable. She had Scott well and truly duped, but- There comes something positive from his point of view. The lack of any romantic entanglement, real or imagined. Certainly Rose displayed no feelings toward him whatsoever. Which is good. He cannot handle it any more! Scott is determined not to be played the fool by women again. Life is challenging enough without having a person manipulating his feelings.

Must be the alcohol making his thoughts a tumble of gibberish random musings. How long was the nullifying drug supposed to work for?

Proceeding along the harbour wall and Scott is experiencing a climate which he now more associates with Scotland: chilly and damp! But this is still more bearable than his time a few months back in

Greenland; another beautiful country, which should swap names with neighbouring Iceland because that would surely be more pictorially appropriate.

Ghostly black shapes with twinkling lights rise and fall gently on the lapping waves of the harbour water, lights cast from the few boats which are occupied.

It is Scott's preference to be on land but he realises they are heading toward a four berth boat. Growing up in Norfolk, an area whose Broads are world renowned, did nothing for Scott. Apart from holidays with family he felt absolutely no inclination toward boating and hasn't really been enamoured with it since. On his journey from Norway to Scotland he felt the uneasiness clutching at his nerves, the power of nature, the fickle greatness of the sea, it's hidden dangers, and the fragility of human existence atop. But there, he muses, we cannot all be Steve Zissou.

Bob clambers confidently aboard and Scott follows more cautiously, not wishing to make a fool of himself! An extra chill runs down his spine when he realises this could be a set-up which might now be leading to his death, but what's the sense worrying about it really? Being pragmatic by realising you are more likely to die in a car crash than by the hands of terrorists is much more logical thinking!

The boat is not unlike the size of pleasure craft back home in Norfolk, it's fibreglass and wood sounding familiar beneath his feet, like a past childhood experience where the fond memories bely truthfulness, because a stupid misjudgement as a child which saw him topple head-first in the murky water of the Norfolk Broads is probably what caused him to lose interest in the water. Not that he hasn't had good times in the Mediterranean, where it was warm, clear and adventurous, on the most part. Not that Scott is going to dwell upon it, of course! That's for another, more appropriate, occasion when his focus doesn't need to be fully on the moment in hand.

Lights blaze briefly against the night as the cabin door to below-decks is opened, and Scott follows Bob, squinting against the harshness of three naked bulbs as his eyes adjust to their surroundings.

The man closing the door behind them is another ruddy-faced Scotsman. This one is long-haired, bushy of beard, and built like the proverbial outhouse. He sports tattered jeans, heavy brown boots and a sensible green sou'wester over a black t-shirt. He may as well have the Scottish flag tattooed on his forehead because, like Bob, he is unmistakably from a long lineage of Highland stock, probably the cattle! An inhuman broad grin reveals crooked, broken teeth, while the face is slashed with several scars although, extremely disconcertingly, his eyes are warm, clear and possess a childlike quality.

A woman is seated at the small table upon which are empty lager bottles, coins, notes and playing cards. The remnants of a poker game between these two and a couple of other people who have long since departed. She is of Eastern European extraction, that much is obvious from her stature, skin-tone and facial appearance, despite a concerted yet failed effort to hide these features through dyed-blonde hair and loose-fitting local clothing of generally drab colours. She is in disguise, and not a good one.

"Who won?" Scott says, breaking the silence, trying to bring brevity to a situation which, judging from the hard stare and expressionless mouth of the woman, is likely to be a tough egg to crack.

Is it a confused silence? Does the woman not speak English? What is it with these people which make them appear stone-faced, probing, judgemental, and plain mean, all at once? Scott wants nothing more than to slap a bit of personality into this woman who...just...looks...at...him...!

50

The big man says something completely unintelligible to Scott's ears which might be a foreign language for all he knows, but the bizarre grin he displays indicates he may very well be the victor in the game of poker and Scott is impressed because the woman clearly has the better poker-face permanently plastered in position. And she just stares at him.

"This is Scott Dalton." The woman asks Bob in a statement like voice, obviously unimpressed by first-impressions, and after receiving a superfluous nodded confirmation she turns her attention back upon the Englishman. "Your records pieces missing." As are words from her vocabulary.

"Phew, that's a relief!" Scott replies sarcastically, the best of all humour.

"What you mean?"

"I was beginning to think every strange weird-o knows more about me than I know about myself."

This response actually produces a grin from within the woman eyes but fail to ignite her face as most people's would when they have a genuine sense of humour! It doesn't last.

"What you want?" She asks.

"Let's not beat around the bush shall we-?" Scott says.

The woman looks at him with what Scott can only interpret as confusion, maybe she hasn't spent much time around English people to understand their wide range of worded expressions.

"Beat around the bush!? She asks predictably.

"It's English-" The big Scotsman propping up the room explains to her before launching into more unintelligible language, which Scott hopes is his way of explaining exactly what the expression means, and then the woman nods, bizarrely understanding the gibberish

- or does he speak her particular European language? - before she looks for Scott to continue.

"You know why I am here." Scott states bluntly. "Because by unseen means information seems to travel pretty darn quick around these parts." He says this with condescending contempt. "I was told there are people here who are sympathetic to the English People's Resistance."

"Why we believe you?" The woman asks.

"For goodness...! I was sent here!"

"So you say."

"Yes, so I say."

"Why you want work with us?"

"I want to make a difference. I have had enough of bureaucrats dictating what's best for me and my country."

"Your country?"

"Yes. England."

"Your country is good?"

"I won't say I disagree with everything that Generation You stands for, I 'm not that hypocritical, because I like St. George's day as much as the Scottish enjoy Burns Night, but enough is enough. Now, am I in the right place or not, because you don't look like the Scottish Secret Police?"

Scott stands defiantly, looking from one to the other, excluding the big Scotsman because his stupid grinning face is starting to get annoying. Bob looks at the woman of European origin and an unspoken message passes between them but Scott cannot interpret what it is, he just has to wait, but that wait isn't long.

"My name is William." The man formally calling himself Bob says. "There's no need to know the name's of my companions here, save to say this guy will be the death of you if we are wrong, and the lady, well, I needn't say where she is from or what her motives are. You will deal with me and me alone."

"Fair enough." Scott replies pragmatically.

"We're a man down."

"So I gather."

"You're the extra. I can't tell you much more for now."

"Fair enough."

"You aren't bothered by much."

"I am. But I learned tolerance."

Since arriving onboard Scott, and no doubt his companions too, have become accustomed to the various sounds of grinding cleats, lapping water and creaking wood. To some these might be restful and whimsical but to Scott they would be annoying if one were trying to sleep. There have been the occasional voices drifting in and out of the airwaves like faint radio signals, a car engine starting and gradual acceleration, plus the other sounds indicative of their locale, but for no real reason the thudding of a car door from up on the harbour wall draws all their attention, puncturing a nerve.

Irrationally Scott's hairs bristle on the back of his neck. A bit like a sixth sense. Like an early warning sign.

The quartet are all silent. Three pairs of eyes are on Scott, and he can feel their accusations even as the big Scotsman standing at the door kills the light switch.

"You brought a friend?" The woman says in the dark, drawing out her chair with a soft creak, a sense of threat in her movement.

"Don't be stupid" Scott says, not panicking because it's the truth, but equally uncertain who has drawn forth their suspicions and aware of the building tension in the small vessel. "Might be nothing."

"Or not."

"Or it might be someone has been monitoring your communication devices." Scott says with exasperation. "And you've sold me down the river!"

"What do you mean?"

"You have been listening into me all night!" Scott says reasonably, irritation steadily rising in his tone. The woman is grating on his patience. "I will take a look for you. Give me a gun." He says to William forcibly. "I presume you have some, and I'm not going down without a fight, if there is a fight."

While the big Scotsman opens the cabin door after receiving silent confirmation that it is alright to do so, a bit of watery nighttime moonlight enters, for what it's worth. William is pulling a gun from a side drawer which he coldly hands to Scott.

"You better be for real." William churns menacingly under his breath, close to Scott. "Otherwise you get a bullet in your head!"

SEVEN

Scott Dalton literally plants a fist firmly into the face of the man who has briefly flashed the badge of the Scottish Secret Police figuratively into his own face, putting the man down hard onto the cobbled street to where this foot-chase has carried them since arriving from the dank harbour of Paltournay.

Yeah, welcome to Scotland!

Thanks!

Initially Scott and William aka Bob had skulked off the small boat onto the slick wooden cat-way, treading silently along the dark boards, eyes slowly adjusting to the milky darkness of mist which has descended like a smokey diaphanous veil, hanging as damp murk in the air, thinner than the trust Scott is apparently forging because this new situation is a jeopardising factor.

It was difficult to make out very much at all, least of all the topmost part of the harbour wall, but shadow movement of human figures wavered in the swirling distance. Undoubtedly the slamming of one car door had been accidental and, Scott muses, had this not occurred there is little doubt these new arrivals would have achieved whatever their goal is.

Be decisive. Stick to the plan. Stay undercover.

Of course, these new arrivals might bear no significance whatsoever to the quartet who had gathered in the boat but some sixth sense tells Scott that this isn't the case, and his companions have agreed with him. He has been lucky, himself, really. For now. William's faith and possibly Rose's too has kept Scott alive. They are a man down. They need Scott. Now he must return this faith to continue ingratiating himself within the organisation he is infiltrating. They must be in desperate need of his services to be so trusting of a newcomer. What is the job they will be sending him on?

Henceforth he and William had climbed the black, rough-hewn metal ladder which is firmly attached by large bolts set deeply into concrete, and offers an alternative route other than the main steps from the harbour up its wall, where, peering over the top, Scott can see four black-clad characters who are anything but innocent tourists. Conspicuously out of place is an understatement. One man is berating another, undoubtedly the rookie of the group, who reluctantly waits with the car while the more experienced men in the team proceed toward the steps.

Scott smiles at his luck, but not too broadly, just in case his teeth give away his position. The rookie mistake has delayed whatever their initial plan had been.

When William is beside him he slips a piece of paper into Scott's jacket pocket.

"I trust you." William says close to Scott's ear, under his breath. "Rose trusts you. This is where you need go next with Rose."

Scott nods his thanks, grateful that he has been able to earn a modicum of trust in such a short timeframe, showing clearly that his training and technique has been successful. He need not ask how to find Rose because the implication is that she will find him.

When Scott leaps the wall he has to take just two long strides up-to the rookie before pistol-whipping him across the back of his head, rendering the man who is having a bad time of things unconscious without knowing what hit him.

Before Scott can rifle through the rookie's pockets one of the more experienced men inexplicably returns through the mist, presumably for something previously forgotten, and clocks Scott immediately.

William has since departed into what is, for him, safely familiar territory to where Scott cannot follow.

So the Englishman sprints way from the wall, feet pounding the road, suddenly very warm in the autumn clothes. The man, who Scott can only presume is Scottish Secret Police, judging from the vehicle the four have arrived in and the general appearance of the rookie, pursues.

Scott shouldn't really be surprised they have latched onto him so soon but still, it's an inconvenience all the same. The airwaves must have been monitored for such an incursion. The authorities do not know his real identity. But all the same, he cannot afford to be captured.

Scott ducks and weaves amongst the restricted cover with little real hope of throwing off his pursuer, but at least he is taking the man away from William and the two other conspirators who were on the boat. He wonders if he shall meet them again. They are undoubtedly making their own successful escape into the darkest recesses of the town. Scott is pleased he had time to familiarise himself upon arrival in Paltournay with the town's layout, not that there is much of a town to remember, otherwise he might be stumbling in the dark. Instead he knows exactly where he is heading, taking the man up through High Street and into the darkness of the National Park where it would be a fool who would follow him. At least this is the plan. Unless he is the fool. He intends to subdue and question this man, find out who has sent him and his team, because their appearance is obviously not merely a coincidence. Someone must have alerted the local state Police, but who and why?

Unfortunately Scott has sorely underestimated his pursuer, and has overthought too much.

The local policeman is fast, in good shape, and catches him halfway up High Street.

Scott strikes first with a rabbit-punch placed in the chest, doing well to knock the big guy and his drawn ID card to the ground, but he proves too big, too tough and experienced for Scott, clearly not a bobby on the beat officer and used well to a brawl, so he simply shrugs off the blow as if it was nothing and stands, grinning, before slamming a sledge-hammer fist at Scott's jaw.

EIGHT

How long was I out? This is the Scott's first question he asks himself. The first thought in his brain after searing pain in his head, neck and- all over, in fact. Again! Although judging retrospectively by the force of the strike he is lucky to have a head on his shoulders and nose on his face. The metallic taste of dried blood is in his mouth. Lovely! He must look remarkably attractive. To an Orc!

Taken into the world of the Resistance and now dumped on by The Law! Check. A shady drinking establishment, a femme fatale, unlawful conspirators, and now being chased by cops! Check. Waking up bruised and battered! Check. A typical life for a Humphrey Bogart character or a fictional British Secret Agent. What's it all about, eh!?

Welcome to Scotland! Yeah, thanks a bunch.

Upon opening his eyes Scott expects to find himself in a police station. Or tied to a chair in some seedy basement. Anywhere other than Paltournay High Street. Yet here he is.

It is obviously the same night, or early morning, so it's not like he has lost time by being unconscious for multiple hours. Curiously, there is no sign of his foe. And so a mystery becomes a riddle: what has happened to the man from the Scottish Secret Police? Why were they here if not for him and why has Scott been left here if they were after him?

Dampness in the air means that the most pressing issue for Scott right now is to get to the Bed and Breakfast before another wave of nausea threatens to take him down. The last thing he wants is pneumonia!

Mustering upon the hazy willpower clouding his brain, he somehow drags himself from out of the gutter and props his body against a wall. This is probably not an uncommon sight in Paltournay.

Or anywhere, for that matter. An apparently drunken man staggering home from the pub after a few too many! So should anyone see him at least they won't be too alarmed.

This humorous thought make him smile, causes a headache on top of his headache, and propels Scott onward, or downward, he cannot he sure.

Welcome to Scotland indeed!

Sloping, stumbling, head down, he drunkenly edges in the direction of his B&B accommodation.

Scott checks his pocket, suddenly remembering the key to his room, grateful that it is still there.

He is pleased too that his memory isn't faded into loss. And Rose. Rose. William aka Bob had said she trusted him. Is she his contact? How will she find him? How did the Scottish law find him? Was it him they were after? Was it the gang of conspirators they were after and his presence was happenstance?

Too many thoughts cause him a splitting headache, just behind his eyes, bursting with shards of white and red light. So that's enough of that thinking lark for now. He needs to concentrate on walking the few metres to the Bed and Breakfast. It isn't far, really, but right now, it could be a hundred miles for how leaden his legs are feeling.

Unsteadily, one hand on the wall, Scott continues the head-splitting, sluggishly unbalanced stagger which will get him back to where he needs to be. Hopefully.

The conspirators were obviously on the Police radar.

Maybe there has been increased activity here, in Scotland, in this precise location. This activity alerted the local law and they struck.

Too coincidental?

Or just routine?

Scott's feet shuffle onward until he reaches the bottom end of Paltournay High Street, the sorrowful wailing of a siren out at sea, warning the unwary of the mist which is thick, eerie, ghostly, distant.

The European woman on the boat had stuck out like an incongruous sore thumb. How long has she been here? What is her involvement in the impending plot which they require Scott for? Is she just an immigrant awaiting a boat home? But no. She was part of the group. In charge, almost. So what's going on here? They need him. They knew he was coming. Still they vetted him. They were baiting him. Trust. Very useful for him. These people, Rose and William. Desperately short on manpower so recruited him hurriedly. Lucky for him. But recruited for what? This was about people smuggling. But now Scott is confused.

Across the footpath in front of the Bed and Breakfast Scott goes. Slowly but surely. Walking, stumbling around the side of the building. Grazing his arm. Grazing his body. Up the road toward the driveway at it's rear where his battered ancient Government supplied hire-car is parked, which he hasn't used yet, and where he knows the door to his room is located.

A hospital would be better. For him.

A flood of thoughts.

Not his people, or William, or Rose, or the man who knocked him out with a single, staggering blow. The blow. A sledge-hammer.

Lights explode behind his eyes and he finds himself on the floor. Scott has blacked out again. Not a good sign. But willpower enables him to get to his feet, somehow, eventually finding himself at the back door of the Bed and Breakfast gripping its handle. Miraculously his keys are still where they should be, in his trouser pocket, now in his hand. They jangle loudly.

"Scott."

A voice from the darkness, from his past, from the dead. Se-ri? No. Not Se-ri Solitaire. She's dead. But-

But the voice is definitely familiar. The woman holds an umbrella to protect herself from the rain. Is it raining? Scott hadn't noticed until he see's it cascading magically, like a beautiful waterfall, from off the umbrella. A woman. Scott passes out.

NINE

Blinding light explodes beyond his vision causing Scott Dalton to blink wildly, eyes watery and sore, before screwing them tightly shut against the pain. His skull aches, his thighs feel hard as stone, his mouth tastes rancid, metallic, and he is both hungry and thirsty but his stomach is tight and painful. Life doesn't get much worse than this. Maximum discomfort with minimum effort. He needs to limber up, stretch, drink coffee and eat a full English breakfast. That will do the trick! But does he posses the motor skills to perform such feats? Although, this said, he seems to be laying in a soft bed under a comfortingly warm duvet while his head is delightfully propped up on an eiderdown pillow. Luxuriously comfortable. So he should be thankful for the small mercy that he is still alive and comparatively well. And he is able to witness another day.

Twenty-five hours remain.

Scott should be thankful. But thankful doesn't take the pain away.

"Take your time." Says the reassuringly familiar Scottish brogue of Rose.

Which poses one questions to enter Scott's mind: Where am I?

Tentatively Scott once more opens his eyes. The blurred darkness which is Rose is moving across the room wraithlike to a window, drawing across the curtains to minimise the early morning sunlight filtering through. Very thoughtful of her.

He can smell coffee. And is good.

Scott realises immediately he is not in his room at the B&B, so asks Rose the question:

"Where are we?"

"Don't worry. You're safe."

"Safe?"

"That's right."

"For how long?"

"Long enough."

"Long enough for what?"

"Stop worrying."

Rose is handing him a glass of water which he promptly and swiftly drinks down, feeling every single drop of the liquid on its journey as it quenches his palette and slides downward to hydrate his body. Splendiferous. He could do with a few gallons more. And some of the coffee.

She refills him and he repeats the action, looking around the bedroom of his occupation, which is clearly one belonging to man much older than himself, possibly a single male judging from the lack of any obvious feminine touches.

"Is it- still the same day?" Scott asks her tentatively, not sure of the severity if his concussion, hoping it was mild.

Rose laughs: "Ye're okay, Scott, just a wee bump to the head! I've seen worse. I've had worse! The Doctor said nothing more than a mild concussion. So yes- its morning."

"Doctor?"

"That's right." Rose says, adding with a straight face: "You can remember what one of those is?"

Despite feeling terrible Scott laughs at the much needed levity, a slight relief at finally being out of immediate danger, even if that relief might just be a temporary event.

"This obviously isn't your home." Scott states.

"No. It isn't." Rose tells him matter-of-factly. "These are- temporary accommodation."

Scott nods, fully understanding the implications of what she is telling him and realising he needs to pull himself together and make a swift recovery. They need to move on.

He defiantly flings back the duvet, wincing as he does so. The sight of the purple bruises on his bare legs, the grazes and cuts take him aback. One might wrongly suspect he would be used to such knocks after his previous missions because they are part and parcel of his job! But he gains no pleasure from receiving such injuries so why glorify the after effects?

"Any word from your friends?" Asks Scott, swinging his legs off the bed and cautiously sitting upright, gritting his teeth as the sparkles burst across his vision, prickly heat burns his face, but both feelings pass without further need for alarm.

"Not since William contacted me." Rose replies, truthfully, watching him nonchalantly ."He told me what was going on. I was already waiting at your Bed and Breakfast while you were at the meet."

"Fair enough."

"You need a hand?"

"I need a coffee."

"You'll get one soon enough. You sure your okay?"

"We shall soon find out."

Stretching his legs, limbering them, Scott stands tentatively, naked but not caring, breathing easily as he awaits the sensation which will tell him if he is going pass out again or not. His head throbs, but it's the not part of passing out. Yet once again it's a temporary comfort/ discomfort ratio and nothing more. Scott is irritated by the fact the person who attacked him took him out so easily, so precisely. Be thankful. Scott tries to tell himself. It could be worse. To hell with being thankful! Be angry!

"And the law?" Scott asks, receiving a shrug in response:

"Dunno what happened te'em."

"Upped and left."

"Seems so."

"Any of your people caught?"

"Not so I'm aware."

Scott spies a mug with steam rising from it and, without asking, drinks it down. Coffee never tasted better.

"Where's the bathroom?"

Rose indicates a door off the bedroom, which he strides to, working the blood around his system to improve circulation and increase his energy. He is thinking more clearly now. He knows their next move must be to get into England, away from the Scottish Secret Police, who might be onto Rose or Scott himself. After using the toilet, he vigorously scrubs his face with cold water, before returning to the bedroom and locating all his clothes on a wicker chair. They are clean. A new set picked from his wardrobe back at the B&B.

"Thank you." Scott says. "For saving my life, and for trusting me."

Rose nods, watching him with silent detachment while he dresses. Scott reflects on her professionalism. This is obviously not the first time she has been in a sticky situation and she is handling it with complete composure, for someone so young. Scott hopes he will find out what drew her into this life. He wonders about her involvement in this organisation, what is her position, her rank in the hierarchy? Will he get the opportunity to ask?

When he buckles the belt on his trousers he pulls his phone out his pocket, amazingly undamaged. The battery life is almost nil and his charger is back at the B&B. The slip of paper which William passed onto him last night is crumpled. Scott smiles. He had forgotten all about it. Scott opens it up and reads the address out loud.

66

"What's that?" Rose asks.

"Our next destination. Our friend William gave it me."

"He trusts you.”

“And you?”

“What?”

“Do you trust me?”

“Ye are here, ain't ye?”

Scott pulls on his shoes. Rose is either pretending to be naive or she is perhaps playing Scott for the fool. He wonders which it is, but cannot blame her. Maybe they are still testing him. Understandable. The organisation were a bit too trusting of him last night, unless he really did pull off his act with expertise. They were expecting him. And yet what have they given him really? Nothing. This address could lead nowhere for all he is aware. And what does it matter? They are people smugglers. Nothing more insidious.

There is a possibility too that Rose is part of the lure, the bait to test his honesty and genuine interest in what he claims. How long until the real task begins?

Rose is young and attractive and might be playing to the base heterosexual male instinct, although in retrospect she showed detachment during his complete nakedness. Maybe Scott's male instinct is being a tad chauvinistic!

"Over the border. It's a village west of the Lake District, near Gosforth." He tells her.

“How do you know?”

“A holiday there. Many years ago. It's quiet. Your people certainly enjoy their remoteness! Good place for people to go unnoticed. Do you have a car?"

"And a fake ID if we have to cross the border. But I know an alternative route. You?"

"I shall manage. Might be tricky. But we have no choice. Your car outside?"

"No. I parked half a mile up the road after bringing you here, just to be safe."

"Any food in this place?"

"There's a fridge in the kitchen."

"Splendiferous. I'm bloody famished."

"Hurry up about it."

"Yes, boss"

As soon as Scott steps out of the bedroom he is alerted to the two men stealthily moving toward them through the hallway.

How are they at this place so soon?

They all freeze on the spot.

These appear to be better trained Secret policemen than those who struck last night, their arrival is completely without warning. Despite feeling like spit Scott is quicker to react than these two men and be pounces forward like a cat, tackling the nearest man to the ground, ignoring the throb in his head, the lethargy magically slipping away.

Ignore the pain. Focus. Concentrate. Remember the training.

Out of the corner of his eye he makes out the figure of Rose advancing on the second man. It takes five seconds for both the Scottish policemen to be unceremoniously rendered unconscious.

"What was that all about!?" Scott asks rhetorically, riffling through his man's trouser pocket for the inevitable ID card which just confirms his suspicions: they are Scottish Secret Police. He holds the official ID up for Rose to see who their attackers were.

"How did they find us?"

"I have no idea." Scott tells her, angry, confused. "But we do need to leave. Now! Before anyone else joins this damned party!"

Rose doesn't need to be told twice.

Following her closely, Scott tosses his mobile phone on the floor as they depart the bungalow without Rose witnessing this action. He knows without a shadow of a doubt that his own Government, the people he is working for, have informed the Scottish authorities of his presence in their Country in an attempt to expedite this assignment. This can be the only answer. His phone was being monitored. It led the police to Paltournay last night.. Thats the only way he and Rose were tracked down here so efficiently. But it's a ridiculous, stupid action! Why would they do something so reckless which might prove to be so counterproductive? Behind his back. Who authorised this? Why can't they just let him get on with this Mission? It's not rocket science. Just infiltration of a people smuggling operation, for goodness sake! Scott can only hope his people haven't jeopardised his entire success so far!

TEN

For some reason this morning Ashley Barber's muscles ache more than they have done so for years, and he is extremely reluctant to part himself from between his bedsheets. His bones are stiff, grinding and popping when he moves. His spine feels as if it has been worked over by a particularly vigorous masseur. And sleep- His sleep had been fitful in the extreme, barely worth calling sleep. There is the residue of a dream upon the edges of Barbs' mind without recalling its extent. No sense of dread is apparent, so it obviously wasn't bad. Probably a dream about a lovely comfortable life floating in a world of cottonwool! And sleep.

Barb's is certainly feeling his age, though, and it is when he hears the sound of his own kettle boiling that he remembers why this is the case. A late night. Junk food. Too much alcohol. Ego boosting exercise to show-off, to prove he's fit.

Claudinalli Tucamkari and her daughter Dee spent the night downstairs on chairs - not what you were thinking, sorry.

Barb's isn't sure if he particularly cares if they did or did not get a refreshing night's sleep, because this morning he knows he is feeling his age as a consequence of their arrival. What brought this feeling about? Yesterday's reunion with this formidable lady and the possibilities for what lie ahead have perhaps been playing on his mind. The aching muscles are caused through the tension and not a small amount of the old excitement returning. Because, however deadly serious his job as a henchman had been - he laughs when he thinks of the word 'henchman' and the image it conjures - there was always the thrill during and after a successful completion. Except for the last time. The final great deed to alter the world according to a megalomaniac. Barb's had always been of two minds about his decision to sell-out

Joseph Tucamkari. Essentially he has been able to have his proverbial cake and eat it. Now he can make amends for that.

If his body is old and tired at least his mind is fighting fit. Barb's doesn't believe in letting the mind lapse into serenity, or senility. A lazy mind promotes a lazy body. It's easier to give up, admit defeat because of the aches and pains, sit around vegetating, ruminating on past glories. But what's the point? Why waste precious time and fleeting life? Now he has a renewed sense if direction, a true purpose to the possibly last few years of his life, or even hours if he over-exerts himself.

Barbs' mind is as clear and focused as if he was forty going on thirty again!

Barb's slides off the bed, saying too hell with his old-man aches and pains, dropping to the bedroom floor and performs a set of push-up's followed by some sit-up's. He would like to claim a successful high quantity of both, unfortunately his heart is racing so hard he is afraid of giving himself another heart-attack. There was a time when this exercise regime was almost a pilgrimage. Barb's is angry at first but soon calms himself with breathing techniques, smiling wryly at his ridiculously high expectancy.

Striding resolutely into his bathroom Barb's must be proudly satisfied that at least something hasn't diminished with age.

While emptying his bladder he tries recalling exactly what age he was when he get first got into the game, reasoning that it was officially later than his actual introduction to the alternative way of living. Alternative as in not a normal education, buy a car, get a job, take sightseeing holiday's, family-man, desk-job, working for 'the man', type of life. No. Young Ashley Barber chose to avoid school, only going when forced by his Mum. His Dad had left them when he was he a toddler. Typical, or stereotypical! Juvenile rehabilitation was called for at age fifteen on account of a beating he dealt to a neighbourhood kid who looked at him the wrong way, or was it a girl this guy had looked at funny? The memory recalls what it wants to sometimes. Selective memory, it's called. Similar to selective hearing, he supposes.

Barb reflects his reflection in the mirror has altered considerably over the decades but the hard, fighting eyes and broken nose have remained constant. His Grandma would say he had the devil in him, but what child doesn't to some small degree to their elders?

While Barb's was in Rehabilitation with other kids who also had a few social issues, he befriended a boy a year older than he, called Job. This was not the biblical figure Job, and there were certainly no religious comparisons to be made although he did claim his Hispanic father was called Jesus and his American mother Mary, but Barb's was never able to verify either of these.

Those, for Barb's, were the good days when he had little worries in life and definitely zero responsibilities. Job was his teacher in the art of crime and getting away with it, while also a wise advisor on how to tow the line for one's own purpose. Juvenile Detention was like an education to Barb's, thank you to this knowledgeable buddy he had made, and would remain indebted to until Job's death ten years ago.

Barb's admires the scars upon his body with total recollection of the actions which caused them, reflecting on the symbolic nature of their existence. Other injuries which are not visible are the healed wounds of broken bones, and he has had a few of those over the years, too. Some of which he received through a nice perk of his job, and they were the hard parties which he and friends in the world of henchman-ship would find themselves at, letting rip and enjoying life because who knew if the next day would be the last? Beautiful women who liked a bit of handsome rough would find their way into his bed, if they ever got that far. Anything went in those days. Wild days. Fantastic days.

He should write an autobiography, really. What an eye-opener that would be. And not just for the public at large living safe in their comfortable homes, not realising what characters lurk there in the world where life of innocents often has very little value and certainly no consideration. It would have to be published posthumously, his revealing autobiography, because some of those who have suffered at his hands and lived to tell the tale are still alive in the world. Also he has to consider his employers, some whom might object to the information he has on them imparted, and may not wish for it to become public knowledge that he worked for them. Now Barb's thinks about it there will be lots of story to tell, lots of life which he has witnessed, real eye-openers.

He has no regrets, really. His wife and children are his legacy. Barb's has lived his life on his terms.

And now, thanks to Claudinalli Tucamkari and her daughter, Dee, he has the opportunity to relive past glories. The thought of aiding her in her quest for revenge against the British Government is not unappealing, they certainly haven't done him many favours, especially in recent months when they tried to purge the non-English elements from their society, dissolving human rights to it's bare bones. The old head of MI6, who authorised the attack on the Tucamkari's base, is dead, as is the agent who was sent to do the deed, but their legacy definitely lives on this new breed of corrupt Government.

ELEVEN

Rose's off-road crossing wasn't available to the duo, which meant going the conventional route. Crossing the controlled border between Scotland and England with it's stringent security checks wasn't as stressful as Scott feared it might be, particularly taking into consideration the entanglements which he and Rose have so far experienced with the local authorities. This apparent ease of passage is a signal to Scott that his own people, his own Security Service, are in collusion with their Scottish equivalent and have told them to let him pass hassle free. They are aiding him but what...? It was too easy! Too convenient. Scott can only hope Rose doesn't realise something is slightly off kilter. Is she really this naive? He doubts it. What explanations can he offer if the question arises? Can he casually enough preempt her?

After the twin-action in Paltournay an image of his and her likeness would surely he circulated to all authorities by now and they would've been stopped at the first opportunity. At least that's the case if he weren't working for a Government organisation. How to explain that? There is another possibility: the Scottish agent's who attacked them were employed by an outside source operating above the law. But this is just silly. And pointless conjecture on Scott's part, and he knows it. The only other hypothesis would be the Scottish Secret Police are after Rose, who used fake ID and a very convincing make-up job, and thus, they have no description of his alter-ego in their possession.

So everything is fine for the time being.

Since passing safely onward Rose has driven silently. They have had the radio for company. Scott might wonder what's going through her mind right now. Is she mulling over their ease of passage, like he is? Does she have an agenda of her own? Has she got to await instructions before killing him, perhaps, once her feelings are made known to William aka Bob? Or should the akabe reversed?

Rose certainly hasn't had any opportunity to be alone and consult William or anyone else by telephone to impart her suspicions since crossing the border so easily. Don't look a gift horse in the mouth, as the expression goes..

So what can Scott do?

Does he take her out of the equation?

He knows their destination. What impact will there be should Scott arrive without Rose? There is a Government safe-house not many miles from Windermere. En route, give or take. Should Scott leave Rose in their hands to extract whatever information she has about the organisation who she is working for? He can pursue the next link in this chain himself.

It's surely his own Government who have placed him in this pickle! Let them deal with her.

Scott is more than capable of concocting some rubbish for the benefit of William and his people to remove suspicion from himself. But what if his plan backfires? So what if his plan fails!? It's worth the gamble. Yes. This is the best option. Get Rose into the hands of the British authorities. Report his findings so far to HQ. Tell them how pissed off he is that they have jeopardised the assignment, then go off the grid to pursue this job which William wants him a part of.

Scott nods involuntarily, which Rose notices. She smiles at him, then averts her eyes once more.

"Lovely countryside."

"Ye can tell we're across the border."

"Yes. Less richness."

"Less water."

"Also true."

75

They are driving through the lowlands around Keswick with the green and orange valley's of the Lake District rolling resplendently before them in the autumnal sunshine, a curiously reassuring sight for Scott. Maybe it's the sign he needs to remind him why he is doing this job in the first place. This beautiful country, his country, is being saved from destruction by terrorists and the unscrupulous destruction being caused by those opposing Prime Minister Alfred McCann and his Government, Generation You. Nature and the countryside is where he grew up, even if that countryside is presently on the opposite side of England, and south a bit, to where he is now located.

It's definitely worth fighting for.

Scott laughs to himself, thinking how much he is sounding like a speech from the people employing him, Generation You and the Prime Minister, or a particularly sunny movie quote.

Rose casts him another brief sideways glance.

"I was just thinking how fickle this life can be." Scott lies, changing his mental tack into something which better suits his undercover profile. "There's a bubbling spring of oppressed people like us in the world throughout history who have stood up and declared that enough is enough."

"And still it goes on."

"Every nation, however great they may claim to be, has experienced rebellion, or an uprising, or revolution. The victors invariably term these losers however they see fit, altering reality to suit themselves, manipulating historical accounts to vilify themselves. And what does that say about those who now run these countries? Their noble goals are often forgotten when they come to rule, discovering greater, more important things come along to distract them. Less noble. Such as money, greed and power. So who are the ones suffering, paying, cowing, to these entities which eventually become like the corporations whose aim is solely to profit for themselves and their elite shareholders? Us, that's who." He lets his impassioned speech hang for a while, the winding country road being ample distraction, before completing his thoughts. "I wonder if we shall be impactful? Shall we be a forgotten cog in a thwarted machine? Not even a footnote in the history written without us?"

"A bit deep for this time of the morning."

"Maybe. Maybe no."

"Definitely maybe."

"What brought you into this type to crusade?" Scott asks; better find out now, before he hands her to the authorities. "Helping the innocent escape the oppressors?"

Rose casts him a sideways glance, her eyes distant, remoteness signalling to Scott that she is doubting his trustworthiness and that he needs to act before she hands him over to...whomever. And vice versa. She displays a remarkably hard exterior for one so young, clearly the experiences she has had, only a small amount of which she mentioned in their conversation of last night in The Prancing Pony, of which Scott doesn't know how much to take at face value, was enough to give a small indication of her past.

"I'm sorry, Scott." She answers. "I want to believe you are...what you say you are, but-"

"But too many things have occurred which have sowed the seeds of doubt." Scott finishes for her, knowing where this conversation is leading. "And I have to agree with you wholeheartedly, which is why I dumped my mobile-phone back at that house. Whoever was tracking me were able to use my phone as a GPS finder. I can only guess my activities were being monitored by Big Brother Britain because the powers that be think I am some kind of troublemaker worthy of stopping before I carry out some conspiracy against them!" He watches her reaction to this information but Rose is concentrating on her driving. "I can only conclude they have an eye-in-the-sky on us right now because we crossed the border too easily for my liking. I should've mentioned my concerns earlier, really, but- so far we are safe."

"Aye. So far."

Scott puts on a look of regretful apology when she casts him a brief glance, and says:

"We should change car if we are to reach our destination without jeopardising William's plans."   And that will be his opportunity, too.

"It's already too late." Rose announces unexpectedly.

As if coordinated simultaneously with Scott turning in his seat the lights of the unmarked police-car behind them begin flashing their intention, signalling a warning to others, perhaps anticipating what comes next.

Scott purses his lips angrily, mentally sending daggers across the space between cars at the driver and his passenger, both who stare determinedly in their direction. Cussing out loud isn't Scott's style but he breaks from character and let's spill. He cannot exactly suggest to Rose that they pull-over.

Their car lurches forward the second Rose drops down two gears while also applying power, pedal-to-the-metal.

Scott can see straight away that their car is not going to be any match whatsoever for the police-car, irrespective of how skilled a driver Rose may be, because their's is a bog-standard family car whereas their pursuers vehicle has inevitably been modified for such chases.

"There's a gun in the glove compartment." Rose informs Scott, she in total focus on the road and her driving.

"Splendiferous."

"Thought you might be pleased."

Trying to remain steady in his seat while the little car takes the bends in the road, speed constantly changing, Scott opens the glove-compartment and pulls out the stub-nosed pistol, flicking off the safety after first checking the rounds - there are only thirteen so he must use them wisely.

"It's a bit compact."

"Size isn't everything."

"Thank goodness!"

Scott doesn't necessarily wish any harm to the officers in the car chasing them down but at the same time he has reached the point of utter frustration at the people who paying them to chase, and also to keep up the pretence to Rose!

Traffic avoids them, blazing angry headlights, motorists gesticulating in an understandably rude manner, but at least the police-car cannot overtake on the twists and turns of the gorgeously scenic Lake District valley pass. It is a dangerous game of cat and mouse which comes to a swift, crashing, rending conclusion at the first opportunity of a shunt from behind, both vehicles coming off the road to a shuddering, deadly halt.

TWELVE

Hiding in plain sight can often be the most effective device for those who wish secrecy when carrying out history-making schemes, although finding the right venue so as to avoid suspicion or unwanted attention can be as equally important as the meeting itself, particularly with Big Brother monitoring the airwaves through any audio device or visual apparatus at their disposal. But find a pokey cafe hidden on the fringes of a no-frills Norfolk coastal village and act as casually as conspirators possibly can, then the freedom to speak without fear of crumbling secrecy can be more readily achieved.

Titchwell Marsh RSPB nature reserve can be reached off the A149 from its tree-lined carpark's or via the beach, but either way it couldn't possibly offer greater seclusion for Claudinalli Tucamkari, Ashley Barber, and their fellow plotters, all equipped appropriately for the venue with undoubtedly expensive bird-watching paraphernalia they shall not use, but it's all part of the facade.

Twenty hours remain.

Ashley has been here before. Twelve months before, in point of fact. Out of respect to a departed work colleague. With Norman. A retired ex-TAMS assistant who used to be a Twitcher friend of their departed colleague. Ashley had enjoyed the peaceful day he and Norman had experienced in the environment of birds. They had visited the commemorative bench which was bought in respect if their departed colleague, Titchwell having been a favourite bird watching locale.

But this moment is different and without melancholy.

With it's promise of big skies, sandy beaches and bird-filled marshes, plus the cafe and a gift shop, this is both an ideal place to watch the wildlife and enjoy relative tranquility without any fuss. Except for the frustratingly stop/start drive here, which Ashley discovered to be quite a chore along the coast-road despite the delightful villages and countryside they passed through en route - great for sight-seeing, which is exactly what he had been able to do when in Norman's company, not so great if you are in a hurry. But, he must admit, it really is a good place for these particular people to meet without raising an eyebrow of suspicion from the genuine visitors, those who are more interested in their own plans for the day than what else might be going in around them: ignorance is indeed bliss!

"William?" Claudinalli speaks first to the Scotsman once they are all gathered around an outdoor circular bench-like table, their Autumnal gear a necessity in the present climate although it's a stretch of the imagination for this imposing woman to blend in seamlessly.

The weather-beaten Scotsman bobs his head as affirmation to the unspoken question. He is the only one of them who might pass as a genuine twitcher in this camouflaged group, his coat, boots and trousers bearing the testimony of time spent in the wilderness for he seems at home in these surroundings. William's big hands hold the entire mug of hot chocolate in them, his fingers cold after journeying from a small rowing boat across the inlet between Norfolk and Lincolnshire, but he doesn't complain, he has experienced worse. Before this meeting began he had expected a phone call from Rose to confirm that she and Scott had gotten safely away from the Scottish Secret Service and through the border this morning, but he has received no such call and hasn't heard from her since last night, so confirming his team's progress to Claudinalli so freely is awkward for him. Embarrassing. This will be first time during their brief acquaintanceship that he hasn't been utterly transparent. William fears a long journey presents itself for him after the conclusion of this meeting, longer if things fail according to plan.

Claudinalli accepts William's response without question. No surprise. This woman has made everyone plainly aware of what success will mean to them and the citizens of this country. This task, a broad statement, has been in the planning for many months and must not fail.

"We're good." The eldest of the two Englishmen present speaks for them both, having coordinated their side of things together with their respective underground organisations, which itself is no easy task considering how tight security has become since Generation You came into power, where all British subjects of a certain age are required to enlist in the Part-time Territorial armed forces, or even become a permanent soldier if their skill-set warrants. These two Englishmen of well-to-do upbringing are twenty-five and twenty-two years of age respectively. The eldest holds a tutor's job at a well-respected University Town, while the other is a student at the same location. Both feel harshly aggrieved by what they perceive as the dictatorship now in power and have been a part of the protesting resistance from the very beginning, seeing a loss of their freedom and wealth instead of the opposite. There are many such factions as theirs, and they hope the events planned for today and tomorrow will draw forth more into the collective conscience who daren't speak up for fear of the repercussions. Not all of those free-thinkers are wealthy brats frightened to lose the stability of the family income, although the even distribution of wealth to English citizens has definitely had its opposition.

The youngest guy consults his watch, grinning like the Cheshire Cat with arrogant satisfaction.

"The first phase is beginning right now." He brags, sipping the filter-coffee with a self-possessed smugness despite the sour taste of cheapness in the beverage.

William tries not to react, his disdain for this type of self-serving, self-righteous, little privileged rich boy might stir up an argument which he cannot be bothered to tackle. Their lot care nothing for the country, just their money!

"And what is this first phase?" Asks the eldest of their motley crew.

"It is something," Claudinalli says cryptically, "which propels us into tomorrow and will be all over the media today."

The man nods acknowledgement even though his scientific mind prefers explanations rather than hidden meaning, facts rather than conjecture. He is the idealistic intellectual academic amongst them whose clothing disguise doesn't sit comfortably upon his frame, shifting awkwardly on the wooden bench. He is definitely not an outdoor person, being more suited to laboratories and seminars, luncheons and research, and the old way, the better way, the EU financed way.

"Is everything prepared your end?" Claudinalli asks the academic.

"Of course," He tells her irritably, not taking a breath, "you know it is I told you what a waste of time it was my coming here but you insisted so here I am but time is precious so hurry along and I can get back to my work."

From the look of controlled anger on Claudinalli's face, Ashley Barber wonders what exactly this man is bringing to the operation happening tomorrow, because its obviously very important, she is being very patient with him. Barbs doubts her calmness would remain such if either of the other men present talked to her with this disrespect. She has only presented a few sketchy details about their endeavour to Ashley, he knows what is happening today, right now, but this woman at their head has obviously kept individual assignments separate to contain the possibility of information falling into unwanted hands. Wisely, naturally. They all know the location of where this scheme is taking place tomorrow because the operation shall require precision timing and coordination: the Humber Bridge.

THIRTEEN

Scott Dalton stands in front of the austere dirty grey pebble-dashed four-storey tenement block with the mobile-phone belonging to the recently deceased young Rose in his hand. The poor girls lifeless body dangling loosely from the car seatbelt will be imprinted forever in his brain. Scott had been lucky to get out of the car unscathed, and quickly, too, because the two police officer's had advanced upon him. Both had been unarmed, signalling to Scott that they had been ill-informed of their quarry, which served Scott well because his red fury at the senseless killing of such a young woman as Rose had sent him berserk. He launched his unnecessarily brutal attack on them and it wasn't until they were on the ground writhing in agony that he finally pulled himself together. After questioning the one who remained conscious Scott could gather no information of true importance - they had been acting on information given to them by superiors, who said they were to transport both he and Rose the nearest police station - so Scott lost his patience and gave up on the questioning, wondering what exactly in the world is going on around him.

It had taken a little over and hour for Scott to travel to this destination, the small village near Gosforth where William aka Bob had sent them, and upon reaching the incongruous tenement building he had touch-dialled the number for William contained on Rose's phone, which he had brought with him, along with her small-calibre pistol with a few bullets remaining. One never knows what dangers one might encounter here.

"Yes, lassie." Comes the familiar deep burr of William's Scottish voice on the other end of the line, clearly expecting Rose to be the caller, and Scott almost regrets the information he is imparting when he tells the man everything that has happened. After a brief silence,

William asks Scott if he is willing to continue with the plan, to which Scott replies in the positive.

"There's a fella called Greg. Tell him ye know me an Rose."

"Is he coming with me?"

"That's the idea."

"Because I don't have a car."

"Then ye better borrow one!"

And then William simply hangs up.

Next Scott dials the number for his Security Service contact but is perplexed to receive no reply whatsoever; the line is completely dead, like it never existed in the first place. His desire to report in is less than theirs to hear from him, obviously. But why? What can possibly be going on that's of more importance than the integrity of this country!?

Scott mentally shrugs to himself, pockets the phone and thinks that he should not be too surprised at the general apathy shown him, considering how many times intervention has almost caused the failure of the assignment. Why was he to be taken into police custody? Had that aim been to remove suspicion from him? Turned out well, that did! Rose is dead!

Ascending the concrete northern-side entrance stairwell of the building which nestles incongruously amongst superior homes in the small village, Scott wonders why this unsightly housing project, which is clearly a quickly erected early-seventies edifice, hasn't been torn down well before now. It is a blight amongst the beauty of the west coast Lake District village and sits uneasily amidst the more modern imitation Edwardian creations that abound it. Perhaps this is another failed and forgotten Government promise, and there have been many similar failures, that is until disaster strikes and lives are lost before note is taken - Grenfell springs to Scott's mind. Prime Minister McCann's promises were handed down from his predecessor, and so on and so forth, but they haven't been actuated here on anyone's pledge. Government's come and go but failed pledges remain the same.

Why the cynicism? Scott must be getting old!

Scott doesn't want to come across like a snob but the sooner he frees himself from these run-down environs which barely classify as habitable the better. Maybe this is like a halfway house for criminals, people cannot actually choose to live here! And these are daylight hours, Scott reflects when he walks along a graffitied back corridor of the topmost floor, sickly opaque light shining through wire-mesh windows. He shudders to think what the place looks like in the dark: what a scar!

Reaching the required door without meeting a single soul en route, he firmly raps his knuckles upon the crumbling painted surface. His other hand in his pocket, reassuringly holding the gun, ready to use it if necessary. Scott looks up the corridor then behind, and the door is eventually opened after much shuffling inside, rattling and scraping on its hinges.

When Scott looks at the occupant he is greeted with doe-eyed indifference by a pallid young woman whose greasy sheen and glazed eyes indicate some psychotropic drug is in effect.

"And?" She slurs without civilised cordiality.

"I need to see Greg." Scott tells her, unsure whether any of the words are getting through, but persisting nonetheless. "William sent me. I was with Rose."

"So?" She responds, her face at least giving some indication that one or some of the trio of names he has just mentioned ring some far-away bells in the farthest recesses of her brain. She sways against the door frame, looking vaguely along the corridor past him. "Where are they?"

Instinctively Scott follows her gaze although he is fully aware the two aren't here and it is this action which saves his life because it is the woman's brains which are blown out by the first shot fired from a gunman who has seemingly ascended from nowhere.

While the first shot still rings deafeningly inside the concrete obscenity, Scott dives over the still falling woman's dead body into the room. He rolls with practised efficiency onto the questionably carpeted floor of the sitting-room. A second gunshot smacks into the door-frame precisely where his head had been moments before, debris landing atop the dead woman, blood from her severe head trauma pooling beneath her.

An undefined smell consisting of mould, damp, sweat, smoke, burnt food, dope and rubber floats in the atmosphere of the room. It clings to the back of Scott's nose and throat as he springs to his feet. He instantly gets his bearings, the room layout doesn't take much digestion. Bounding over the tacky green stained and battered sofa, Scott slips on something on the floor the other side of the sofa which doesn't bear thinking about before he skitters into the flat's confined tiled hallway and pushes open the door nearest.

The smell wafting in the air in the bedroom is unprintable here because it's disgusting enough without describing it and makes Scott gag.

Upon the bed the dirty sheets speak volumes, while the woman atop them is in a naked spaced-out state of self-pleasuring frenzy that she doesn't even register his presence. The man kneeling at the foot of the bed, who might very well be the Greg whom Scott is looking for but doesn't have time to ask, watches the woman with uncontainable enjoyment. Neither seem bothered about this new arrival or to have heard the commotion in the corridor, making Scott wonder if intrusion isn't so new to them.

Aware of the probability that the gunman is not too far behind, Scott strides over the woman and bed, flings open the only window whose ancient metal frame creaks in protest at the unfamiliar action yet yielding to his weight behind it.

Scott recklessly cares not about the precarious height but he is grateful for the rickety wrought-iron fire-escape ladder which he had prudently made a mental note of when he had reconnoitred the perimeter not more than ten minutes ago, while he is equally pleased the window is so close to it. He swings onto the ladder which pulls away from the wall with sickening ease under his weight, the ground rushing upward at him.

FOURTEEN

Prime Minister Alfred McCann slumps in his chair in the stateroom of No. 10 Downing Street completely broken by the news he has just received. He has gone sick to the stomach. Mouth dry. Legs heavy. Hands shaking uncontrollably. Shock. Dread. Foreboding. Anger and frustration. He cannot get his head round it. He must avoid knee-jerk reactions. But how? How? How can he avoid acting upon this news? But think logically. First of all, is it real? He hopes not. But he knows it is. Denial. Proof. Facts. Facts in his hand. A picture of the facts in his ice cold hand which cannot stop shaking from anger, from shock. What more proof does he need?

When the rumblings of non-hostile protests had begun at Oxford University the information was filtered through the usual channels. Quite unhurriedly as per protocol. Mostly because other Governmental departments were in place to deal with such scuffles, and the Prime Minister of Great Britain had other important memorandum's today to attend regarding progress in certain sectors of the utilities, which, since leaving the iron clutches of the EU, had been placed back under state jurisdiction, benefitting customers who have saved hundreds of pounds since. This had been one of his promises upon taking power, one of his first successes implemented, and he was scrutinising them intensely to ensure avoidance of what was once termed the "Fat-Cat's"; namely those money-grabbers greedily lining their own pockets at the expense of the general public. There is nothing wrong with free enterprise so long as it isn't utterly unscrupulous. For too many years the needs of self-made shareholders playing golf on their off-days, which were numerous, had been better catered for than those less privileged. It had taken time for a younger, more innocent, Alfred McCann to fulfil his dreams because of the elite establishment, so he knows exactly what it can feel like to be opposed from those with money. The tide of change is very slowly reversing.

It has been ten minutes after the first footnote about the protests in Oxford before peaceful did an about-turn. The local police were called, which subsequently alerted the Security Service's at Headquarters who then informed the Prime Minister that these events had begun to escalate, to gain a certain amount of media attention.

Instinctively McCann had switched on the television to the London BBC station he had become accustomed to, preferring their liberal, Government approved broadcasting method rather than the other more scandalous, scare-mongering alternatives which relied heavily on shock, awe and hyperbole. Adverts now paid for the BBC, not those once forced into paying an archaic licence fee.

This is the University which his daughter attends and the inflammatory reporting possibilities of this fact are not lost on McCann. The haters would love the story if she were to be involved directly in this latest skirmish, especially if it is voiced against some Government legislation like the previous protests of this nature. This would not be the first time his daughter has been involved in such a scandal, and the less scrupulous media had a field-day. But the strap-line running along the bottom of the television screen points to something more deep-seated and troublesome occurring. There is the declaration, which McCann expected, that this was a soured peaceful demonstration which rapidly descended into chaos when opposing factions clashed.

Universities are prime institutes for passionate debate and differences, they always have been and they always will be, no matter how much of the behaviour is structure enforced, but to McCann's professional gaze he can see immediately this is a coordinated conflagration. But by whom?

The First Minister, McCann's most senior Government supporter, stands silently by the door, watching the Prime Minister. He is the bearer of this news. He feels responsible for his chief's turmoil, now, the tears tightly concealed in the twisted features of the young man in charge.

On the television the newscaster talks to her on-the-spot reporter, a man whose voice is solemn, trained, professional, precise. Statistics scroll along the ticker-tape banner which splits the screen near the very bottom. Statistics of injuries. How many police are on the scene. The number of emergency vehicles. Ambulances at the scene. Behind the reporter an orange, strobing, smoky gash in the skyline which itself is behind an old University building, its clock a white, sad face, harsh against the reds, tangerine blaze and grey smoke.

"Students were seen," the reporter is saying, "letting off makeshift Molotov cocktails. This is as near as we have been allowed to get and you can see the devastation. The number of casualties increases by the minute. We have a number of confirmed fatalities. While the police have yet to disclose what has caused this tragedy, there are reports of involvement from several members of the so-called Resistance. "

The Prime Minister sighs deeply. Concern sits heavily on his dark eyes. His brow is furrowed. He has aged in the past ten minutes. The Resistance. Hard to believe such an organisation lives in England. This would be bad enough as it is. Innocent lives once more snatched early. Possibilities killed. Ideas quashed. Bright futures nurtured before being obliterated from existence. Caused by a movement of resistance here, in England, in a Land of Hope and Glory, led by Generation You, a force for good.

Why do these acts of wilful terrorism continue? What more can McCann offer to protect his people?

Tighten national security further?

Create a police state?

These are unthinkable even to one such as he who has risen to his position through support from those who extol worse wishes for his enemies. But these dead people aren't his enemies. These dead are citizens of this great country. They are his people. His loved ones.

"Is this-" McCann stumbles on his words limply, desolately, brandishing the photograph in his hand as if they are infectious, emotion crushing his larynx like a vice and he has to draw forth upon his great composure from some hidden recess of his mind to continue. "Is this...known to anyone else?"

The First Minister slowly shakes his head: "The photographer is one of ours. Nobody out of this room but him has seen it, but-"

"Time is of the essence."

"Yes, sir."

"And I need to make a call."

"Yes, sir. Sorry."

There is no need to continue. The Prime Minister knows it is just a short matter of time before someone else makes positive identification. If the connection isn't already made. This kind of news doesn't stay private, not in this or any age.

McCann gulps. Finally the suppressed tears spring out. He cannot control them any longer.

The First Minister politely and respectfully busies himself with a shirt button, straightens his tie, anything to give the chief some modicum of privacy in this grim narrative.

Through teary eyes the leader of England looks upon the grainy colour photograph, a broken man.

His own daughter!

The photo. The eyes closed in death. A peaceful face.

Milena must be told. His wife must hear it from him. Not from some loose-talking paparazzi. His own daughter. What will her brother think? Where is he? Is he safe? Where is Milena? Is his wife safe?

Panic takes over from logic. And anger replaces composure.

He bangs a fist on the top of his table. Someone is going to pay. Someone is going to wish they had thought twice about this! Almost twenty years he has been in the political business! There has been turmoil. And before that. McCann has dealt with many things. But this is the worst.

For some reason he looks to his aid. A man who he has known since getting into Government. Not before. Not a lifelong friend like Giuliano, but a political aid. Quite randomly the thought pops into his head. The recollection of the day it was decided he should consider pursuing this new path into the political arena, one on a distinct tangent with the movie business he has long left behind.

FIFTEEN

On the stage of Screen Number One in Leicester Square's most prestigious of cinema's, the Odeon, stands twenty-six year old Alfred McCann addressing his colleagues and their families. This in 1997. Winter. McCann is the wunderkind entrepreneur who has built up the successful Hammicass Studios from nothing into a respected British movie producing company. His Italian wife and their two children, one an infant, the other a mere babe, watch proudly front and centre amongst the glitterati. This evening is about celebrating past achievements and lauding future releases, but most of all it is the pride McCann shares with all who endeavoured upon their latest release, premiered that very night not thirty minutes ago across all screens of this fabled establishment to great and justifiable acclaim.

Hammicass Studios were officially christened as a movie and television production company a mere three years previously, in 1994, with future Prime Minister of Great Britain Alfred McCann as it's co-founder and Chief Executive Officer, along with his business partner and best friend Giuliano Badalamenti as Production Chief. Their company set-up produces in the lower echelon of what might be termed modestly budgeted horror and action films, having already established markets for themselves in Italy and Japan for these products, building a solid financial springboard from which to create movies which the established elite could deem acceptable, and increasing their profile while remembering their roots. With determination and the right connections this duo with their mutual passion for movies gradually edged their way into the snobbery which had formally sniffed condescendingly at the upstarts who they saw as riding the coattails of their successful Italian benefactors.

94

"Three years of hard work from you all has brought us to this moment." Alfred McCann says with sincere pride into the microphone when he addresses the gathered men and women in the auditorium.

A rapturous round of applause follows his remark, everyone knowing it is really the duo who has transformed their own fortunes with insight and unrelenting passion, reaching the point where this highly-praised feature called A Crazy Life registered through-the-roof preview scores a month ago and now, just twenty-minutes after the first official press screening, this contemporary comedy drama is already causing a buzz. Yet despite this move into mainstream fair, McCann and Badalamenti are not moving away from their core independent sector, their roots, where they have successfully nurtured previously overlooked British and European filmmaking talent overlooked by the snobbery.

"Thank you." The CEO says once the applause dies down, his smile one of genuine pride. "Its true. If not for the commitment to our vision and the confidence from our families we might have failed where others stumbled. We might now be nothing more than a footnote in the annals of movie making history. For this, my sincere thanks goes to all of you." Another round of applause ensues, with McCann clapping too. "When Giuliano and I entered this business we were sneered at by the established community. Some of those gathered in this very building today scoffed at our proclamations and declarations for achieving success on our terms." He adds with a sly, knowing grin: "And my friends back in Italy dealt with the hardened detractors severely!" This gets a laugh. "Together we have done what others claimed was the impossible. But it is your faith and not inconsiderable skill which has continually proven them wrong. We have kept a stiff-upper lip when faced with adversity and have prevailed on all fronts. And I do not just mean just commercially, because now, with A Crazy Life, I think I can confidently say we have the critics on our side for a change."

A ripple of laughter fills the auditorium from the knowledgable people within. For three years those self-proclaimed movie critics who consider anything but art as tasteless, who have condescendingly deemed Hammicass product to be unworthy trash solely marketed toward the lower-class, turning their noses up at each and every release like they know best, have acknowledge A Crazy Life is more their cup of expensive Earl Grey. Based on an acclaimed stage play always helps and made with a renowned director, pedigree cast and the studio's usual reliable crew, this production, poetically No.100 on the Hammicass Studios' roster, is set for a swift change in critic opinion- pretentious bowing of heads by those who know best finally seeing the light. The publicity has already reached a greater level than the ninety-nine film output thus far from Hammicass, so exciting times and untold possibilities indeed beckon.

"We are shaping a unique success within the British film industry today." McCann continues. "By thinking outside the stoical box of traditional English film-making heritage, while also respecting those who have come before us, our films are reaching further across the world, finding greater audience acceptance, bringing us in line with the upper echelon's of our business. If A Crazy Life is the success we anticipate our expansion plan shall be two-fold, while our continued investment in British talent continues and your personal dividends increase in worth."

While the auditorium erupts with the expected cheering there is one man who watches Alfred McCann with greater pride than most, an Italian whose eye for talent spotted the young man first of all, and only a short span of seven years when Alfred first came to his studio with his nephew, Giuliano. He notices how the crowd lean into Alfred's every word, drawing inspiration from the charismatic leader up on the stage and their loyalty is clear, passionate and devoted.

"I thank you all sincerely," Alfred says, "for your support when enforcing and focusing on this vision for Hammicass. We have already gone beyond what I first envisioned this studio to be when I was just a novice entering the movie world with my friend, and business partner, Giuliano Badalamenti. It began as a flight of fancy and if not for him I should not be here today, and as he has family business back home in Italy so is unable to be here, I think we should all extend our gratitude to his Uncle, my Godfather."

The clapping begins slightly awkwardly this time because of the stereotype many people have toward the Italian use of Godfather as patriarch, but under McCann's guidance they realise it is a heartfelt expression of love and gratitude, rather than an overbearing Mafia-type figure who expects supplication. The Italian plays along, standing, turning, bowing gracefully, and despite years of experience he cannot help but marvel at Alfred's ability to put them in the palm of his hand so easily, thinking that such power could be a useful tool if the young man were ever to consider entering the world of politics. This is the moment.

SIXTEEN

From the very brief undercover experience Scott Dalton has had as a Hollywood stuntman he is fortunate enough to know how to control his body when falling uncontrollably; relax the joints so they don't break, which might seem obvious but if it were really that easy there would be fewer broken bones at A&E; roll naturally, using momentum to avoid serious injury; and practise with your team, have an airbag ready for high falls, stacked empty boxes for low dramatic tumbles.

Unfortunately these things don't allow for zero preparation time in real life so when the rusty ladder crumbles at its joints from the wall and a shower of dust drops onto Scott, grit and shavings in his mouth, he is sailing through the air without the knowledge of a safety net below him. In point of fact he recalls there is going to be very hard concrete for a landing pad, which from four-storey's up will definitely cause injury unless a person possesses superpowers!

Life doesn't so much as pass before his eyes because the sheer ugliness of the building which he falls from is full in his vision, along with a lingering image from the room he has just departed. Neither pretty images to die on! And nor the kinky sex act, but a thing which shouldn't have been in the bedroom, incongruous with the prevailing surroundings yet perhaps in bizarre synchronicity. Who can tell? Will he get the opportunity to find out the answer himself?

A second before his heart figuratively leapt out his mouth Scott Dalton saw something arguably more dubious than the drug-fuelled sexual shenanigans he left behind.

Completely out of context with everything else, in fact.

And not dubious: terrifying!

It was a clean and shiny aluminium or stainless-steel case, brushed metal, roughly the size of a large briefcase - or small suitcase.

Upon its side was a yellow and red hazardous material warning symbol emblazoned unmistakably upon it. No writing, just the symbol. Could be nothing. Might be something.

It was a brief sighting but enough to make Scott's sixth sense blare a loud warning signal itself. He hadn't imagined it. It was real. Under the bed. And contained what? Toxic waste in a druggy sex-den? Not an impossibility if one considers the gruesome aspects!

Might be nothing. Might be something. Worth investigating.

His fingers and palms scream hot, painful, as he grips the sides of the ladder. His body takes the direction of gravity, the downward swing quite rapid yet slowly surreal. Like dream of falling. Or nightmare. The breeze an imperceptible brush upon his face and hair, like the whispering voice of death welcoming him into it's kingdom. His fingers bite. His grip is hard. Rust particles and concrete dust falls into his face, grit in his eyes Daylight above, the building a view from a blur of pendulum motion.

This is it. Is this it? Life. Death. Crippling injury followed by a bullet to the head to eliminate the pain? That sounds nice!

Instead an abrupt but shocking, jarring halt, metal reverberating through his arms, bouncing upward an inch or two from momentum only. Shuddering through Scott's bones, forcing him to lose his grip, bracing himself for broken ankles, remembering, remembering.

Was the drop only two feet?

Still painful but no time to stop and think, thank his lucky stars instead because the gunman is now in the bedroom looking out.

Scott's CIA-trained reflexes snap into action!

A roll protectively behind a car, bullets splashing hot lead against metal, brick, concrete, ricocheting in a deadly dance of sharp shards. Shattering glass.

Catching his breath at last, Scott blinks the dirt from his eyes. Don't wipe them, that only makes it worse and might scratch his corneas. Blink away the unforced tears. Stinging. The blur clearing.

Held at the topmost point of the fire-escape ladder, Scott see's that he was saved by the brick bunker where residents of the flats store their dustbins. The dangerous ladder is resting upon it, still attached to the building but only just. Should he be surprised by the lack of health and safety?

Silence.

Scott takes this as his cue to make a run across the forty yards between him and the entrance to the tenement building. The shooter is obviously changing his magazine, clipping in another, hoping to catch something flammable next time. With this in mind Scott grits his teeth to suppress the pain and tension which courses through him and leaps like a cat before sprinting full-pelt toward the building. He skitters on some indefinable debris. Almost falls. Almost fatal. But eventually he reaches the wall, pressing hard against it, panting, heart pounding in his chest, dodging one more bullet.

A new determination sets in. He checks the pistol, Rose's pistol. Six shots remain available to him? Scott has lost count if how many he has loosed at the unmarked police-car earlier that afternoon, now he knows.

There is no time to think so Scott doesn't.

Wrenching open the same door by which he entered the building barely five minutes previously he bounds up the flight of concrete steps, ascending rapidly, noisily, but there's no point in pussy-footing around now, trying to conceal his intentions, being overtly cautious is wasted. The gunman will be expecting him so Scott needs to get into position quickly.

When he reaches the upper corridor all has gone eerily quiet, the calm between the storms!

And still no tenants.

Positioning himself with a clear view of the open door, bare female legs projecting grotesquely from it upon the ground, Scott wonders for the first time who this gunman is, exactly, and who sent him. Is this just another repeat of events from earlier, only with a more deadly purpose? Scott shakes his head. His own people want to fast-forward events, not put a halt to them. But the man is a trained killer. Who would hire him? William's people, perhaps? The Scotsman has informed them of Rose's fate, told William to eliminate the Englishman, and this is the result. Or is Scott clutching at straws? Reading too much into the situation? The question must be: can Scott take the gunman alive and actually find out some facts about these people? Any nugget of information is better than being totally unaware of what the hell is really going on! A mouse being chased by too many cats. From here he will go to London, to the Security Service headquarters, confront his chief, discover the motives and end it once and for all.

But that's for later.

The first bullet smashes into the ratty plaster wall about two-feet in front of and above Scott's head, showering him with ancient dust, forcing him back, eyes watering again, cursing.

A second shot whizzes past his corner of the wall, exploding against the stairwell, creating a crescendo of sound. Between the two Scott was able to loose off a single, ineffectual shot of his own, before retreating back out of sight.

Blinking furiously to clear more grit from his eyes, Scott sucks in a breath. His last? Before throwing caution to the wind. He takes two clean strides to the opposite side of the hallway, shoulder hard against the grimy wall, milky light shining in through the dirty, mesh-filled glass, while he simultaneously aims at the open doorway, senses impending movement, squeezes the trigger and pegs the gunman the instant he exposes himself from cover, knocking the man off-balance, his gun arm smacking hard against the door frame, weapon spinning onto the floor into the hallway.

A stupendously lucky shot.

Scott grins, satisfied. Now for the denouement. He says:

"Step into the open."

And the man complies, clutching his bloodied sleeve, pain contorting his face. Good.

The gunman is slight of build, quite short, stocky, about five seven, dressed in combat trousers and bomber-jacket in matching camouflage green, and Doc Martens. Scott would estimate he is in his early forties. His finely cropped military-style haircut is greying, his dark face etched with life's wrinkles.

"Unless a gunfight is a common occurrence here," Scott says, thinking with irony that perhaps it is, "then someone will have alerted the police already. Now...I don't know about you," he continues, advancing toward the gunman, gun unwavering, "but I shouldn't like to get caught up in a lengthy series of questions and the subsequent investigation- places to be, and all that." Scott stops ten feet in front of the man. "There's time for us both to leave. Your wound isn't fatal, but you probably know that, right? So...who do you work for?"

The gunman purses his lips, realising the futility of their situation and understanding the sense in Scott's words, plus not particularly wishing to ruin his career by ending up in prison.

"I was hired to kill the first visitor to this flat." The gunman explains. "I don't know by whom and I don't know who you are." He tells Scott, the look of pained sincerity difficult to disbelieve. "All I know is- they paid well, told me to keep schtum like I usually do, so it's obviously someone who has benefitted from these services before." A shrug is attempted but discarded with a wince. "And that's it."

"When were you asked to get here?" Scott asks.

"Not much before you arrived." He says. "About an hour ago."

Scott nods thoughtfully, frustratingly still none the wiser. He wants to ask if this gunman has been used by the Government but doesn't want to give too much away himself. He seems to be truthful in what he has said. What does he gave to lose?

Yet more ambiguity. Scott frustrated, once more.

"You spoke to the person?" Scott asks.

"Sure."

"Did he have an accent?"

After much thought, the gunman shakes his head.

"Not particularly." He says.

Trying his best to show zero emotion, Scott gives a small open-palmed gesture to signal the gunman can go now, and, clutching his wounded arm, the grateful gunman departs.

Scott picks up the superior gun from the floor, tossing his own, Rose's pistol, away. How long will the police take to arrive? He hopes the complete waste of time questioning hasn't ruined his own possible escape.

Crossing through the sitting room Scott goes straight to bedroom without further ado. The woman on the bed and her male companion are both dead, otherwise they have matching 3-D bullet-hole tattoos in the centre of their foreheads. Before bending to examine the suspicious object under the bed, Scott glances out the window. All seems peaceful, as it does inside the building. Maybe there are very few tenants. Which doesn't particularly surprise him. There are no sirens. No panic. Nothing but the rooftops, chimney smoke, birds in flight, distant noise of a car, a boat, the wind. All is good.

103

Scott tentatively pulls the finely corrugated aluminium suitcase-sized container out from under the bed, its hazardous material warning signs vibrant against the brushed silver. It has twin combination locks. Feeling its weight, Scott picks it up. Its not heavy. What to do with it? Phone William, tell the Scotsman he has retrieved it, arrange a location to meet up? This was obviously going to be Rose's objective. Maybe the plot will be revealed more after this action? But Scott needs to know what it contains. How can he get into it without William or his people discovering it has been tampered with? There is one possibility. One person he knows who can be trusted to help. It means getting to Nottingham without a car, for the time being, and with the potentially hazardous case in tow. No time to waste. Scott sets out upon his way.

Shorty after the hitman exits the ratty building the Observer steps out from her car, engine running, binoculars still aimed at the grey tenement. She wonders if Scott Dalton came off better or worse than the injured hitman. But the man looked angry. Not just in pain. And he jacket was flapping open like there was no gun. Maybe he dumped it. Maybe Scott took it.

She wonders too who paid for the hitman's services. Certainly not her own people. She would know. He has done jobs for them in the past, but not this one.

So who? And why?

For the reason she has been asked to keep close watch on Scott?

Possibly.

Since the word got to her that British Agent Scott Dalton is working undercover and may or may not have gone rogue her entire network has been alerted. She has been told to take him out. Maybe the job has already been done for him. But something else is amiss. She cannot kill in cold blood without hard facts.

Scott Dalton eventually appears from the building. His looks around furtively. In his right hand in an aluminium case. Curious.

She climbs back into her car, not taking her eyes of British Agent Scott Dalton.

SEVENTEEN

Prime Minister Alfred McCann is in his family home in Oxfordshire with his wife, son, and several security personnel to ensure their continued safety after the cessation of the politically charged events at the University, concerned these might be a precursor to something larger. Events which has resulted in the loss of McCann's daughter's life. The family have converged on their home, inundated with condolences from various luminaries, but they need this evening away from the spotlight to properly grieve because such a thing is virtually impossible to do when every paparazzi and their editor in the country wants a scoop. A scandal hurts real people. A death hurts real people. But real people forget about those whom they see in the papers or on other media because, to real people, these celebrities exist only to entertain, to pity their latest extravagance, sneer at their newest quirk. Because celebrities, to real people, have no feelings and therefore cannot feel grief.

Not true, of course.

People are people no matter what their station in life.

And this is McCann's family. His own family.

Eighteen hours remain.

This first family are grieving like any other family grieves when such a huge personality is taken from their collective. And such a young personality. A personality in its stage of growth from childhood, out of the teens and into adulthood. A young life. One barely twenty years of age. Learning, developing, becoming the adult. It is easy to assume that such a person from a high-profile family who lives in a spotlight has the privilege to live more affluently and to do more, exist more, experience more. Which is certainly true to an extent, especially for ordinary people who rely on media for their filtered, glossed up, or salacious tabloid information. Yet to her parents, losing their daughter who was only three months shy of turning twenty-one, a supposed milestone in one's life, it is unbearable to contemplate.

A child.

Dead before their parents.

Who will never experience becoming a parent of her own.

And Alfred McCann sits in his favourite chair shifting uncomfortably, unable to settle, unable to motivate himself to get up, to do something, anything. The glass of brandy, the best brandy, does nothing to nurse his mind. Whirling ice around the bottom of the glass. A whirling mind. Confused. Why? Why his daughter? Why his family? His poor, poor, broken wife. And what is the boy, their son, really thinking or feeling?

And his best friend too. Giuliano. Such an important member of their extended family. He offered help. Help from the family. What sort of help? The implications of that kind from an Italian family might speak volumes.

But nobody can help. Nobody can bring his daughter back. None of the others with all their power, all their wealth, all their best intended wishes can reverse what has happened. Powerless. Money cannot buy the life he has lost.

He swigs a drop of brandy, its warm, powerful taste igniting angrily against the dryness in his mouth, on his heaving hard chest, and wallowing in his empty stomach.

Nobody can bring her back. His baby. A gift in his gifted life. Alfred McCann: successful businessman and Prime Minister, he thinks cynically. Now, he is nothing. What does it all mean? What was it all for? If not for family, what's the point? Why go on?

Another burst of alcohol adds twisted fuel to his fire and he knows it isn't helping, just making things worse, masking clarity, creating false truths and lies, but Alfred McCann doesn't care.

Milena is in the kitchen.

He can hear her preparing a delicious dinner.

With their son. He is being helpful, strong like his mother. Strong like his daughter.

McCann knows he himself is to blame. He put his family in this position. It was his decision alone that has taken his daughter's life.

EIGHTEEN

His children kiss him goodbye as they board the school bus on their three-mile journey into town because, despite his wealth and very good fortune, Alfred McCann wishes for their first informative years to be as normal as possible before sending them to a better, private school, for education. Milena protested at first, naturally, but only because their safety is her most paramount concern. Alfred was able to convince her this was a good way to keep their offspring as grounded as possible in the realities of life which, she eventually admitted, is exactly the kind of lifestyle she herself has tried to maintain at their home in England, and when in Italy, however privileged they might be.

The key word is: grounded. A difficult thing to attain when success and money and power are involved but Alfred is determined his children will not be spoilt brats in a world of increasing celebrity nobody brats, those who ride the coattails of others without achieving anything by hard work for themselves. In reality he knows State schooling unintentionally fails too many children with uninspiring parrot fashion conditioning, but this fitting-in to the drone society is what they are setting out in the curriculum. Alfred's life soared well above the expectations of his moderate upbringing despite latterly the elite classes attempting to thwart his charisma and achievements.

Milena remains less enthusiastic about these benefits of placing her children amongst 'real' children. She would prefer to home-school them into more rounded human's but her family agree with Alfred and in the end, if it fails, she can always get her way eventually. She wants what is best for her children and sometimes a parent doesn't quite know what is truly best so need guidance. Milena also worries about their safety as her husband's recognisability is increasing, and this might endanger their safety in Public School from the more unscrupulous members of society.

But this is just part of the risk of living in their world.

Mum and Dad wave proudly at their children in the departing bus until is disappears from view around a bend in the road.

Taking his wife's hand, Alfred and Milena walk slowly along the footpath toward the avenue where they live, in a desirable property in an affluent part of an Oxfordshire village. She squeezes his hand.

"You know I support you one-hundred percent?" Milena says to her husband in Italian.

Alfred McCann's chest swells with pride as he looks at his wife, the love radiating undeniably from her eyes, and he smiles. This enthusiasm he had as he matured from boy to man has never left him. He feared it might, however much he resisted. Life often takes the joy from people. But not him. In the world of Italian business he has flourished, possessing their spirit for life as his own, learning and improving and channeling his passions by inspiring others. Alfred owes a great debt to Franco, and his nephew, Giuliano, Badalamemti, over these past years, and their friendship is as strong as ever but as his enthusiasm for the movie business continues, so does his outlook tor the future, particularly within the community that is the English film industry. Which is primarily why has chosen to make his home and base in this country. England is the place where he grew up, it is the place he holds in his heart with almost as much emotion as he has for his family. Through his connections in filmdom, he has discovered such a talent-pool which has been suppressed by the so-called self-appointed elite, where success is inherited rather than nurtured, he decided long ago enough is enough.

Too much red-tape and protocol restricts a corrupted system and unless you operate within the system you have restricted access.

This is true not just in the film business, but it has been Alfred's nurturing of young people who were in similar situations to him in his early teens, that with his own success flourishing, he was able to change antiquated ideas for the better, achieving a small victory, recognising where the country is lacking.

Nurture is the buzz word in his company.

Petty bureaucrats have often been the most obstructive, particularly when it came to expansion of the Hammicass Studios complex. Trying to convince the local councils as to the extent of business brought into the area by the studio already and the various positive implications for greater profits in the region, has been a frustrating task. Many businesses have flung open their arms, welcoming the film community and its money but the near-sighted MP's, old-school Lords, and self-aggrandising experts who run the country seem to stand in his way. It's like the English aristocracy don't like success in their own country from their own people. Which, to Alfred, seems utterly ridiculous, not to mention frustrating. So the money which began his company came from Europe, from an Italian conglomerate, but since the swelling of Hammicass's dealings full ownership is now British, with monies benefiting the United Kingdom.

Through his own success, Alfred has been asked to join many multi-national business seminars and lectures where he has extolled and promoted British products and values, gathering around him such a culture of change that, passingly, several influential figures have suggested he enter the world of politics.

Initially he dispelled the notion but gradually, slowly, as he sought advice from others including his Italian and English families, he gained inroads into political discussions, airing his views on television programs and bringing a new, youthful, approach to old ideas. His popularity simply grew and grew from there but it wasn't enough for him to merely join a staid political party, he needed more.

With the help and support of Giuliano and family advisors, he devised an agenda for a new party, saluting the past within the present while pushing into the future, a new future.

"Generation You." Alfred says to his wife Milena in a voice which is barely a whisper, a reverential tone that signals intentions and goals, enjoying the sound of this new name in politics which is to be officially announced that day, that very afternoon, to great fanfare in the Houses of Parliament, by his representatives, while he himself is conducting a press conference immediately after the declaration of intent has been made. He shouldn't be excited, he should be a stoic Englishman, but he cannot help himself.

"Still perfect." Milena responds.

Alfred grins like a school-boy before kissing her on the forehead, thinking how fortunate he has been to have such a supportive person in his life, a woman who loves him, encourages him, and challenges him daily to be a better human. Milena is the foundation upon which he shapes his life, and he is the skyscraper reaching for the heavens.

"Ten years ago," Alfred says wistfully, "I could never have dreamed I should be married to the most beautiful lady in the world. Uncle Franco's best gift has been my meeting you, lovely Milena. Is all this really possible for an ordinary boy from England?"

"But you are not ordinary." She tells him, her eyes watery with pride, entwining her arms about his neck and kissing him firmly, lovingly, reassuringly, and passionately, upon the lips.

Melina steps back, face red, neck flushed, but not at all self-consciously.

"Now, now, Mrs McCann." Alfred pretends to berate her. "Such displays are quite improper for an English politician and his wife, don't you know?"

"Then when you become Prime Minister," Milena says, embracing him once more, "I suggest you change policy!"

NINETEEN

Their daughter, and sister's, presence hadn't been felt here for too many weeks. So what if they didn't see eye to eye all the time, what family truly does? She and her father clashed often. Alfred doesn't expect everyone to bow and scrape to him. His wife doesn't. Neither does his son, although he shares the youthful enthusiasm which Alfred had for movies at his age. But their arguments were about politics and ideas, never breaking down the family, while nearly always ending amicably. Despite the feeling which Alfred had that she was keeping secrets about how deeply buried her feelings were. Secrets which came out through sources he had at the University. But he never mentioned them to her, never interfered in that aspect of her life. Alfred always respected his daughter's opinions. Even if he did not always agree with them. He was watching her to protect her, like any father would, not to interfere in her life.

Senseless. Meaningless. Wasteful.

Hurt beyond anything Alfred has previously experienced. An equalling of balances? Maybe. His life was going smoothly. Too smoothly? Something had to happen to redress this lucky-streak imbalance. This good fortune. It couldn't last forever.

Why was Alfred not able to do more to protect his family? Keep all of them safe? He of all people is fully aware of the dangers rife in the land. They cannot help. It is the nature of people, of humans. They cannot be trusted. Their influence can corrupt. Will corrupt. Twist the knife to inflict more hurt.

But- his daughter?

Angrily Alfred McCann empties the brandy glass, the beverage barely hitting his tastebuds, and despite the knowledge the alcohol is doing more harm than good, he pours himself another.

Despite the harm? To spite the harm? To spite himself. Perhaps even to deliberately increase his hatred for those who have caused his daughter's death. Alcohol will do that.

Who are they-?

More importantly: why do they exist?

The protest was a peaceful demonstration of differing opinions, a classroom debate gone mainstream. But it wasn't the protestors themselves who incited the violence, this much has been revealed by the preliminary reports from his own Security Service, and backed up by the surprise resonating through the University itself in the aftermath.

So who, then? Was his daughter targeted? Was it someone determined to undermine this new era for England? To undo all the good work he and his team have done thus far by instilling fear in the population. Fear. Terror. Why do these terrorists think they can continue these acts of fear without retribution?

Pathetic!

Enough is enough!

McCann isn't going to be frightened off by some stupid, reckless ingrates who believe in a helpless cause. Idiots who cause wilful death under the falsehood of misplaced religious conviction.

Alcohol be-damned.

Tomorrow, he will show these mongers of hate that he is not bowing down to them. They probably want him to cancel his visit to York Minster. They expect him to cower. Their gloating will be short lived. And what better place to show them he is making a complete stand against terrorism by appearing in public at York Minster while simultaneously grieving for the loss of his daughter. Such strength he can convey by doing so. His team, his people, will show solidarity to wipe these bigots off the face of the earth once and for all. This is the British spirit. The Bulldog breed. Enough is enough.

TWENTY

Internet search-engines are all well and good but they haven't been much help to Scott Dalton when he tries finding out exactly what the hazardous material symbol on the aluminium case might mean. All the results are simply too ambiguous, ranging from toxic waste to raw plutonium to Dead Mutants video gaming! All three are possibilities, the first two of which he hopes are not presently in his possession on the train seat beside him. The only thing he has learned from Rose's phone is the media reporting on the Oxford attacks this very afternoon, and the death of Alfred McCann's daughter, with quotes from the Prime Minister and her elder brother.

A tragedy which the media are loving to bits, their own condolences smacking of desperation to be the first with a scoop.

But this media operation is none of his business.

Scott does wonder if these events in Oxford might have been avoidable had his people not interfered with his own trail. He might have alerted someone before it happened. Or not. There might be no connection whatsoever. Or maybe there is. Maybe William aka Bob is the kingpin. Maybe that's where he was when Scott phoned earlier in the afternoon.

Scott laughs at his own speculation. Can he be any more ludicrous?

Yes. Easily.

Such as boarding a public train for Nottingham when persons unknown are after him! That's pretty ludicrous. It stands to reason that whoever is following him can easily locate him on public transport. So-why not use it anyway? What does he have to lose? Not much. Except maybe his life should there be something explosive in the case. Nobody is following, of this he is certain.

He pulls the mobile phone out of his pocket once more, considering his options. If he contacts William now he shall undoubtedly be prematurely forced into a rendezvous before discovering anything further about the case contents, and perhaps lose the advantage should some scheme which requires said contents be imminent. So Scott needs them examined first, by an expert, whose home is not many miles from his destination. But if he fails to contact William, the Scotsman's suspicions are bound to be aroused. Or are they? What excuse might Scott concoct?

The countryside flashing by the window offers Scott no help, and no comfort, either. Fields, trees, hamlets, cows, sheep, flowers, cars. Nothing. Wiling away the time worrying isn't the best course of action. The only good thing to come from this opportunity is drowsiness which turns to light sleep filled with noises of the train, voices floating in and around, muffled familiar mixed with unintelligible new, dark red eyelids flecked with flickering light, images of the now and the recent, broken not long after by slowing, rattling, stopping.

Scott blinks away bleariness, wiping his eyes. Looks around. The municipal station is like any other; steel and concrete and frosted glass. Just outside the Nottingham limits. A short walk to his friends home.

He tentatively picks up the aluminium case wondering, only briefly, if he should leave well alone and curl up into a ball to sleep into next week. He needs the bedrest to get rid of the headache which has plagued him all day, and the aches and pains, and the hunger and thirst.

The carriage is almost empty. There had only been four people aside from himself in the entire compartment during the journey anyway. It was their voices he had heard, intermingled with those imagined. Rose and William and the hitman. Their words going around his brain. Along with his own unanswered questions. Of those there are many.

Curious.

Curious how this part of the journey, where nothing is really happening, the calm between storm's, or the exposition during the action, Scott is expecting something, anything, to happen. Really, he should be enjoying this relative tranquility. If carrying a potentially hazardous material container genuinely offers tranquility. Scott smiles. Perhaps the case is empty. A hoax. A MacGuffin? He muses.

Scott disembarks the train, grinning at everyone and nobody like a fool, wondering who amongst these unassuming characters going about their lives in a trance is that one unique person, that spanner in the works of the machine which follows him like some unrelenting drone. A drone? Is that what he, Scott Dalton, has become? At the moment he doesn't feel like he is a drone, more like the living dead, a zombie. Self-pitying tiredness. If this is the case he should blend in well! He is operating very much outside the system. Or is he? Scott must pretend he is. But is Big Brother watching him how, smiling arrogantly upon his false sense if individuality? Smirking at the illusion of freedom which he and millions of others blindly assume?

Looking about the small municipal train station there are no apparent cameras.

Nobody appears out of place.

No helicopters circle.

The plain answer, then, to Scott's own fears is simple paranoia on his part. Yes, that must be it. Surely? No-one is after him. All the stuff in Scotland, with Rose and the Lake District hitman, was linked through consequence of the previous action and now Scott is on his own meandering path there is little or no reason for 'them' to pursue. William can wait, too. Scott can breath more easily for a while, relax, enjoy this

119

delightful village in the Heart of England. Meet his friend. Chat. Eat. Sleep. Sally forth once more.

Sunset casts long shadows along the narrow unmade track from the dense, overgrown hedgerows. Bowing trees splinter fiery, dancing light, creating a colourful strobing effect against which Scott has to blink rapidly as he passes from dark to light and back again in an instant. Golden and green leaves litter his way, hard clods of earth remind him how far he has come off the main-road, and Scott randomly recalls the day's from his youth amongst the fields and tracks of Hoveton, their newly turned smell, the Autumnal breeze, dampness, cooling air. Innocent days. Fun times where the only care was school - if that! - and the only fear was being caught by the farmer whose field he and his friends would be trespassing upon. The games they played. Make-believe. Discovery. Developing social skills, learning hierarchy, discovering girls!

 Weariness causes the ruminations.

 Those days are long gone, a distant memory playing in the back of his mind like a half-remembered favourite movie rendered more fondly through the passage of time. Because this is what maturing does. Growing up should create memories. Becoming an adult should offer greater challenges. When we are in our later years we can reminisce the so-called good old days - but is reminiscing admission to old age? Unless there were no good times. One must not forget those others while thinking selfishly of oneself. Some people suffer in childhood and carry those scars with them throughout their life. While other's rise above these early trials. Scott, on the other hand, has seemingly experienced a rose-tinted thirty years before his life has been launched upon the real world with a vengeance! Strewth. How long ago was it since Operation Retrieve? Five years, tops! Another sign of getting older: memory loss! Yet it's the making of memories which is essential to living.

Hedgerows part to his left, a sturdy wooden gate six-feet high with solid concrete posts to reenforce the sense of security reveal a gravel driveway. Fine stones, more noise to alert occupants of trespassers. The old single-storey cottage with its thatched roof, white pebble-dashed walls, dark brown oak beams, encircled by a flowery border losing their summer bloom. A rickety lean-too shed against the northern wall, a path down the southern side, all surrounded by spectacular well tended topiary ferns.

The tail of a Mercedes 4x4 is barely visible behind the branches of a weeping willow.

Scott can understand why his friend from the Ministry of Science would live in relative seclusion from the hustle and bustle she faces in London. The place is calming to the senses from the outside, a restful home which might settle the thoughtful, intricate mind. A cottage for meditation and cogitation.

Attached somewhat lazily, an afterthought perhaps, to the concrete post nearest Scott is an intercom. He presses the call button, remembering his purpose, sorting out in his mind what he needs to say to this woman to gain an audience with her, knowing her time is precious and even though they are friends, if she is working, he must impress the urgency of the matter without preamble. Why didn't he think of this earlier? He might be utterly wasting his time.

Now he realises this!?

Before he can press the intercom button a click emanates from the gate, indicating the lock is open.

Scott smiles, not just to himself but to his friend who has obviously been observing his approach. He wonders where her cameras are. Does she have audio surveillance? Motion detectors? There should

121

be no surprise if she does, considering the very specific research she tends and some of the more covert work carried out for the Government.

Opening and closing the gate, Scott's walking boots crunch noisily upon the small stones of the driveway as he approaches the house, a favourite sound of his, but this time rattling his teeth and brain.

The front door opens well before it is necessary.

Naomi Maxwell watches him studiously over the top rim of her rose-gold spectacles, frowning at him gravelly, unimpressed by his slightly disheveled appearance. Her silver hair is tied back without any real thought, while her clothing of red slacks, loose-fitting sixties-style flowery blouse and bare feet, could be seen as an uncoordinated mess to some, uniquely quirky to others. Naomi possesses her own style, far from the sheep-procession crowd!

"Been to war?" Naomi asks pointedly.

"You might say that. Sorry to disturb you."

"Rubbish."

"Okay, I admit it, I'm not that sorry."

"Better be worth it, young man."

"You're not wrong there, too."

"Well come in, young man, before you drop down dead!"

Scott follows Naomi into the bespoke kitchen with it's central large oak dining-table looking like it has been hand built by the woman herself, which is a distinct possibility.

He closes the door.

"What's that you're carrying?" Naomi asks.

"I was hoping you might tell me."

"Put it on the table." She instructs. "I'll put on a pot of herbal tea. Fancy a sandwich?"

"I could eat a horse."

"Will a pig be enough?"

"With mustard?"

"Of course. And proper butter, too."

With due care Scott places the aluminium case atop the dining-table as if the contents will somehow choose this specific moment to react after the jostling, while Naomi puts a rustic steel kettle on the stove then loads some herbal teabags into a big gay yellow china pot.

"It's good to see you, Scott." Naomi says seriously, facing him once again, studying his face. "You need some rest." She states pointedly. "Is this anything to do with young McCann's daughter?" She asks, while running her fingers over the top of the ridged case, raising a quizzical eyebrow at the hazardous warning symbols, eyes twinkling at the prospect of discovering it's contents.

"No."

"You know they are looking for you?"

"Really?"

"Yes. They contacted me. Told me to report immediately if I saw you."

"Will you?"

"Have you done anything wrong?"

Scott shakes his head. It's a half-truth, really, because he isn't sure, but with enough truth to fool anyone. He has had suspicions about his own people but they were theories only.. There were indicators, yet he really did not want to believe. It seems his own people have informed everyone in the service who he might come into contact with to keep their eyes peeled. But what, exactly, has Naomi been told?

"Don't look worried." Naomi tells him. "I'm not about to say that you can trust me because to a man in your business that is tantamount to a falsehood, but, if it's any consolation, you need not worry about my discretion."

"What have I done?" Scott asks, grinning wryly.

"They didn't say. I concluded it has something to do with the Oxford thing and McCann's daughter, hence my question. But I might be wrong jumping to conclusions." She tells him flatly, picking up on Scott's lack of more knowledge on the matter, she adds: "She died in the troubles."

"I know. I saw it on the internet."

"The wonders of technology."

"But that has nothing to do with me."

The kettle whistles it's anguish at reaching boiling point so Naomi removes it from the stove.

Scott rubs his eyes, the ceaseless pounding behind them worse now. He is reminded about the concussion. Was it last night? The night before? He suddenly feels tired. Exhausted. Like he needs to lay his head down. But he cannot, not yet, anyway. Not until he fills Naomi in on the details about the case, drink the tea, eat the sandwich. He knows unequivocally that he can trust her. Why are the Government after him? It's too ridiculous to think they would tell Naomi. Maybe they're calling him to assist.

Maybe, maybe, maybe, what if... He could on forever with such speculation.

While they take tea together Scott tells her about his day, which sounds farfetched even to him while he is running over all the events, skipping some, embarrassed by others. He concludes:

"I can't see how immigrants are this big a deal."

"Maybe the thing in Oxford partially explains why you haven't been contacted?" Naomi suggests feasibly.

"Could be." Scott agrees. "But if so, who has been constantly standing in my way, and why? Nothing makes sense anymore!"

While they sip silently at the herbal tea, they both regard the aluminium case curiously, like it will unravel the truth to all this mess.

Scott jumps with a start when the phone in his pocket starts ringing. Rose's phone. He thought he had switched the thing off. He pulls it out. William is calling him at last. He takes the call, listening intently to what the Scotsman tells him, explains to the man there is no way to meet until the morning, after sleeping, he was concussed, Rose helped him, and he needs to procure a car for himself. William hangs up the line once in agreement with Scott.

"It seems I have to be in York by seven tomorrow morning." Scott tells Naomi. "With this. Can you get into it?"

Naomi smiles reassuringly: "Of course, young man! And nobody will be any the wiser. But what do you want me to do once its open?"

Scott doesn't need much time to answer:

"Disable it." He states. "Whatever is inside is important to these people and any delay in carrying out their plan might help me. It's clearly not being used for getting illegal immigrants out of the country."

"You better get some sleep, and I have just the pill for it."

Eleven hours remain.

The Observer drives furious, overtaking when it's dangerous to do so, forcing power from her car like petrol is water, eyes staring straight forward. The M1 is her racetrack and she doesn't care who she upsets. She has been summoned to London for a meeting. Her cover has been scrapped. The Joint British Security Force have new plans for her. The undercover operation which she has spent months on, not including the prep landing stage, has been superseded by a new task.

A new task!

She has questions to ask about the old one. Such as why another agent was dispatched alongside her without her knowledge.

Scott Dalton. A newcomer, no less. Undercover to do essentially the same task as her!

Why?

Had they lost faith in her ability to deliver results?

This is why she is driving furiously. Not because of the urgency behind the message to return to base, but because she is, quite frankly, pissed off.

TWENTY-ONE

Why do people rarely go out for a plain and simple coffee these days? Why are we brand crazy? It's not as if Scott can tell any significant difference between the coffee he is drinking presently from the road-side stop, with it's "Hot Food n Drink on the Go" slogan emblazoned upon the side of the van, and a Costa. At least not at seven o'clock in the morning. He doesn't care what it tastes like, really, so long as it's hot and got plenty of caffeine in it! Trendy coffee shops serving overpriced beverages have replaced the pub. It's the Government's fault, really. They banned smoking in public places. Scott never was a smoker, it hasn't ever appealed to him, but part of the atmosphere when going to a pub was the odour of smoke and beer. They alone lent character to a pub. People who claim they don't go to pub's because they are too expensive are lying if they go out for a coffee or tea because these days there is very little difference in price between them! It's a fact. Some designer coffee's cost more than an alcoholic beverage, for goodness sake! How? Why? Complain all you like but it is we, the general public, who condone such establishments. And don't get Scott started on the pretentious in-home coffee machines, they are as pointless as dish-washers!

It can be good to rant about something. Takes the mind off reality. And a serious situation.

Two hours remain.

Okay, Scott must admit upon greater reflection that this particular coffee in it's cheap recycled cardboard cup has nothing on a black Americano from Costa. But the important thing now is that it's hot and wet, and that is all that matters to him right now while he leans against the rear of the borrowed Mercedes 4x4 parked in the broad lay-by on the outskirts of York while awaiting the arrival of William, the

Scotsman, who is expecting the component in the aluminium case which Scott has stowed in the trunk. Actually, upon even further reflection and study of the murky liquid in it's flimsy container, Scott would kill for a large Americano right now, it's superior flavour, quality and caffeine content cannot be beaten!

He tips the inferior liquid onto the road disdainfully.

Naomi told him before leaving her cottage in the early hours that morning what the thing in the corrugated aluminium case is. In great detail. Most of which went straight over Scott's head because he didn't really understand the technobabble terminology which she had use. But he most certainly grasped the basics. The facts hit home. Hard! The component by itself is not harmful, just copper, steel, diodes and various electronic components. Quite innocuous. There is no real reason for the warning signs on the case except to deter those who might be nosy. But if linked together with various other components of a similar technology it can form an explosive jigsaw puzzle.

A very large, powerful, deadly device of immense destruction.

No exaggeration.

That much, Scott most definitely did comprehend. Naomi had insisted that he should contact their own people, tell them of this probable threat. The implications are phenomenal. He said he would see to it before departing, suspecting she might too. But he hasn't yet. He doesn't know why.

And it's too late now.

Seemingly from out of nowhere Scotsman William aka Bob appears. His weathered brown complexion creases with fatigue, the clothes on his back bear the unchanged appearance of a man who really doesn't care what people think of him. Scott chastises himself the instant he has the thought that William fits right in at this greasy-spoon truck-stop lay-by! Stereotyping didn't used to be in Scott's nature.

William's face is grim, a bit like the overcast sky, which doesn't really bother Scott because he also is none to happy about the situation he is in right now, and the condition he feels in doesn't aid his temperament. Tired in a hung-over way, pain in need of pills! He truly has had enough of being used and abused, knocked around, concussed, battered. If that isn't enough to cause one to be ill-tempered than there is no hope in the world!

"Morning!" Scott says with sarcastic joviality - if there is such a thing.

"Ave ye got it with ye?" William asks bluntly.

"I'm fine, thank you for asking! Which is more than I can say for poor Rose, or do you have no feelings in that matter either?"

"I do."

"Just when it suits you?"

"I've know the lass for years, boy!"

"Then show some compassion. She died in my arms."

William seems slightly dumbstruck at Scott's blunt harshness, stopping quite literally in his tracks, locking eyes with the Englishman. Scott can see a visible shift in the deep brown pigment, satisfied that he has hit home, hoping the Scotsman will now not dare ask how Scott himself has fared. At least there can now be no questioning of Scott's loyalty and commitment to the cause, a doubt which was inevitably fomenting in the Scotsman's brain yesterday, and this morning too. Scott now has control, at last. He knows what William is after even if the actually plan is still out of grasp! Scott knows too this resentment isn't solely directed at the organisation which this man represents. Whose to say they aren't doing good work? Perspective can often be oblique.

"She knew the score-" William says with unconvincing candour, before adding: "-and I shall mourn her- but not until after this job is finished. So I don't need no lecture from ye."

"I'm pleased to hear it!" Scott tells the Scotsman brusquely. "Mind telling me where we're going with your case?"

"Aye." William replies, checking his wristwatch for the eighth time since arriving. "Who's car is this?"

"That," Scott says, "is none of your business."

"Fair enough, boy."

"Stop calling me boy. It's almost as patronising as young man!"

Tipping his empty coffee cup into a litter receptacle Scott opens the drivers door and sits in the car, only half pretending to be angry with William at the man's aloofness surrounding the death of Rose. It seems bizarre to Scott that such disinterest can lay within even the most hardened criminal toward a woman who has died so young for the cause. Maybe this is the business William and, to a degree Scott, are in. But Scott wonders if he could be so cold in his actions. Of course not, he has been brought into the world on an altogether different moral path. Rose and the Prime Minister's daughter have both been cut down before their prime, their ages not far apart, unlike the opposing upbringings. All for what?

William gets in the passenger seat alongside Scott, drawing out a snub-nosed Police Special, spinning the small barrel. Intimidating. If Scott could care less. He knows that William might have a loaded weapon pointed at him but he, Scott, still has the upper-hand.

"Lets head south to the bridge." William says.

"What bridge?" Scott asks despite knowing the inevitable answer.

"Don't play stupid, laddie." William says. "The Humber."

"I won't play stupid," says Scott, pressing the Stop/Start button of the 4x4 which growls into life, "if you stop using predictable Scottish colloquialisms!"

Scott eases the gorgeously smooth car forward, the automatic gearbox seamlessly changing as he accelerates onto the main A-road southward, brushing the very outskirts of York, it's Cathedral spire briefly visible when they mount an overpass incline. Silence is not golden so Scott activates the DAB radio which is preset to the wonderful timbre of Beethoven on Classic FM, much to William's obvious disdain, which adds to Scott's delight, temptation to turn up the volume resisted. This must be Naomi's preference. Scott now realises he was so enthralled by his own thoughts on the journey from her home to York the lack of radio accompaniment had gone completely unnoticed. He grins to himself. This music genre isn't his present taste but it is tolerable.

"What are we carrying in the case?" Scott asks casually, knowing the answer but searching William to determine the amount of trust and transparency he can expect. A reply isn't forthcoming. "I'm assuming it's not highly explosive otherwise I should he dead long before now!"

"Its part of a bomb." William tells him frankly. "But ye needn't worry yerself with details."

"Why not?"

"Cause it's none of ye business."

"Touché."

"Aye, lad."

"Dying in an explosion is my business, though."

"Then there won't be nowt to worry about after, will there?"

Reflecting upon the fact that the furthest couldn't be true, Scott indicates to join the right-hand slip-road off the outer York ring-road, signposts clearly defining their route that nobody could possibly go wrong on their journey to the Humber Bridge. Scott smiles. He recalls a very rudimentary mistake which his blowhard Uncle made on a family excursion to Skegness many years ago. He was approaching Kings Lynn from Norwich, saw a signpost to Cromer and took a round-about in the direction of that particular seaside resort simply based on the fact he recognised the name. Unfortunately as anyone who has made this southbound journey from Norwich, Cromer is almost a U-turn back upon oneself. But never mind, it gave everyone the opportunity to remind his Uncle of this mistake on every possible opportunity, and nobody is perfect, but at least here in Yorkshire there is no room for such stupid mistakes.

Scott remembers what William has just said to him and gives the Scotsman a brief sideways glance.

"Presumably I am to be miles away upon construction of this bomb?" Scott asks in a facetial tone of voice.

"Like I said," William reiterates more firmly, "it's not your concern."

"Okay. Thanks."

Pondering the likelihood of there being any truth to William's words, Scott drives in silence, listening to the powerfully robust William Walton sound now resonating through all the speakers in the Merc, triumphantly Imperialistic in its splendour. Rousing stuff on a morning of dull English weather with the long winter ahead to look forward to. But what is there to stop Scott taking a holiday of his own once this assignment is over? Sunny climes, a relaxed beach, alcohol and swimming. Sounds pretty good right now. Not to mention attractive female company bettering his surly male passenger!

William checks the time on his watch then his mobile-phone.

Perhaps twenty-miles ahead of them, beyond the trees, houses and concrete, the support spires of the Humber Bridge are visible. They are quite an awe-inspiring sight, rising out of the land, touching the clouds, a manmade structure of magnificent achievement. A monument to man's accomplishments. Or a blot on the landscape! Depends on one's point of view.

"Are we proceeding according to schedule?" Scott asks.

William nods and murmurs an affirmative without thinking.

Scott grins. At least he has something to go on, however flimsy. He wonders if it hadn't perhaps been prudent for him to come here without first communicating with his people. Its almost as if he has gone off their grid. He feels like a rogue agent. But why the guilt? Is it not they who have remained uncommunicative? Have they not been the one's whose interference has been endangering his task? Could they not perhaps answer a few questions? When this is over, they shall. Or perhaps Scott should go above them and directly to the main man himself. It was Prime Minister Alfred McCann who recruited him in the first place. Could he not shed light upon this? Tell him what's been going on.

Smiling ruefully, Scott realises that an audience with the very man running this country is not going to be an easy task unless summoned. The man running the country is mourning the murder of his daughter. How is he feeling? What measures are being carried out by McCann and his team to bring forth justice? Is he seeking revenge for the killing? Is that the real reason why Scott hasn't been able to communicate with his own team, because they too have been reassigned? Is this why Naomi was contacted ahead of his arrival?

Off the sweeping curve into the wide boulevard of the Humber Bridge toll stations, the structure is a foreboding, awe-inspiring, metal giant stretching its huge limbs across the great expanse of land and water, joining north to south.

"I presume you have some cash?" Scott asks, adding a silent doubt about stereotypical tight-fisted Scottish folk.

A jangling of coins silence's Scott's thoughts, and he touches the control to buzz down his window. It is with retrospect minutes later that Scott registers the van which draws into the next booth and an unusual amount of conspicuous joggers attempting to be inconspicuous.

But for the present time Scott is focused on drawing the car to a suitable position before dropping the money which William has handed him into the metallic receptacle. The barrier rises and all hell breaks loose as a succession of events take place...

Black-clad and armed people burst forth from the rear of the van.

The joggers spill out along the roadway, blocking the paths of oncoming vehicles, loosing ammo spraying the surface to discourage rashness.

Car tyres screech, brakes apply, screams stifle from within.

While Scott drives onto the Humber Bridge under instruction from William, caught up in who knows what melee.

TWENTY-TWO

There are very few cars ahead of Scott Dalton's borrowed Merc as he slowly trundles the vehicle up the slight incline of the foreboding metallic giant which is the Humber Bridge to it's apex - three-quarters of a mile, hard to believe until one is there, the vista is breathtaking. Both shores. Miles and miles of coastline and water. Miniature houses, toy cars, model trees in the middle distance. Clouds wishing below the main grey body. Bridge struts lost above, hundreds of feet below. A four-lane miracle of engineering.

On a normal day.

But not today.

Instead, this bridge is going to be a terrorist sacrifice unless someone can stop it.

At this moment Scott realises the bomb is most likely to be assembled and detonated here, destroying the proud structure to make a political point as is the usual case in these particular situations - these people do not seem to be backed by any religious fanaticism or more altruistic motivations, but Scott has so far only scratched the surface, who knows what backers are financing this operation? He is now encountering something far more insidious that people smuggling.

A small cloud of smoke or dust billows from a two-car shunt on the opposite lane back at the tolls, the traffic of various sizes is backed up a further fifteen vehicles, their passengers remaining safely inside. Scott wonders how safe those people really are and if the civilians will be spared or sacrificed, depending on the whims of this organisation, he supposes.

There are no other vehicles tailing the Merc, the toll apparently blocked successfully by however many are involved in this attack. This is a big operation involving many people, a well organised group. Scott wonders why all cog's in this machine have been allowed to work systematically undetected by any law enforcement agency in the country. His own people are trained to identify such a threat before it occurs. Occasionally something small slips through the net, but this is potentially huge. It's normal for someone to slip up somewhere. A misplaced communique. A word spoken in haste. But not this.

How long will it take for these terrorists to undo his friend Naomi's work? Will they have an expert who can identify the tampering? Fortunate for Scott that he had the foresight, although he never anticipated something happening so soon. Is this linked to yesterday in Oxford?

The road ahead has emptied. It seems those car's who may have been in front of Scott have been spared, let off the bridge.

Scott wonders if he too will be sacrificed. Why? What's the point? What message will blowing up a bridge send?

William taps a number on his phone:

"Is he here?"

Scott cannot hear the reply but he can see the grin, a frighteningly uncharacteristic, horrible grin from the Scotsman beside him. Who? Is who on here? Scott gets a sinking feeling in his gut. The phone is deactivated with an unnervingly satisfied tap.

Who?

Is who here?

An automatic glance in his rearview mirror confirms what Scott already knows, so whoever William is asking about must be in the traffic on the opposite lane, ahead and to the extreme right. But who is it? Someone significant, obviously. Someone worth exploding a large bomb on a bridge for. Or is it a ransom? Is the bomb a decoy? Possibly. That might he part of the explanation. The explosive device is somewhat excessive for just a bridge, at least according to Naomi's analysis. What then? Or who? Someone worth a bomb and ransom. Travelling up North. Who?

"Stop as near to the middle of the bridge as you can." Instructs William.

Scott nods slowly, trying to absorb everything. Take everything in. Don't miss a trick. He is afraid of losing track of events as time swiftly passes. Don't let things get out of hand. Scott has a definite advantage. He knows the bomb cannot be activated as soon as William and his organisation perhaps hope. This is a good thing. There are other factors, too. This person mentioned. Will they ransom him? Can they really risk hurrying their timeline along? No. Any delay will be favourable to Scott, surely? Will he have the opportunity to-?

"This is fine." William says suddenly.

Easing to a halt obediently, Scott pulls on the parking brake and switches the engine off.

"Get the case," orders William, "and follow me."

The gruff Scotsman is out of the car first, obviously not concerned that Scott might be a security risk, there is no threatening gun, no obvious distrust, just focus on the plan.

As casually as he can, Scott pulls out the pistol taken from the hitman, which has barely a five rounds remaining but might be if use, from the glove-compartment and slips it easily into his right-hand pocket along with Rose's phone, while simultaneously popping open the truck which smoothly arises like a casket on hydraulics.

Stepping out of the car Scott looks along the opposite lane and back, trying to not be too obvious by doing so. He assess the vehicles queued back. They are mostly family cars, a hatchback, and a mini-van. Nothing too pretentious. No high-roller worth a ransom. Just innocent civilians caught up in who knows what, never anticipating in a million years that when they left home this morning they would be unwilling participants in an act of terrorism. Because that is surely what this is. A show of force by a cowardly organisation whose sole goal is destruction, claiming they are actually doing it for the people, when in fact it is the lives of those people who are affected, lending falsehood to their preaching. If a point is to be made. Freedom from oppression can be won another way. If there are enough people with the same voice then the collective can be heard. Yet time and time again, violence is the great leveller. It becomes the voice. And yet it is a voice we are hearing too often, repeating the same thing, a distant voice, whether for a religious cause or political power, we have become accustomed to it, anaesthetised against the actions taking place elsewhere. Even those acts of killing which take place on our home soil soon become forgotten history, our initial reactions muted by the repetitive commuting of our own lives.

But Scott Dalton can make a difference. He must make a difference here.

He hauls the part of the explosive device which Naomi has professionally tampered with last night to slow these criminals down. Scott must make sure he uses this benefit to his advantage.

Banging down the trunk Scott follows William, the Scotsman striding towards a maintenance gateway between the opposing lanes of the Humber Bridge, opening them and passing through. Scott isn't far behind, joining this man who now walks south on the north-bound carriageway. There are cars, official cars, and two vans on this side of the toll-barriers, while on the opposite side the queue of traffic builds up from the south. The great British pastime, hey: queuing!

A cool breeze atop the bridge forces an involuntary shudder from Scott. Is it really the cold or a touch of shock at the situation he has found himself in?

The clouds are low in the sky, the vista is undeniably wide and spectacular, the structure he is upon is huge, ominous, and the situation...troubling, to say the least. He must keep his wits. Not become overwhelmed.

There are other access points like this. There must he places to hide. Ways off the bridge. How soon before real anti-terror police arrive? Helicopters? The Ops Tower are only equipped for basic emergencies. What will their effectiveness be? Boats. The water is quite shallow but boats could gain access, could be a drop-off for hostages. Could he use a car to ram the vehicles blocking exits? What will happen when the police arrive? What will be the reaction of the terrorists? Can he possibly contribute toward saving civilians? Can he learn more about these people? Scott must find out more.

Two official cars. Shiny. New.

How many terrorists are here?

Scott must that find the exact number, too. How many would it take to maintain this operation to its ultimate conclusion? Twenty at a guess. Maybe thirty? That seems like an impractically high number, too much opportunity for pre-plan slip-ups. But not impossible.

Official cars. Black. Armoured. Government.

Strewth, the bridge is some length! Unappreciated in a car. Further on foot. It would take many minutes to cover the entire distance, for Scott or any other physically fit person.

Government. Official. How official?

Closer, now, the black car's are new. Shiny. Governmental. And there is Mike Jones. The Prime Minister's chauffeur. Why is he now standing near the car conversing with the Scotsman William?

TWENTY-THREE

From the suddenly uncomfortable leather backseat of his chauffeur driven Parliamentary approved car Prime Minister Alfred McCann gets the sense of foreboding one is told to expect immediately prior to the loss of one's life. Not that this situation has precisely reached this fatal point just yet, but all the same, the eternal optimist that is McCann is now having doubts about the future. His future. Maybe the previous day's events have impacted upon these trains of thought, altering his perspective somewhat, but walking into an ambush does have the effect of making one feel abysmally foolish.

Mike the Chauffeur has parked their car approximately a quarter-way up the curvature of the southern end of the Humber Bridge, passing under the magnificent, now ominous, support pylons with their invisible honeycomb interior, which tower above, linking the astronomical 44,000miles of suspension cable. They are dark shadows overhead. Mike switches off the engine and turns about in his seat.

"You're free to use the phone, sir." Mike says pleasantly.

"Thanks, Mike."

"But please stay in your seat."

"Whatever you say."

"Its for your own safety."

"I'm sure it is, that is, after all what you are paid for, my safety and protection."

McCann glowers disdainfully at this man who is one of the components in this hijacking, and whom the Prime Minister believed he could indeed rely upon to protect him. How could have been so stupid and naive? And how could this have happened? Why has a man close to the leader of Great Britain been able to conceal his true intentions?

"What do your people want: money?"

"Not for me to say."

"Whatever it is, I hope you can live with yourself afterwards."

Mike shrugs, opening the car door while extracting the key from the ignition; "You'll have to wait and see, sir. I'm not high enough up the chain of command to be privy to all the details, sir, but once I am, I'll let you know how I will manage! For now, sir, look at this as if it were a scene from one if your crappy old Italian B-movies!" And he bangs shut the door, not bothering to lock the car because where can the Prime Minister possibly go under the current situation, over the side?

Sinking dejectedly in his seat, McCann's first instinct is to activate the emergency distress beacon, which he does, even though after this act he realises it is probably superfluous because the alert has undoubtedly already gone out from his lead car, which is not fifty-feet in front of him, another one of his own people holding the other two inside at gunpoint. He shakes his head: this is like the statement which Mike the Chauffeur made about this situation being like some stage contrivance from one of the movies his company made in days gone by.

The London studio is now under the control by his best friend and long-time business partner, Giuliano Badalamenti. Alfred McCann sighs almost wistfully for those days to return. Can it really be just over half his lifetime ago that he set upon the adventure?

1990

Alfred McCann stands awestruck by the shimmering clear blue sun-speckled swimming pool out back of Chateau Neuf du Menti where his college friend Giuliano Badalamenti has brought him during their summer break. And what a break. What an amazing place. The young man's back is to the magnificent white three-storey building, drinking in the splendiferous view across the Tyrrhenian Sea. The modern Chateau belongs to Franco Badalamenti, Giuliano's uncle on his father's side,

141

and it is in the beautifully diverse Santa Maria province of Italy on the South-west coast of the country. On a clear day such as today it has the most magnificent view across the graciously undulating sea to the island of Sicily, a great swathe on the horizon, and offers a panorama worth drinking in for the duration.

Alfred McCann's English middle-class background permits him to be suitably impressed by the property, it's land and surroundings, taking nothing for granted because this is the sort of luxury which great wealth can buy and is certainly beyond the means of his own family, and beyond his wildest dreams. This is also the sort of occasion which only great success can bring into a persons life, with a glittering assortment of celebrity personalities shining brighter than the sun itself on the property.

So, who lives in a house like this?

Franco Badalementi is a tall, dark-haired, barrel-chested, jovial red-blooded Italian male in his fifties who has persevered in his quest to become a successful and well respected figure in show-business. This charismatic man is also a hotelier, political supporter, an advocate of social equality and all-round philanthropic bon vivant. One is instantly drawn to him because he exudes the natural familiarity of a lifelong acquaintance, making everyone feel welcome with his exuberant friendliness and personality. Even the most cynical of cynic cannot help but hang on his every word, drawn as if magnetically attracted.

From afar, young Alfred McCann watches this big man interacting with consummate ease and wonders in awe if some day he himself could possibly command even half Franco's respect, as well as the genuine admiration of others which exudes around him. Franco's personality dwarfs even the palatial splendour of the Brose designed Chateau Neuf du Menti, an early twenty-first century construct typical of the region yet functional in its appearance too. It has sound-proofed plastic windows, powered by self sustaining solar-panels, has its own water and waste source, and is fitted with state of the art Wi-fi, surveillance and alarm system, yet the natural flora has grown up it's walls so this ecological marvel almost blends into the very grounds which surround it, and disguises the modern contrivances. A covered carport attached to the side is discretely positioned at the end of a circular gravel driveway which loops through natural woodland.

As well as the clean lines of the swimming pool and spacious patio area at the rear, there is a beautifully maintained meditation garden, hidden tennis court and a maze for the many children in this large Italian family. Behind the garden, a manmade pathway wends it's way down through the orange coastal cliffs to a private beach and sturdy boathouse. Because of it's prominent position on the coast, which receives it's fair share of battering weather, everything has a robust quality about it.

But now, at this present time, the climate could not be more idyllic.

A feeling of euphoria clutches at Alfred and he cannot help but smile at his miraculous good fortune, while catching the eye of a stunning red-haired young woman in the process, who returns the smile with one of her own. He sips the red wine from the glass in his hand, the exquisitely expensive flavour dancing over his tastebuds. Alfred is no connoisseur and has never drank wine as divine as this particular beverage whose name escapes him for the moment, but it is an Italian variety costing in the region of one-hundred pounds a bottle. One-hundred pounds! This is indulgence at its finest and his glass is soon empty, the alcohol warming him inside as the very essence penetrates his system, aligning his confidence with his euphoria.

Alfred wonders what his college friends back home would think of him now if they could see him. He is in an almost surreal situation amongst surreal surroundings, a complete world away from the comparatively humble environment where he grew up in Oxfordshire: here there be celebrity! His English state education wasn't anything spectacular and offered him little opportunity despite good grades, because his real passion drew him to media entertainment which, to his way of thinking, allowed freedom of mind and artistry. Alfred pursued a path to college which had a very limited course in film studies, while seeking employment as a trainee projectionist, when there were still such people in existence, at his local flea-pit to earn money of his own. It was at college where he befriended Giuliano Badalamenti, an obviously Italian exchange student the same age as himself. Between them and their mutual passion for films and film-making they created a film club which would extend from college hours to leisure time, and along with other likeminded students they began making their own movies, inspired by late-night viewings of films from all genre's and countries. They were gradually able to acquire better equipment than the college could supply through Giuliano's Italian connections back home, thus creating better than average product. The duo became an inseparable, inspirational team to their peers, who flocked to their improvised 8mm Festivals and seasonal events, sometimes utilising the outdoor back-wall of the college as a screen to display lavish productions of their own, sometimes idealistic protests on current affairs in their own naive youthful enthusiasm. Although they were both popular and committed students they soon discovered the Elitist British Film Industry at that time offered very limited opportunities unless one fit-in to their clique or possessed family connections, and College wasn't quite University, in their eyes. Passion and enthusiasm will only get a person so far in this industry.

So how could Alfred McCann possibly refuse the generous offer from Giuliano's family to spend the seven week summer break in Italy surrounded by the very people and craft he loved?

This is the place where Giuliano's own proclivities were nurtured and encouraged while growing into the teenager he has become, whose parents had been a positive influence on his pursuit to learn more, hence requesting the placement in England as a cultural and creative experience. Giuliano's parents, although a part of the wealthy clan, live a more grounded and realistic existence that gives the young man an endearing and approachable quality sorely lacking in the the more elite upper-classes of England. Which is probably one of the many reasons why he and Alfred hit it off right from the bat.

"Ciao, Al."

Alfred turns from his daydreaming and smiles at the familiar, deep Italian voice of his friend Giuliano, his bronzed features more natural than McCann's red complexion which indicates he has already consumed a considerable quantity of alcohol, and it is only one o'clock in the afternoon. This handsome, dark-haired young man is resplendent in casual flip-flops, smart beige shorts and a crisp white short-sleeved designer shirt.

"That is Anjou, il mio amico." Giuliano informs Alfred with an approving bob of his head toward the young woman in the pool whose eye he unintentionally caught moments ago. "Anjou is twenty-one and she is the daughter of Ennio Leone."

"Spectacular."

"A rare beauty indeed."

"Devine."

Alfred gulps theatrically before glancing once more at the beautifully streamlined figure of the woman swimming gracefully from one end of the pool to the other, her lovely black hair a flowing train behind her wavering to the top of her bikini thong. She is a rare beauty who is unquestionably out of Alfred's financial ballpark, but that is a mental barrier which can be overcome if required. Not only that but she is the daughter of Italian cinema's most preeminent male box office draw. A young woman who could have any red-blooded male she chose, so Alfred's admiration might be nothing more than visual. Her father, all six-foot four hunk of a man with a massive personality and oozing charisma is surrounded by a bevy of beautiful people of both sexes lapping up the very aura of his presence, undoubtedly regaling them with inspiring stories of grandeur which Alfred can only dream about. Yet here he is, this boy from England, his skin gradually soaking the colour of the European sunshine and its air, loving every minute of it.

"I can introduce you." Giuliano whispers in Alfred's air.

"More wine first."

The young Italian claps his friend on the shoulder and they walk to the gazebo where finely attired servers are dishing out the most exquisite food and drink imaginable. The place is dotted with chic trying to compete with itself yet seeming to be the norm so the ability to stand-out from the crowd here is virtually impossible, although Alfred is having a good try, dressing down in borrowed flip-flops, light-blue High Street shorts, and what he considered up-to the here and now to be he best ochre-coloured shirt. He passes by luminaries from English, American and European cinema, some he most definitely recognises, while others only vaguely. Of course not all those gathered here today are necessarily faces one should recognise. There are bound to be Producers, Directors, business folk and other's from the Badalamenti world, plus family members too. Alfred is a quite confident young man yet even he would hesitate to introduce himself to someone like Sean Connery, seated inconspicuously at a table with his wife and other adoring females, unwilling as he us to encroach upon an unfamiliar scenario - something which over the ensuing years he shall overcome.

A wine waiter refills his glass with a knowing familiarity that amazes the Englishman, making Alfred relax into the occasion, perplexed by such natural ability.

"Anjou." Giuliano says from behind him.

Alfred turns about in his best casual suaveness which he hopes doesn't appear futile. Standing before him is the most beautiful creature his eyes have ever been blessed with. Anjou Leone is indeed eye-catching. Her wet black hair is pulled back from her face, she is holding a towel loosely in one hand which has dabbed away some of the swimming pool water from her wonderfully lustrous skin, and her clear brown eyes regard him with such a pure radiance Alfred is afraid he might be consumed by stupidity.

"Alfred McCann." Giuliano gestures to his friend.

"Ciao, Al." Anjou says in her heavily accented, sensual, husky voice.

It takes a brief moment for Alfred to fully align himself to the reality that this enigmatic beauty it actually talking to him before he musters a reply which is spoken more confidently once he has cleared his throat:

"Hello. Ciao. Anjou. It is indeed a pleasure to make your acquaintance."

"And you. What do think?"

"Spectacular."

"We are blessed."

This beautiful Italian woman raises an approving eyebrow, clearly impressed by something he has said, maybe his English accent or gentlemanly manner which maybe she is unaccustomed to.

"I shall throw on some clothes." She tells him in English without once taking her penetrating eyes off his own, as if summing him up. "And perhaps we can have a drink?"

The stunned young Alfred cannot possibly refuse such an invitation and nods gracefully, determined not to mutter something foolish, receiving a dainty smile in return before Anjou walks away, hips swaying gaily, evocatively. Alfred has no time to be stunned.

"Ah, my favourite nephew!"

Franco Badalamenti clutches Giuliano by the shoulders and kisses him on each cheek, before appraising the younger man.

"You look well." Says their host, nodding, naturally bringing Alfred into the conversation with a gesture at his nephew. "The English weather has done you good. But not the food." The old man pats his nephew fondly on the stomach. "Not that I can talk! Your Aunt's pasta is the best there is. Have you tried some?" He looks from Giuliano to Alfred then back. "You should. It's the best. Plenty to go around." Franco turns his attention fully to Alfred. "And who are you, my fine friend?"

Alfred stretches out his hand: "Alfred McCann, sir. Thank you for inviting me."

"Che cos'e questo?" The big man says, dispensing with the traditional handshake and going for the more familiar shoulder clamp and cheek kissing which Alfred has yet to become accustomed to. "Benvenuti nella famiglia. You have looked after Giuliano, I shall look after you. Are you enjoying the wine? It's produced from my own crop in the northern mountains. The grapes should not survive, yet they do, and this is the result. How are you enjoying my friends?"

"He has a date already." Giuliano says.

Alfred silently wills his friend to say no more, to no avail.

148

"And who is the lucky young lady?" Franco asks the blushing young Englishman.

"Anjou Leone, no less, mio zio." Giuliano offers.

Franco steps back, eyes and arms wide with impressed approval.

"I like your style." The head of the Badalamenti clan says respectfully."Have you met her father? Such a powerful man, strong heart, strong back. Or maybe you have had a chance to meet one if your fellow countrymen, Brian the Blessed. He is inside. You can hear him? A delightful man. He is working on my next picture. Filming begins tomorrow in Rome. You are a student of the art, like my nephew?"

Giuliano tells his Uncle in Italian that Alfred is the best young filmmaker in England right now and that all he needs is a break into the industry.

Franco nods, stroking his chin thoughtfully.

"How many weeks have you got?" Franco asks. "Six?"

Alfred nods, but explains that he has only three in Italy because that is all he and his family could afford.

"You shall have six." Franco says in a stern voice which doesn't allow for misinterpretation. "I shall pay your expenses, both you and my nephew. Report to my studio in Rome at your convenience Monday morning. I shall tell my Assistant Manager that she is to place you under the wing of Sergio Marque, he is a fine director, up-and-coming, as they say in this business. You can study with him while you are here." He pauses briefly. "As long as this pleases you?"

Both young men are stunned into silence by the offer which clearly they are not about to refuse.

149

TWENTY-FOUR

Scott realises it doesn't take a Hercule Poirot to deduct that Mike Jones is part of this hijacking/ransom/suicide-pact and that the person in the car is inevitably none other than Prime Minister Alfred McCann. Yet still this realisation comes as a slap in the face to Scott. The main man is being held to ransom by a group of- No...not terrorists. Not the right description, just Scott's deluded assumption, a pigeonhole for everyone these days.

These are freedom fighters.

And Scott realises his assumptions were misplaced all along. The Prime Minister has nothing to do with causing recent events. Why would he?

Terrorists wouldn't hold someone hostage for a mere ransom. Not like this. Terrorists would detonate the bomb, wiping out themselves and the Prime Minister of England without concocting some elaborate plot to attract media attention. Because attention is what they will be getting pretty darn quick. So the bomb is merely their safety net. A way to keep the authorities at a distance.

What would Thomas C. Match, his old, dead friend call this situation: Die Hard on a Bridge? Scott smiles briefly to himself at the thought of his often comical friend who was capable of brightening any deadly situation with his humour. He misses his friend badly.

The presence of the British Prime Miniater puts an altogether unique perspective on the situation. Alters the purpose and the aim of these freedom fighters, in Scott's mind's eye. There is more than death and terror on their agenda. Freedom fighters it is. Scott must remember that. Because these type of people are open to negotiation. And the more stalling there is the better for Scott. Can he get to chat with-

Oh no.

The Prime Minister. He will recognise Scott. And will Mike Jones?

The chauffeur glances casually backward at Scott as if a sixth sense tells the man he is being looked at, but the glance lasts a lingering second, not too long, no recognition factor.

No, is the answer. Not Mike. Scott breathes a sigh of relief? Just the PM.

The chauffeur continues chatting with William.

Scott hasn't been in circulation long enough at the Security Service for someone like the PM's chauffeur to recognise him, so there should be no one else here involved Scott need concern himself with. Although the fact the chauffeur is in on this act is enough to alert Scott to the likelihood that others in the service, and Government, are also a part of this operation. It's logical. Otherwise how would these people know the exact time the Prime Minister was taking this particular journey? Its fortunate for them this trip wasn't cancelled after yesterday's protest, coupled with McCann's personal loss. But if one thing has been made clear from the very beginning of his reign as Prime Minister and that is Alfred McCann doesn't give up or cow to such acts. Several other questions remain unanswered.

"You can give the case to Mike." William tells Scott when he reaches the chatting duo, peering casually through the car window, it's frosted glass not too dark so that Scott cannot see inside.

When Mike takes the case he locks eyes with Scott. Still not a flicker of recognition lies behind them at close range. But he does nod knowingly, sensing kinship somewhere, on some level, the mission they are both on, perhaps? Another thought for Scott: if the Security Service have been trying to prevent him reaching this destination, does someone already know who he is? Do they now not care? Is Scott a threat no more?

The chauffeur walks toward an unmarked long wheel-base white van, Transit-sized but a foreign imitation which is between them and the now blacked southern side of the Humber Bridge. A train of traffic stretching as far as the eye can see behind a sixteen-wheel furniture transport. Some of their civilian occupants are on phones, pacing, shouting. Horns bursting impotently, pointlessly.

Scott cranes his head toward the smoked glass window of the black car, squinting for Williams benefit, before facing the Scotsman with an impressed wry smile on his lips.

"Can I- give him a piece of my mind?" Scott asks.

William replies without hesitation:

"Be my guest. None of us are goin' anywhere. Don't touch him, mind."

The Scotsman strides after Mike, Scott watching the very trusting man, not feeling an ounce of regret at the betrayal he is going to be dishing out as soon as he gets the opportunity. This man William and his band of freedom-fighters, terrorists, whatever, are jeopardising innocent people and Scott must try to stall their plans further than he has done so already. Scott must forget his own anger at the situation his Government have gotten him into, maybe his manipulation was merely a small part of this entire operation.

When William is out of earshot Scott casually opens the drivers door to the Prime Minister's car and drops into the seat, arm across the headrest, grinning at his chief's chief. The recognition is instant, along with a certain amount of relief.

"Dalton!"

Scott holds up a cautionary finger, and is frankly surprised the country's main man recognises him and remembers his name.

"What are you doing here?" Prime Minister Alfred McCann asks in a conspiratorial tone more suitable to the atmosphere, but the initial look of hope is subsiding from his face fast when he remembers something important, and is replaced by uncertain acceptance of the fate now upon him.

"I am on the undercover assignment which you authorised!" Scott replies, trying his best not to show terseness because so far the assignment hasn't exactly gone smoothly! "The one to root out the organisation causing all the problems to your administration. The illegal immigrants." He explains irritably. "Which is going really well, thank you for asking, because its led directly to this moment. I am trapped here with you."

The Prime Minister opens and closes his mouth like a fish, sceptical, yet wanting to believe. Dalton seems genuine. The big man is rendered speechless for once. He should be berating this young man for his insubordination but he cannot, not under these circumstances and with the knowledge given him this morning in one of the numerous report dockets - should he reveal anything about the report he received to this young agent? But this young agent is contradicting the report, unless this conspiracy with McCann is just a part of the act. This knowledge makes him angry. Such a contradicting trajectory of emotions this morning.

"A bit of respect, man!"

"Respect is a two-way street, sir."

"Apparently not! What's this all about?"

"What's what all about, sir?"

"Your new found insolence?"

"Maybe if I was told that I was being thrown into the lions den on this assignment I might be more understanding, but so far I've not exactly been helped by your own security services."

"I know nothing of this, Dalton, so show some respect."

Scott looks away angrily, his eyes scouring back and forth along the bridge, making sure they aren't soon to be disturbed while also trying to figure out exactly what he can do in this situation. The Prime Minister isn't helping matters. Why should Dalton bother? The odds, frankly, are not really in his favour. Scott needs something to shift the balance. But what? The boss is angry, upset. His daughter. The man cannot think straight. And Scott hasn't helped.

"I'm sorry for your loss, sir." Scott says, and the pained expression behind the Prime Minister's eyes speaks volumes. "This must really cap things off nicely." He adds pragmatically, then continues almost apologetically. "But it doesn't mean I'm pleased! They have a bomb. These people. I don't necessarily think a ransom demand is on the cards here, but who knows? What do I know, after all? I am barely in the loop with these people or mine. They've gone to great effort to coordinate all this if it's just for the money. These people are no mere terrorists. Their beliefs go beyond that, I'm certain, while I sincerely believe they think they are as right with their aims as you with your policies."

"Do you think-" McCann's words catch in his throat, he cannot say what he wants to say but he need not, for Scott deduces the rest for himself.

"Yes." Scott tells the Prime Minister bluntly. "And I think yesterday was part of an inside job, too. Like this. Your abduction."

"But that's ridiculous." The Prime Minister looks hard at Scott, assessing through his years of experience to discover the nature of this young man, an agent in his Security Service, but a relatively unknown quantity just the same.

"Is it really, sir?"

"Of course it is."

"As ridiculous as this right now?"

154

Alfred McCann nods slowly with resignation, in Scott's eyes he appears to awaken to the realisation - but something niggles, makes the Prime Minister reluctant to entirely trust this man. Knowing he was stupid to think that his chauffeur is the only member if his team to be part of this whole terrorist plot. Abduction. No ransom? Now a bomb?

"It was too easy." Scott says.

"You said-" McCann starts, his brow creased with the loss of control, the confusion, the fatalistic words of Dalton, while also playing along with this agent, remembering the report. How true can it be?. "A bomb?"

"And a big one, too."

"But that's...impossible."

"No, sir, it's reality."

"How?"

"I don't know how they got it here or who supplies the parts or if it's genuine, but it's here. And we have assume it's real."

"Good grief. How much time-?"

"I had someone on your staff fix it so these people cannot set it up as quickly as they probably hoped. It might allow enough time to-" Scott's attention is abruptly drawn to movement from the Transit-like van, and William, who is now striding back up the bridge toward them with an older man in tow. "Blast. Times up for now. But don't worry, sir, I shall try everything in my power to diffuse this situation before we are all blown to kingdom come and, should my luck hold, I will be back."

The approaching Scotsman does not look happy but this is nothing new. His hand is inside his pocket - holding a gun? The other, older man, comfortably brandishes a gun like its a fashion accessory. Scott checks his own weapon, wondering if his luck finally over?

TWENTY-FIVE

Prime Minister Alfred McCann watches as the two terrorists converge upon Scott, overwhelmed by the sheer magnitude of the Humber Bridge, which itself seems to mock the insignificance of his plight. So what is it with Scott Dalton? He ponders the agent's words. They rang true. Dalton seemed genuinely aggrieved, to the point of insolence. The man was sent on a mission, which has been officially sanctioned, and his own people, McCann's own people, have interfered in its expedience. Maybe he is irritated because he could have prevented yesterday attack in Oxford, or warned McCann about today. Can the report he read on Scott Dalton not much more than an hour ago really be true? Has this young man truly defected to the enemy cause in such a comparatively short space of time? Was he plotting the Oxford job with his cohorts? It seems ridiculous. But if someone had told him his own chauffeur was radicalised, McCann would've laughed that notion away too. So no. The report has been planted by someone in his Government, some other unscrupulous traitor. Scott had said there were more people in his Government under their influence. It has to have been one of them on the inside who planted the false accusation against the young agent. But once more, doubt raises its angry head. Was Scott merely trying to enhance the Prime Minister's suspicion's to divert his own guilt. A person could go crazy thinking such things. He needs a voice of reason to balance his mind. Someone who he can trust to give him solid advice.

McCann picks up the in-car satellite phone, touch dialling directly to his most trusted friend.

"Ciao Al."

The deep Italian voice of Giuliano Badalamenti is like a soothing elixir to the Prime Minister's ears, instantly on the other end as if expecting the call, comforting in it's familiarity, conveying the maturity of the forty-six year old. McCann should have perhaps telephoned Milena first, his wife. Let her know he is safe. But contacting his friend first is a way to ensure his wife is taken to safety before she too might possibly fall into the hands of his enemies. Giuliano will get her and their son out of the country.

"Giuliano. My friend." McCann's voice is breathy from relief, urgent, tense. "Go to Milena. Get her to safety. Please. Trust no one."

"What's wrong, Al?" Comes the reassuringly calm response.

Alfred McCann, the British Prime Minister, screws shut his eyes. He realises he should order his thoughts so they don't tumble out in-cohesively. Why is such a simple act which comes naturally to the man in charge of a nation so difficult to achieve right now? He cannot get the image of his wife, his son, his dead daughter, out of his head, Focus of mind is what is required. He takes a few deep, settling, breaths, before continuing.

"I've been hijacked." McCann states, his voice as steady as possible. There is no reaction on the other end. "On the journey to York. I am in my car, the fanatics responsible don't care if I phone out. They were- I think, they were also responsible for yesterday. They have a bomb. I am stuck- that is, I and several civilians are being detained upon the Humber Bridge. I don't know how many." McCann tries looking out the window but he cannot get a clear line of sight. "Likewise, I don't know how many hijackers there are. This is a nightmare, Giuliano. My own people are involved. I don't know how deeply. That's why I need you to ensure Milena and the boy are protected. You also need to find out why this is happening. But-" McCann sighs. "I don't know. That's not a good idea. Get away. Get Milena, the boy, and yourself away. Don't ask questions of my people, Giuliano. I don't know how many are involved. Good grief, my friend, how could this have happened? How could I have been so blind! How could I have been...manipulated into this situation?" McCann hears breathing on the other end, his friend is obviously trying to absorb all this information. "These...fanatics are not the usual terrorists. They have a...a bomb. Who knows how much devastation they can cause. They will obviously ask for a ransom but- I don't know, Giuliano, I really do not know."

His friend is silent, processing the information, McCann is sure. He has know this Italian man for years, since college, since their early days in film, but even from their first production together Alfred McCann has never felt so out of his depth.

Youthful Alfred McCann strides exuberantly through the concrete boulevard between twin white sound-stages 3 and 8, squinting against the sunshine which glares off the buildings which are as broad as they are tall, behind whose walls anything imaginable can, and does, happen for the purposes of the silver screen. These are the historic Velucci Studios in Rome, formerly the Cassiari Studios, which are based close to the Corviale District. They are located on the opposite side of the great Italian City from the old workhorse studios at Cinecitta, then and now the largest such production facility in mainland Europe. Velucci Studios are honourably named after Franco Badalamenti's wife in 1981, and have grown from strength to strength, doubling it's outdoor space for backlots and transformable acreage of hills and pasture, while offering the most state-of-the-art facilities in Europe during the 1990's comparable with some of the finest in Culver City - aka Hollywood.

Gucci sunglasses protecting his eyes, Alfred McCann cuts quite the figure in his designer shoes, tailor-made white cotton shirt and light grey Armani trousers, feeling exceptionally comfortable despite the early morning hot wind carrying its preordained dust! There really is no escaping the elements even amongst the many dozens of buildings which form the studio's concrete and steel soundstage facilities, but at least he isn't sweating yet, although he surely shall be soon because this is Alfred McCann's first Associate Producer credit working for Uncle Franco, albeit on a B-picture, and tensions sometimes rise in this volatile Italian environment. Cool under pressure, show them who is in charge.

Since the previous summer and it's fateful introduction to 'Uncle' Franco Badalamenti, Alfred and his best friend Giuliano have both share the privilege of being granted a prestigious internship as recognition of their multi-tasking movie talents. This has been a totally eye-opening revelation for McCann after the rebuffing received back home in England, his home country stale in the nurturing department: England belonging to the do your best but we will enjoy failure more, kind of school.

But their loss has been McCann's gain, because the young Englishman has discovered a great many new talents he heretofore never believed he possessed. During his tenure alongside Giuliano, he has also been developing numerous friendships along the way in this business of show, and in other areas of esteemed society too! It was comparatively easy too achieve, getting caught amongst the whirlwind that is the wonderful Badalamenti family, their various businesses of operation and the importance of loyalty, while enjoying considerably the numerous parties which are of great significance to raise one's profile in this high-time, fast-paced world, where remaining relevant is essential.

On this particular summer's morning there is so much minutiae to juggle which McCann must try to remember that if not for the invaluable assistance from his secretary he would surely be lost at sea. The young woman has efficiently armed him with a complete itinerary for the day which makes him feel more organised than his brain feels right now. The list has something resembling order. And to think at first he had been somewhat dubious as to the necessity of a secretary. At his young age!? He's twenty, for goodness-sake! What could he, the confident arrogant young fool, want a secretary for!? But he soon came around to the notion because what a notion and revelation she has proven to be in his life, while their time together and acquaintanceship has resulted in many wonderful fringe-benefits as she seeks to further her own movie career - her idea, before you get onto the sexist abuse discrimination etcetera bandwagon!.

Yesterday's pre-production party at Uncle Franco's beach house was a glittering affair and an excuse to really unwind and relax before the gruelling schedule ahead, and it also presented Alfred McCann with the opportunity to practise his oration skills - another facet which will be honed and improved upon over the ensuing years. He had confidently delivered a grand speech to his cast and crew which probably sounded very much off-the-cuff owing to his alcohol induced delivery, but in fact it was memorised spiel which his verbose secretary had created for him, to accompany the A4 expectations memo which is to be circulated this morning. The memo of intent for this production is uplifting, ingratiating and bears a definite authoritative quality too, which he is especially proud of, and McCann duly paid his gratitude to his secretary - and she loved every minute of it!

Indeed McCann has learned much about the movie industry and himself in particular over the last twelve months, his strengths and weaknesses, and has been champing at the bit to get this kind of elevated opportunity, so when he enters Stage Four at the studio this morning, the one designated for his production's use during four weeks of interior filming, he is rightly buoyed on a sea of excitement.

Lighting blazes upon the nightclub set which is abounded by ply-boards supported by two-by-fours, with the open steel rafters high above and swarming personnel mock the illusion in the highly detailed filming area. These are the wonders of the silver screen, creating believable illusion from industrial spaces.

Giuliano Badalamenti is talking heatedly into his mobile-phone just inside the doorway, illuminated by a fiery orange stage light which is positioned as part of the ambiance of the first scene to be filmed today: a nighttime scene. Giuliano holds the latest flip-device telephone which fits squarely in the palm of his hand and possesses an extendable aerial of about four inches in length, only he and McCann are in possession of such modern wonders. When he see's the arrival of his English friend he hurriedly concludes the phone call, ending on a demand for alacrity in the matter, causing McCann some concern because his friend is usually the most optimistic person he knows: problems already? Hey ho.

During the requisite amount of businesslike kissing on the cheek, McCann is able to take in what is happening on the busy sound-stage.

"Ciao, Al." Giuliano eventually vocally greets the young Englishman with a degree of nervous anticipation. "I've just been on the phone to our leading man's agent."

Preoccupied with appraising the calmness at which the set-decorators, lighting technicians and cinematographer are setting up the first scene to be filmed today, it takes a brief moment for McCann to re-register the concern and subtly hidden message Giuliano is trying to convey in his lowered voice.

"Nobody knows where he is." Giuliano tells Alfred with a hint of desperation.

"Who?"

"Pierro."

"Seriously?"

"Si."

"Our Star?"

"Si."

"Pierro Pasolini. Essential to this scene. The man whose participation is crucial for our backers?"

"Si."

Thanks to much practice and surrounding himself with the country's people, McCann's use of the Italian language has increased at an impressive rate, including quite a variety of expletives and colourful metaphors, one if which he now mutters under his breath.

"Everyone else is here?" McCann asks.

"Si. But no star!" Giuliano says helplessly. "I haven't the nerve to tell our director. He's a bit, you know, focused, at the moment."

This definitely isn't the way Associate Producer Alfred McCann had envisioned his first day of production going, yet above all this he must rise despite the panic building in his chest. So he remains as calm as he possibly can, collecting his steadily fragmenting thoughts, showing off his own acting abilities. He knows the first scenes involve their leading man but can they can work around his temporary disappearance? Is it going to cost the production money and time to do so? How late will he be? What if he doesn't turn up at all!? That notion doesn't bear consideration. No star, no production money, no movie.

There must he some perfectly logical explanation for this, so no need to panic just yet. Or perhaps the title of this modern crime noir film is somehow prophetic: No Way Forward.

"The first scene is half way through our movie." McCann says with a certain amount of rhetoric while his mind plots the details. "The audience by this point will be aware of the main character and his

162

qualities. He's a shadowy private detective with authority issues. Perhaps we can add a bit of excessive noir lighting to the night-club scene but hiding the detective in full shadow. Filmed from behind. This way we can use his stunt-double for the entire day if we have to. No-one will be able to see the difference."

"The director won't like it." Giuliano states flatly, impressed by his friends guile.

McCann simply shrugs his shoulders: "We can feed him some nonsense about the star having a family issue or whatnot. Who cares, really? As long as he starts shooting and we don't stand around wasting money. Make this seem like his idea, if we have to. He gets a few creative flourishes to put his distinctive artistic stamp on our cheap B-picture. This way Uncle Franco doesn't fire us before we get properly started in this business!"

"What's the expression?" Giuliano searches the rafters with his eyes for inspiration. "You are full of spit!"

"Close enough." McCann nods and grins, pleased to have his friend on his side, slapping him confidently on the back with youthful exuberance. "There is another expression I prefer." McCann adds. "Where there's a will, there's a way."

That challenge of the distant past now seems tame to McCann when compared with his present predicament upon the Humber Bridge. Older, wiser, but more susceptible to being dealt painful blows. More avenues of fear for the unscrupulous in the world to deliver. Giuliano, his reliable Italian friend whose presence has been with him for almost thirty years, will alleviate McCann's dread. His friend will offer level-headed advice, a positivity which he needs right now. Unfortunately for McCann, this is not the case.

"I am sorry, Al," Giuliano Badalamenti is now saying to the older Alfred McCann, the one stuck in a hostage situation on the great structure which is the Humber Bridge, "but this is where your life is going to end!"

TWENTY-SIX

Claudinalli Tucamkari sits in back of the van awaiting the arrival of the final piece to the jigsaw puzzle which will see the fruition of her revenge on the British Government. Years of plotting and scheming and recruiting has resulted in this moment. This will be the vilification of her life. The culmination of hard work, determination, and being married to an idiot whose legacy was curtailed by a lucky British Secret Agent stumbling upon their hidden volcano fortress.

This formidable woman surveys the orchestrated chaos which surrounds her. All these gullible fools are totally expendable. She doesn't share their idealism. None of them really know her true intentions. Only Dee is set to survive. Her offspring. She will tell the true tale. Deliver Claudinalli's words like a good daughter. Using her wiles to fool men.

With ease.

Men with wealth and power listen to pretty young women.

Claudinalli cynically believed this scheme would fail abysmally seeing how she typically underestimates this wayward English society with its Union-based subculture. She half expected those she hired to refuse overtime work or complain about the unsociable hours during plotting and executing this act of terrorism. The stupid English! Complaining, grumbling, lazy people who cannot take any responsibility whatsoever for their own actions. Letting their land be governed by corporations. Well, after this grand show which she and her team are going to put on there will be plenty of families claiming and blaming!

Alongside her on the partly carpeted metallic floor of the van made in China is Claudinalli's daughter, Dee. She is dressed appropriately for the dreary weather and somber occasion: brown combat boots, Khaki hot-pants barely containing her cheeks and a green tank top bursting at the seams! Little wonder the heterosexual men in their company volunteered to escort the payload and Dee.

Everyone else has their own agenda but Claudinalli's is the only one which possesses resonance. Even her faithful old new recruit is in the dark.

Ashley Barber's old, craggy face appears in the open partition window, pained and uncomfortable for having sat in one position for such a long time, but his eyes are bright with renewed youthful exuberance.

"Is it okay to stretch my legs?" The older man asks Claudinalli pleadingly.

If the situation were not so serious the villainess would laugh at such a request, but they have reached their destination so she nods permission.

Barbs needs not to be told twice, banging the door shut immediately behind himself, stamping out the cramp in his old thighs and the pain in his foot from a stab wound received many years in his past, a constant reminder of youth. He once counted up how many injuries he has sustained in his lifetime of action but frustratingly is now unable to recollect the exact amount, only that at the time of a drunken pub comparison thing he was on an equal footing - no pun intended - with the world's biggest movie star: Jackie Chan. Lucky him. Not a mean feat to be amongst that great man's survival success rate.

Barbs doesn't feel lucky right now though, because his body is protesting at the sudden relaunch into the stresses which his muscles had long forgotten. Maybe he will put his memory to the test when writing his autobiography.

The old man sucks in a breath of fresh air, filling his lungs gratefully while taking in the new, unfamiliar surroundings. Barbs has

166

seen bridges as large, and larger, than this construction before, but there is definitely something impressive about mammoth structures which makes him feel proud to be a human. The cabling is impossibly thick, the spires tower impressively , while the concrete, metal and length are nothing to sneer at. The architects who create such things are both scientists and artists. It's a shame they are likely reducing it to rubble but that's part of his job, as has been the case for more years than he cares to remember. How many insurance claims has he been responsible for? Barbs doesn't consider the lives which have been lost doing his job - fact is more people die in car accidents per week than he has claimed in his lifetime, not that he excuses himself. But on this occasion nobody with die, just this structure, according to the Tucamkari woman.

Anyway, he is getting away from the present moment with these reminiscences. Focus is what is called for and focus is what Barbs will do...once he has stretched his sore old legs.

"Hello te ye."

The now familiar Scottish lilt of William, which is not at all as cheery as the greeting might indicate, catches Ashley's attention and he see's the feet of the Scotsman at the open rear doors of the van, the rest of the man obscured.

"Give it to my boys." Claudinalli replies in her nasal American drawl, which used to be much clearer, before her near-death explosive experience.

Barbs catches sight of an aluminium briefcase being passed upward. The final piece to the bomb, although he knows more setting up is needed, with the securing and initialising before the device is activated and they get off the bridge. Six separate components have been sourced out across the country so as to eliminate the possibility of quick discovery, or someone spilling the beans. It has been assembled during the night under tighter conditions that they have here this morning, but this is not wholly unexpected to the operation. Claudinalli reckoned on this. She and Barbs discussed this yesterday evening when the meeting of all factions was concluded. They have no real time from hereon out. They have the advantage. Nobody can upset their plans now.

Media frenzy.

Countdown.

Evacuation.

Confusion.

Fame.

These are the steps which Ashley Barber has had outlined to him by Claudinalli.

"Who is he?" Claudinalli is asking William when Barbs ambles around the side to within sight of the back of the van, wonders where they are looking and casually looks toward the unguarded car of the Prime Minister. Is there any point to guarding it? Where can the man go?

"He's okay." William tells her. "He's okay."

"He'd better be." Claudinalli responds.

William looks to Barbs, then the Parliamentary car.

Barbs feels a tiny bit sorry for the Scotsman. Clearly the man isn't used to being a secondary player in an operation of this importance and is reluctant to secede his power to a woman. There is no further protest, though. No masculine posturing. Maybe a hint of resignation in his slumped shoulders. It is highly likely that he and they are not going to leave this place anonymously. For Ashley Barber he is resigned to the fact his days are numbered. This is definitely his last hurrah anyway. And what a way to go out. But the Scotsman- does he suspect imminent capture, the infamy, the inevitable execution?

"What!?" Claudinalli says irritably, almost doubtful of what she is hearing. "How long?"

Barbs hears a reluctantly mumbled reply from within the van. He watches the woman for her response. She is doing well to contain her emotion as much as she is, based on her past. Barbs thinks how Claudinalli has mellowed in her wiser age. In the past she would've exploded at the person who delivered some news she didn't wish to hear, which is what has obviously just happened, probably even dealt a devastating blow resulting in death without a second thought. Or asked a henchman such as Ashley to carry out the act. It was clear to everyone in those days who was in charge despite her husband being the face of the organisation. Back then people did not take female leaders seriously, they never respected women of real power, they were only a threat to the male ego. Things have changed a lot indeed. Time moves on.

"Deliberate?" Claudinalli is asking, receives a noncommittal response. "Get him out of that car!" Claudinalli finally says, pointing toward the Prime Minister's car. "The new guy, I mean. Bring him here. I need a word!"

William nods, turns on his heel and strides off toward the Prime Minister's car.

"What's wrong?" Barbs asks his boss, Claudinalli, with casual interest, not wishing to rile her up.

She doesn't answer at first, measuring her thoughts carefully, too calm: "It's just a delay. A minor setback. I want to know if the Scotsman's friend has anything to do with it."

Without hesitation Ashley Barber follows the Scotsman, eager to stretch his legs plus be a part of the action, feeling the adrenaline rush of yesteryear.

TWENTY-SEVEN

Scott Dalton stands by the open door of the Prime Minister's official car wondering if there is any way of locking both himself and McCann inside the bullet-proof vehicle for their protection against the two armed and dangerous men purposefully strolling toward them. The key is still in the ignition. Surely he could drive them off the Humber Bridge? Would these people kill the Prime Minister of Great Britain so soon after his capture? Hasn't he himself been successfully defying death for the past forty-eight hours, why stop now!?

But Scott immediately banishes these trains of thought because he knows the ignition is finger-print operated to it's driver, who isn't going to lend a hand, so to speak!

A slow-moving train, model like from this distance, catches Scott's eye momentarily, moving eastward like a metallic snake along the coastline.

The Humber Bridge looks down at him, the immense cables grinning forebodingly, smirking in their impossibly obscure knowledge which isn't real, but is mocking Scott's imagination nonetheless. How can this all this be real? How can the past two days be real? Is he still concussed upon the damp concrete in Paltournay? That small Scottish village which lingers in his mind like a surreal vision. A memory from the depth of his very mind yet only too recent. He has the aches to prove it. Why is twenty years ago more vivid than twenty minutes ago? This is real. It isn't his fevered imagination. He must draw strength from experience, from training, from the moment.

Scott still has no idea who has been trying to prevent him getting to this juncture. They have failed, obviously. Or have they? Was there another motive? If so, what is it? Was it someone, or multiple someone's, in the corrupt Government? Duplicitous Mike the chauffeur is only one of a network. How many more lay in waiting? How high up does the corruption reach? Scott smiles wryly: corruption in Government, there's a first!

Unfortunately the time for answering these questions isn't now because as the two men advance for who knows what purpose, his own options are slowly narrowing.

Running isn't exactly an option at all. Disarming the two men is an option if it comes down to it. There is a delay mantling the explosive and they think Scott has something to do with it. That stands to reason because he would feel the same way, no doubt. But also, don't act hastily. They have no actual proof. Scott can simply say the item must've got damaged en route. Or it happened in the junkie kinky sex slum flat - now there's a description! Who can say the component arrived there intact? Who can prove it wasn't damaged by the...whatever kind of people they were!

Feasible.

Thinking more sensibly, rationally, Scott realises he has nothing to worry about at all yet. He still has time to formulate a plan for saving the innocent victims who might otherwise get caught up in the blast, if it gets that far. But why go to all this trouble just to blow everyone up?

"He's okay." Scott shouts.

William and Ashley are now in closer proximity, their faces readable only if you are fearful of being killed. He mustn't overreact. Scott mustn't overthink himself into a corner. Overthink? Scott!? Overthink should be his middle name.

"The boss wants to see ye." William says bluntly.

"Splendiferous." Scott replies as nonchalantly as possible but not seeming to be unnaturally fake.

Ashley looks Scott up and down as if assessing him, reading him, working him out. Scott grins back at the older man without humour, similarly appraising him, getting back into his undercover mode. Scott can see the old man is experienced but out of condition. Competent yet missing something which Scott cannot pinpoint. Whereas William is alert, in his element, reserved, composed.

Scott follows the pair without looking back, his eyes drawn to the rotating blue lights of the emergency vehicles as they eventually converge onto the scene, their way hampered by the queues of disorganised traffic on the southward motorway leading up to Humber Bridge. Their sirens pound the air. How long will it take for them to completely break through the chaos? How many miles will they need to be away from the explosion when it comes? These people surely have no intention of ransoming the Prime Minister of Great Britain. They are going to kill him in spectacular fashion. Make a real statement which shall be remembered for years to come, not easily forgotten. Which happens too often. Small attacks forgotten in a week, a month, a year. People rally against these acts, sound-off on the radio. They used to spill their feelings on social media until stronger sanctions and regulations were put into place to curb those doing them harm, and conveniently reducing the freedom of speech. People would protest on social media but do nothing. Impotent rants. Activity is for other people, they would say. Faced with doing something, the actual act of physical activity, these people would use excuses. So these atrocities were replaced by the next atrocity, the next fashionable thing to protest against, the latest in a line of events to keep the population from questioning who might actually be behind the events. Distraction as propaganda. The terrorist in a foreign country, far away from harming their cotton-wool padded world, being fought by the laws of the land who know best for the common man as they always do because heaven forbid that the average politician has an agenda of his own.

No pressure for Scott. Just prevent a Government catastrophe with collusion from within the very establishment. He wonders if he will get the chance to tell Alfred McCann his own fears. If he will be able to do anything more about them?

Time for speculation later.

The boss looks very much like a plastic-surgery enhanced woman in her fifties trying to recapture her looks from twenty years ago - which doesn't really surprise Scott because women have always been more than capable of evil! In fact this woman looks vaguely familiar too him. Maybe he has seen a picture of her likeness in a Security Service file? Or a late night horror film which his friend Thomas C. Match once put on while they were getting drunk! Either way, she is tall, stern, not at all fragile, with an air of gravitas about her. Maybe her natural features were attractive back in the day but these enhancements are anything other than generous. Her skin shines of plastic, giving her a more masculine, transgender appearance.

While the younger woman beside her is the exact opposite: bursting with feminine appeal which strains at the very fabric of her clothing!

"Morning, boss." Scott says as amiably in his role of freedom-fighter as he can be, aware that this is now a very testing moment, one where he will soon learn his fate.

"Hey, fella." Claudinalli replies in her Texas drawl, not concealing her nationality as some others might who reside in this New Great Britain. "You know anything about this?"

Following Claudinalli's gaze to the aluminium briefcase which he brought, it's contents being manipulated by a stereotypical be-speckled white haired man in a laboratory coat, Scott firmly fixes his expression, removing any trace of guilt on his part. If he fails now what has been the point of all the training? He is amongst a den of wolves and preservation of his life is imperative.

"I'm not- er-" Scott says. "That is, I'm not terribly electronic minded. Sorry."

"Okay." Claudinalli responds. "Let me put it another way: it's been tampered with and I wanna know if you had anything to do with it."

Scott immediately responds with his best bewildered shrug of puzzlement.

"Who you really working for?"

"William and yourself at this point in time."

"And who before that?"

"You know already. William told you."

"Tell me yourself."

"Do you want to know what school I went to? My first crush? I'm here with your thing and I'm here now and I'm working for you."

"Ye get it straight from the place?" William aka Bob asks. He too is evidently aware of being under suspicion by this formidable villainess so must now serve two masters.

"Yes, absolutely." Scott replies, adding with a condescending laugh: "Although said establishment left much to he desired, to say the least. Anyway, what's this Spanish Inquisition all all about, huh? I got it here! How many hands has it passed through? If it's damaged or not working properly it's not my fault." He doesn't wait for a reaction. "So where do you want me? I don't mind watching over his Lordship McCann," he says with hopefully the right amount of contempt, "before the cavalry arrive."

While strained silence passes between them the distant sound of an approaching helicopter can be heard along with the persistent

174

police sirens, both north and south. The marked cars having broken through the frontline traffic, coming to a stop many yards from the machine-gun toting people awaiting them at the tolls on the Northside and lorry barricade on the Southside of the bridge, swiftly assessing the seriousness of this situation. Although they received word from the Humber Bridge Authority outpost. The enforcers of the law desperately need someone in charge to organise them, to draw back the traffic, create a safe cordon for the civilians, make some sense of the chaos. It's too late for those already caught up on the bridge unless Claudinalli and her people release them, but if the suicide pact ends sooner rather than later then more lives will be lost unnecessarily.

Claudinalli stretches her long, lean legs, eyeing each of her team with equal consideration, before she slides out the back of the foreign van. They all watch her, waiting patiently. She survey's the scene, aware of her importance. Aware of the significance. Knowing they await her command, and she loves it. Claudinalli loves the power she possesses over these men. Her advantage.

All eyes divert fleetingly from her and she knows without looking that Dee, her beautiful, captivating daughter, has followed out the back of the van.

"William." Claudinalli at last addresses her rapt audience. "Go to the chief officer down there." She is looking at the southern end of the bridge and the police gathering steadily there, organising themselves, trying to make sense out of the confusion. "Tell them our ransom demands...and our deadline." She turns to Barb's next. "Take a car to the other end of the bridge. And take Dee, too. Give her something to do. Make sure everything is secure their end." Then, finally, to Scott. "Go look after your Prime Minister. It don't matter about this minor delay anyway, our plan still goes ahead, if you are working for us or him."

Scott nods his head slowly, realising these people don't have the prerequisite walkie talkies and obviously aren't using mobile phones for communication purposes. Maybe it's to minimise risk, prevent any confusion. Surely the ransom is a ruse, but who knows. Hopefully it isn't, hopefully this really is about holding the Prime Minister for ransom because that would mean Scott has more time to formulate a plan. What is their agenda? And how much time does Scott have? And can he act before it's too late?

TWENTY-EIGHT

Alfred McCann could cry from the utter despair he is feeling right now after the bombshell delivered by his best friend Giuliano Badalamenti. This realisation of being alone, isolated, in danger and betrayed is overwhelming. Bugger the fact that he should be a hardened politician! A stiff upper-lipped Prime Minister of Great Britain. A businessman man of power who is always in control of his faculties. None of these facts make any difference to him now. How could he be betrayed by his life-long best friend? It makes absolutely no sense to McCann that this could possibly have gone unnoticed. It's like some movie plot concocted by a hack writer. A gag pitch. But the words of doom which Giuliano said down the airwaves were no joke. This was definitely not his friend winding him up. There was no sense of duress in Giuliano's tone, no indication that he was being forced into saying the words by gunpoint, which means, to Alfred McCann's way of thinking, that he has been hoisted into the position of Prime Minister of Great Britain by some insidious organisation who are now dropping him like a stone martyr. Betrayed. Used. Discarded.

But how?

"It's for the good of England," Giuliano had said with barely disguised sarcasm. "My family require your death so our organisation, and your Government, can continue the good work. You will he pleased to hear that most of your successes have not been in vain. Your brutal murder in this terrible act of terrorism shall force the hands of your allies to rally against their opposition. The anger won't be confined to England, no, my friend, not by a long shot. There will be repercussions stretching further than you can possibly imagine because our organisation has more global power than even you envisioned. More than I comprehend. Ours is an organisation within another inspired by

177

wider truths. We have learned, adapted and gained by others. Especially financially. Remember Zaire?"

McCann doesn't need to think back too hard:

In 1987 an estimated $1billion went unaccounted for from the evidently large coffers of the Kleptocracy otherwise known to the western world as Zaire. The African country's leader, Mobutu, has since been described as the 'archetypal African dictator', certainly appropriate for a man who placed money which was destined for his country's economy and populace into his own Swiss bank account. Mobutu became the Military Dictator and President of the Democratic Republic of the Congo in 1971, removing democracy from the country, which he renamed Zaire, to become a single-party state. Like many dictator's of the seventies his victory was popular with the more developed nations, the promises he made seemed acceptable, and the natural resources he possessed were great, until it soon became apparent that those who opposed him would be dealt with harshly via extreme means of brutality, and the prospects of impoverished citizens failed to improve over time. He would relinquish his power in 1991 when soaring inflation in Zaire sky-rocketed, forcing him to eventually share power over the people, although this action did nothing to stop him from bleeding dry the country's finances which, despite everything that had happened, had been bolstered with donations from richer countries such as the good old US of A and France, who sought the many exploitable resources available in Mobutu's country. Some estimates state that he, himself, embezzled over $15billion during his time in power, much of which was still unaccounted for after his death in 1997 from prostate cancer. One of Mobutu's closest confidantes during the last years of his dictatorship had been Franco Badalamenti? The faith and trust which the African leader put into this Italian businessman was almost legendary, while Interpol and other world security agencies suspected the money lavished by Mobutu on his quirky proclivities was in fact finding its way to a benefactor, they never discovered the identity of this benefactor.. So even the most thorough investigation using global recourses could not prove the whereabouts of the missing billions, a phenomenal sum which seems impossible to 'lose' in the system, but these are the facts as they stand today, where such funds could he hugely rewarding if used for good, whereas in the hands of a terrorist organisation they could result in catastrophe.

"Remember other bureaucratic corruption in Africa, across Asia and Russia? Their financial losses have been our gain." Giuliano chuckles. "Oh, I'm not the man in charge, if that's what you are thinking, no. I am just one of the many people benefiting from this new world order. Who knows who is really in charge, or if there is a true leader, in fact. I just know we possess the same desires and my family, my Uncle Franco, was a benefactor of these collapsed nations as I too inherit his goals. We don't want much, just complete control over all Government's, all military and all trade, which is within our very grasp and your murder by a band of radicals shall compound."

Disturbed beyond comprehension, Alfred McCann had truly thought he could not possibly hear anything worse than all the Top Secret information which his Security Service gathers from global resources. But this Italian, this friend who he shared dreams with, ambitions with, success with, is telling him there is an fractured organisation spread across the entire globe which seeks ultimate power over...everything? A World Terrorist Organisation? The anti-United Nations? It's not as if there is a unified faction of terrorists bowing to a single leader with a common goal, a scattering numerous disparate groups whose purpose is ultimately to achieve the same ends. And their means are pay-rolled by finance from the very Governments who fight these acts. However unfashionable the scope may seem, however deeply improbable something like this level of corruption, hidden, sewn deeply within the fabric of nations, it is not impossible for a man of intellect to conceive.

Corrupt Government. Failed Governments. Greed and power and wealth.

These are the devil's which idealistic Alfred McCann thought he was warring against.

Anarchy can be the only possible outcome should these acts of radicalism continue unabated. World anarchism. Not just a single country thrown into turmoil, which has become a too common occurrence anyway, and is easily ignored by those in the supposed civilised world. Anarchy doesn't happen at home. But if these people succeed that's exactly what will happen. Government's shall he forced to have tighter strictures for their citizenry. Borders will spring up in countries where free passage was once allowed.

Xenophobia has existed for over a hundred years since the advent of passports, restricting the freedom of movement, the freedom of identity, but with the tightening of power, the monopolising of utilities as Giuliano has inferred will occur, citizens will become prisoners in their own backyards.

"Goodbye, my friend." Giuliano had said finally before hanging up.

And now Alfred McCann was alone at sea, as it were. His daughter wrenched from him, his Government soon to follow and then, conclusively, his life. His heart aches for Milena. The love of his life, the woman of his dreams. Milena and their son. What has become of the them? Will he ever see them again? Will he ever step off this bridge?

TWENTY-NINE

Life doesn't get much better than this and there has never been a dull moment! At least if you are barely into your twenties and called Alfred McCann. Much has happened in his life in the two extremely short, swift, years since his executive producing credit for No Way Forward for Uncle Badalamenti's film company. He is Chief Executive Officer for the company he and Giuliano have begun together: Hammicass Productions, London, and on the very morning of his wedding day he is nursing the hangover from hell.

Splendiferous.

But it's worth it.

Not only has the Badalamenti family gifted him incalculable career opportunities, grooming him into the man he has become and helped him forge many acquaintances in the world of celebrities, alongside the greater friendships he has been lucky to enjoy, the best of all has been Milena.

Milena is the niece of Uncle Badalamenti, and turned nineteen years of age a week prior to this very day, their wonderful wedding day, which has been a culmination of twelve months of planning. Alfred McCann has only known her in the context of a relationship for eighteen months but then as now he knew she was the one for him, and her feelings for him were mutual. Some might frown upon their swift decision as the naive impulse of youth, but they know otherwise. Their connection was instant, prophetic almost, bordering on the spiritual, like they exist to temper the other, possessing complimentary characteristics which are repelled yet attracted like magnets turning and meeting in an endless, continuous maelstrom. They are they perfect fit for each other.

Milena is an understated classic Italian beauty with dark brown flowing hair, full green eyes, tall, classy, hour-glass figure. She is a passionate realist, artistically inclined toward poetry and painting but openly acknowledges her desire to tend a successful, self-sustaining home and raise proper, healthy children.   Alfred was drawn to her pure laughter, the way Milena's delight in something funny was natural, infectious. Also she has no hidden pretensions or falsehoods: what you see is what you get. Milena enjoys the fine things in life which her privilege has provided yet she doesn't flaunt these things like others might, enjoying good fortune mixed with simple tastes. She definitely helps to balance his potentially troublesome ego in a way which tempers Alfred, because he could easily lose his way amidst the glamour and razzle-dazzle of his new life.

He needs her in his life.

Right now the only thing he desires is something to soothe his throbbing headache and an ice cold shower.

Last nights revelries were magnificent and he will certainly not knock his good fortune by being angry at those whose company he enjoyed until midnight and encouraged his present condition - they were very disciplined to actually cease their fun at the time agreed upon before they began. And however exquisite the taste of expensive wine, it still leaves a sandpaper dry mouth come the morning. Alfred lost count of how many glasses and bottles were consumed amidst the canapés and other finger-food brought to the pool and garden area of Chateau Neuf du Menti by scantily clad servers of both sexes last night, all very tasteful, but fun nonetheless.

They had begun the day on the yacht, fishing and drinking and eating, Italian style. More than once Alfred had to pinch himself to believe the various male celebrities that had joined them through-out the day on his stag-do, with wives and girlfriends joining them during the evening frivolities. There had been no pranks, no incriminating situations, but plenty of Italian-style fun mixed with the genuine, unpretentious religious blessings. Alfred has encountered such a powerful religious spirituality in this family which he thought only really existed in movies - namely The Godfather series - but whereas these beliefs were a curio, now they are part of his own time in this country, which he fully respects is a large part of their culture. Family and religion breed respect all over over Italy, a deeply ingrained societal desire for freedom of spirit and mind. This is quite a different experience from England and something Alfred felt awkward in embracing at first, similarly to the touchy-feely greetings and partings. These routines have informed and tempered his business dealings and the way he works, opening Alfred's mind to a variety of belief systems and philosophies, listening to these colourful characters, absorbing facets of their received wisdom and patterning aspects of his own life upon them. Once more, were it not for these things opening his eyes, Alfred may very well have missed the presence of Milena when she entered his sphere.

And all this is after the most amazing week of Alfred's life. The four week's worth of honeymoon ahead for he and Milena will see much needed recovery and preparation for the challenge awaiting them upon their return. Upon completion of his fourth picture for Uncle Badalamenti Hammicass formally came into existence as a real entity just this week, followed by a succession of celebration parties and lavish press junkets to announce both events.

It has been hard getting to this point in his life but now Alfred is here, despite the pounding skull, he would not want his life to be any other way.

Somebody is now pounding their wooden fists inside his skull which he knows lots of coffee will eliminate, but just the same, he wishes it weren't present. Coffee: the great healer!

The knocking persists as he walks across the luxurious hotel carpet from the bedroom into the main room of his suite. He cannot recall getting here but assumes one of Franco's people brought him. The hotel is near the church where he and Milena are to be married that afternoon, which s probably a good thing.

Alfred reflects that it is curious how many tricks the mind can play, like films, where the audio is either out of place or accentuated to symbolise something that the on-screen action cannot capture, because now he realises the knocking is coming from the door to his suite and is not in his head. He wonders if room service has arrived to deliver him from this evil hangover.

Franco Badalamenti stands in the hotel corridor eyeing him with curious bemusement, he himself showing no signs whatsoever of the revelries or lateness of hour which said revelries ceased.

"My boy!" The man's jolly voice is like a booming megaphone to Alfred's tender ears, without mentioning the European hug and kiss. "I am happy to find you awake so early!" He looks curiously into the room. "And I am impressed you are alone, eh, my boy!"

For the first time in quite a long while Alfred McCann actually flushes with embarrassment. The one thing he would most definitely never do, despite what is on offer to him on a daily basis, is be unfaithful to Milena, the woman he knows he truly loves and adores, but this being the morning after his stag-do in Europe, anything and everything apparently goes!

"But you need coffee." The old man says, studying Alfred's face. "So I won't keep you long."

"I am feeling a bit tender."

"No worries. You feel better soon."

"I certainly hope so. Your wine is quite potent."

"Today you join my family." Franco clamps a hand on each of Alfred's shoulders. "And I am happy beyond compare. We are indebted to all you have brought us, and you take on the responsibility inherent in this occasion. I have opened my arms to you and in return you have given much more than any man can expect."

"It's nothing, truly."

"Family loyalty means a great deal to us and I want to assure you that if you are ever in need of anything, do not fail to ask."

"Thank you." Alfred replies sincerely, genuinely touched by the old man's blessing and warm words. "But it is I who am grateful to you, and should be thanking you and your family. The opportunity and faith bestowed upon me by yourself is immeasurable, and such kindness humble's me."

"I see great things in your future, my boy." Franco says, nodding sagely, knowing he has made the right choice with this Englishman, how malleable the young man will be.

One more set of kisses to each cheek, and Alfred watches the old man as he departs cheerily, humming a happy tune. Franco could be a man in his forties, thirties again. Alfred thinks himself truly very fortunate, undeniably lucky in life and, thinking of Milena, lucky in love too.

He yawns and suddenly a memory pops into his head which causes him to speed up: his parents are arriving from England at 8 o'clock this morning and it's already 7 o'clock! He curses, makes a phone call, knowing that it is impossible for him to get to the airport in time but he can rely on Giuliano.

THIRTY

Scott Dalton's equilibrium falters and he forces himself to not panic. Deep breathing always helps. This is what he does now. Inhale for five seconds, slowly expel, repeat. The situation has caused this irrational feeling. The mind dictating the actions of the body. Knowing how lucky he has once again been. Capitalising on this luck is crucial. Scott tries to casually walk with Ashley Barber and Dee along the blacktop up the Humber Bridge south-side incline, blood whooshing loudly in his eardrums, the yellow fog of dizziness threateningly on the periphery of his vision. He ponders his options, trying to refocus his brain, while also absorbing the unfolding scenes of noisy bedlam taking place all around him - the emergency vehicle sirens with their variety of nee-- naw pitches; the first media-circus helicopter whipping up the air, curiously swift in their arrival at the scene, tipped off by the perpetrators perhaps; voices shouting, ordering, baying at the sky in despair; aggrieved drivers sounding their horns to add nothing but more noise to the confusion; and the wind on the bridge, it's force having risen as it drives the clouds of doom into the already foreboding maelstrom.

The woman in charge whose name he still doesn't know has instructed William to delver her demands to the police on the south side of the bridge. So as far as Scott can tell this is to be a ransom demand after all, with the bomb acting almost as a deterrent. Scott at least needs not worry too much about the civilians as long as the demands are met. Will they be met? Or will the still operational SAS intervene as they have successfully done so in the past?

"How much is she asking?" Scott asks smoothly, followed by a grin. "I just want to know how much my cut will be."

"None of your business." Ashley says, the seasoned pro revealing nothing to the unfamiliar upstart, Scott assumes.

"Fair enough."

"Yes it is."

Scott shrugs as if he doesn't really care anyway, instead giving his best ladykiller smile to Dee when she looks sidelong at him past Ashley. Scott hopes to have some impact on one half of this bizarre coalition. He nods to her to indicate Ashley, silently asking her what his problem is.

"When this is over, Dee," Scott says in the hope of engaging in some form of conversation, "how about you and I hook up for a drink?"

"Sure thing, hon." Dee replies, her accent strong, like that of the older woman who-

"Are you the bosses daughter?" Scott asks.

"Yup."

"Best I watch my mouth."

"How 'bout I do that sometime?" Dee says, just in case there is any confusion adding without need for subtlety: "Watch your mouth, that is."

"Sounds interesting."

"Yeah, don't it?"

Scott nods. He knows exactly what she is flirting about! Who says harmless banter cannot provide results, although one should be more careful in this age of sexual harassment claims!

"You like Chinese?"

"I prefer English."

"Hot or cold?"

"Hotter the better."

"Splendiferous."

They are upon the PM's car and Scott regrets having to stop. He wouldn't mind pumping the young American woman for information. Her loose tongue and corny dialogue is refreshing amidst all the cagey Radicals. These people only trust Scott to a point, which is fair enough, but where can he go with any information he might gather? A mixed up bunch of multi-national terrorists and corrupt Government staff who have all the exits covered except for upwards and downwards and neither of those routes are appealing right now.

What use is all this to Scott? Squat!

When he reaches for the flush door-handle of the official Government car Scott pauses instinctively. In the backseat sits the Prime Minister sobbing into his hands. This is definitely not a situation he has been trained to handle, and there is no experience he can draw upon to relate to what the man in charge is possibly going through right now - except for the loss of his parents. So he gives the PM time to sort himself out, compose himself.

But not much time because it is very much of the essence right now.

"Just me, sir." Scott says with formality upon finally opening the door, swinging his backside into the drivers seat, feet still on the blacktop - Mike the chauffeur has kindly left the starter key in the ignition, so no need for his hand!

The Prime Minister stares at Scott with angry red eyes.

"Are you with this lot?" McCann asks through gritted teeth, his rage and anguish in his voice barely contained but blatantly evident upon his face.

Scott shakes his head.

"How can I be sure?"

"You cannot. You just need to take my word."

"Your word?"

"That's right, sir."

"And what good will that do me?"

"It might save your life."

"Or it might shorten it."

"People in the Service-" Scott begins with an impatient sigh, but catches himself, not really knowing where to begin or where to go with this because the PM might not believe him anyway. "I have been strung along on this assignment but- I think I am in a better place now to assess the situation we are in. I wouldn't mind finding out who has been trying to kill me because it's someone in the Security Service, but that's for later."

"Someone has placed you in a very awkward position, Mister Dalton."

"I realise that, sir. And I admit at first I thought they were acting under your orders."

"Mine?"

"That's right."

"Hmm. I can understand your train of thought, Dalton."

"Oh?"

"They tell me you have turned."

Scott nods and says with a wry grin:

"Then the joke really is on me, sir."

Scott laughs humourlessly before continuing.

"Right now, we just need to bide our time until the hijackers make their ransom demands. I heard orders being given to that effect. I'm sure I think of some way for getting us out of here, or waste their time until someone with a plan to rescue you arrives."

The Prime Minister shakes his head solemnly, his haunted eyes blood-shot, hollow, tired, full of sorrow with the weight of the world on his shoulders.

"It's no good, Scott." The PM tells him with uncharacteristic informality, forgetting himself, pursing his lips regretfully. "There is to be no ransom. There will be no genuine rescue attempt. They are setting up to detonate this bomb no matter what."

Scott is about to ask him how he knows this but doesn't get the opportunity.

"My- best friend has told me I am going to die here!"

THIRTY-ONE

People live in a bubble-wrapped world of complacency snuffling amongst the consumerism troughs without realising they have been brainwashed by corporations. War and violence is something unreal to the people. It is on television which is a fictional environment, much like the arguing factions on soap operas that sully themselves to beautify the lives of its viewers. This world is meaningless. Social media has forced people into viewing all their friends as complicit rivals in life, an offering of trivia and exaggerated truths using base symbols or the highest prose. Fake. Zombies walk the streets, entombed in their own hollowness. Leaders are weaker imitations failing to improve on their weak predecessors. Historical lies are propagated as gospel truths in schools.

But today?

Today all this changes.

Claudinalli Tucamkari smiles at the words she has just typed into the iPad in front of her - realising the irony. She is satisfied with how these words sound, there is no hidden meaning, no unnecessary reading between these lines. They are the conclusion of a two page explanation for those who might be interested in what has motivated the rebellion which begins with the death of the British Prime Minister and destruction of the Humber Bridge - a literal and symbolic divide.

Events before today have stirred the media but this will blend the masses.

Here is a positive message to everyone borne by these actions.

Plus a soul stirring speech which will hopefully motivate others into action while vilifying those already engaged in this cause.

Her daughter will be safe from the explosion. Claudinalli secretly instructed Ashley Barber to whisk her away along with a handful of lucky civilians. A ruse. The car with a supposed innocent businessman sits a car's length back on the northern exit. A story is already worked out for them. They have plenty of time.

She isn't concerned by the arrival of any Special Forces or SAS or whoever the powers that be will throw in their direction - those on the inside couldn't exactly stall a rescue mission, how bad would that look for their own future.

Not that Claudinalli Tucamkari cares either way what happens after she has delivered her message and set off the bomb because revenge is truly her motive. Yet to be a part if something else, something more, and a success after the numerous failings of her husband, would indeed be special. The icing on the proverbial cake.

The world needs shaking up. The chemical attack seems to have faded from memory, and how quickly, too. Hundreds of thousands of people were affected and still businesses operate as if nothing has happened, citizens go about their mundane routines like it's safe in the world. Their bubble-wrapped, cotton-wool cushioned world with bills to pay, family to feed, friends to appease, the taxman to keep happy, the banker's to whom they grovel placated.

Ridiculous!

Where is the freedom? Really. Where?

What is to be enjoyed by being a drone?

Because this is what the human race has become. They are contained by the restraints imposed upon them by the self-serving money-grabbers. The bottom feeders who care nothing about the public at large, using them, discarding them, programming their miserable lives.

Claudinalli prizes herself off the floor of the van, shivering in the chill air, yearning for more sunny climes. It's going get warm here soon, she thinks wryly.

192

"How much longer?" The woman asks.

The studious scientist look from his work, a smile in his eyes not transferring to his mouth.

"Fifteen minutes tops." He tells her.

"Good."

Claudinalli sighs happily, like a child does when presented with a long anticipated gift. And that's what this is: her gift to mankind.

THIRTY-TWO

A milky sunshine is barely visible through the morning clouds which are thin and patchy, breaking into wisps of blue sky upon the horizon, giving some on the North Sea a glimpse of colour. This September morning is typically British: unsettled. A moderate temperature means taking a jacket with you, just to be on the safe side. Prepare for rain because the hours a long. Travel for every eventuality. But most of all be prepared for the unpredictability of it all with a stiff upper lip.

Welcome to England.

For those on the Humber Bridge this morning the unpredictability has taken a very swift turn indeed. Their plans have been scuppered irrespective of what they may be. A simple day out. A business trip. Making a delivery. Visiting friends. All those variations of journey with unique mindsets who organised their route according to individual requirements, scuppered. Upended with the same unpredictability as the weather.

Even Scott Dalton couldn't have foreseen exactly what was going to happen to him, despite the device he was transporting. Who could have known except for the radicals themselves? In this topsy-turvy world their scheme is a logical step: destroy a symbol of man's endeavours along with a man whose impact is arguably greater than those he comes after.

The Humber Bridge and the Prime Minister of Great Britain. Two larger than life symbols.

But what of the innocent victims? Why more senseless killings? Does their deaths make this a relatable situation? Will the public decry the murder of those who could be themselves? Will this atrocity be the straw which finally breaks the camels back?

For Scott Dalton this could be the most important moment in his life. He must save lives. But how?

What can he do?

He looks at the Prime Minister in the backseat of the Governmental car, it's upholstery smelling like new, for some sign of inspiration, a divine encouragement. But the man is merely gazing out the side window, lost in thought, looking but not seeing.

The Humber Bridge looms dauntingly above and below, stretching its giant arms across the grey water of the Humber estuary, both sides of the land giving the appearance of a miniaturised world, an unreal Lilliputian society stretching for miles yet curious unreal. Unreachable yet within touching distance. A heightened reality because of the scope and scale, no doubt. A world where Scott cannot see too many options opening up for him.

"You need to get off this structure, Scott."

It takes Scott a millisecond to register the voice as that if the Prime Minister because at first he thought it was his subconscious mind stating the obvious.

McCann continues talking but doesn't turn to face Scott, instead his wet eyes regard the Estuary with unseeing vagueness.

"You need to get off here and fix this. This is larger than the here and now. More essential work awaits you. You need to- You need to find my family, find Giuliano and try to fix this whole mess. I am giving you a direct order. You need to make sure Giuliano and his family don't succeed." Not long ago Alfred McCann himself was a part of that Italian family. Not any more. "By whatever means you deem necessary. You understand?"

"Yes, sir, but-"

"I need your assurance, Mister Dalton."

It doesn't require a sixth sense to ascertain the Prime Ministers sincerity, and it takes barely seconds for Scott reach his conclusion.

"You have my assurance, sir."

"Use whatever means necessary."

There is such vehemence in the Prime Minister's eyes that Scott simply nods, not willing to point out that his Italian friend might just be another pawn in the broader scheme.

"These people get their financing from corrupt Government's. I can see that now. I was blind to the truth. My own Government are corrupt."

"Not all of them, sir."

"We finance terrorism, Scott."

"But you also do good, sir. Try not to lose perspective."

"Perspective. Yes. You're right, of course. But the fact is I let this happen right under my own very nose."

"It wasn't your fault, sir."

The Prime Minister doesn't respond, consumed by his self-pity, and nothing which Scott can say will change this so he must try a different tactic.

"I can't see too many options here, sir."

This seems to snap McCann back to the here and now.

"Both ends of the bridge are heavily fortified."

"So driving off is out of the question?"

"That's right, sir."

"Couldn't you climb up?" McCann's eyes drift to the encircling media helicopter. "Get off on one of those? The police will probably send one of theirs soon."

"I would still have get to one end of the bridge to make an attempt."

Scott painfully strains his neck to look directly upward, sceptically thinking he would rather take his chances jumping off the side into the water than climbing to the top of his monstrous construction. He isn't afraid to heights but even he draws a line somewhere. Only a complete fool would seriously contemplate making a climb without safety equipment. A fool or a suicide!

"How about jumping off the side?"

Scott almost tells the Prime Minister to stop making stupid suggestions and think of something sensible. Secret agents aren't impervious to death! But, no, the man is only trying to help, narrow down the options, discard the ridiculous until something plausible arrives.

"I don't have a parachute."

"And if you did?"

"I would probably drown or be shot up with bullets."

"Okay. But what about if you jumped onto a boat?"

"I should break my legs most likely. And then there's the question of direction. Without a proper parachute and enough height I would miss the target."

"How about above land?"

Scott regards the Prime Minister with his best quizzical eyebrow raised, thinking he really has lost the plot.

"The bridge passes directly over woodland on the northern side. Can't be more than a forty feet drop."

"Would you care to try it yourself, sir?"

"Don't be facetious, Dalton."

Scott shakes his head, straining his eyes in the direction of the north side. The neat shoreline with its die-cast traffic, thin roadway, miniature trees. Just like a model village. The one in Great Yarmouth which he frequented on holidays in the seaside resort town. Crazed his parents until they gave in just to keep him quiet. Strewth, he must have been annoying. Too late now to apologise.

Jump from a Brobdingnagian bridge to a Lilliputian village? There are worse ways to die.

THIRTY-THREE

"I have a picnic blanket in back."

The Prime Minister announces like it's the most natural thing in the world to suggest: jumping off a bridge using a square of cloth as a makeshift parachute.

Scott regards the notion with understandable scepticism. He is no expert on the matter. In point of fact Scott Dalton has never actually performed a parachute jump for real, with a genuine chute much less something not designed for such an act. Jumping from a plane has never been on his Bucket List. That's not to suggest he wouldn't do it, just that the opportunity hasn't occurred yet. Scott can understand why people would want to do it, the exhilaration and rush of adrenaline while plummeting to the earth must be fantastic, but these daredevil types use specially designed equipment to attain their kicks.

Even professionals don't use a picnic blanket.

"I'm no expert on such things, Mister Dalton," says the Prime Minister of Great Britain, the man in charge of millions of live, but nature a job requiring intellect and common sense, "but the dynamics should be quite favourable. And besides, you only have thirty-feet to travel."

The reverse psychology makes Scott smile: it was forty-feet not much more than five minutes ago. The great Politician's of our time have always been able to bend the truth successfully to suit them when they need. But this is Scott's life - or suicide - being discussed. Would it be suicide or enforced homicide?

"Sit tight, sir." Scott says, opening the car door. "I shall make a feasibility study."

The fresh oxygen is welcome after the dryness in the Governmental car. Obviously the seals are checked regularly for imperfections which is why it became stifling inside. Air-conditioning must be constantly on to prevent tiredness. Makes sense. If there is a chemical attack made upon the vehicle it would need to be sealed tight. But all the same, the lack of oxygen was making Scott feel slightly woozy and susceptible to ludicrous suggestions!

And he might deliberately be wasting time.

Time he doesn't have.

Scott closes the door and holds onto the roof sill for balance. Yes, woozy. The sparkles flash behind Scott's eyes. His eyes are strangely heavy.

No time for concussion.

He needs to stay alert. Being in the cosy confines of the car has done him a disservice. A lethargy has been created when the opposite is called for. Scott needs to do something physical, stimulate his body to engage his brain, like jumping off a bridge!

It's difficult for Scott to get a true perspective of size and distance upon the Humber Bridge but he believes Ashley and Dee have almost reached the northern side of the bridge. He can just see them under the strut, stark figures on the usually busy structure.

Behind him William can be seen conversing with a representative of the law. Giving out false demands to stall for time. Making the authorities believe they have a hope preventing tragedy.

Scott's stomach grumbles hungrily at him.

The wooziness explained.

He knows where there is food. There is a picnic basket in the trunk of the Prime Minister's car. And a blanket.

A picnic basket! How the other half live. Only the rich and privileged would have such a luxurious item packed and ready for them on a daily basis, just in case one wishes to stop off wherever one wishes. Scott wonders cynically if it is from Fortnum And Mason's, realising the likelihood is practically assured.

No expert required!

Thirty-feet of air to free-fall through. Four corners of a blanket. Like a kid. Yes, it's child play, really. Scott and his mates would do something similar to this in the woodland near his home when he was growing up. Half an age ago. If the treetops cushion his fall, the blanket might very well snag upon a branch, slowing his descent to the ground. So long as all the ne'er-do-wells are kept occupied on the bridge he should have ample escape time, although that in itself is of the essence.

Yes, definitely child's play. But first things first, as they say.

Take the basket. Get as far away from the bomb as feasibly possible. The northern end would be logical. Assess his chances of survival. Then jump. One way or the other the odds are against him getting off the bridge alive anyway.

To himself:

"Get on with it then!"

Pulling open the door Scott smiles hauntingly at the Prime Minister.

"I'm feeling peckish and someone informed me of a picnic basket in your car. How do I pop the trunk?"

"Button on the ignition key."

"Thank you."

"Good luck, Mister Dalton."

"Thank you, sir. If there's a chance..."

Prime Minister Alfred McCann waves away any further chatter, smiling his best practised fake Politician assurance.

Scott nods, popping the trunk.

He was right about the basket. It's a plush wicker hamper straight from Fortnum And Mason's. So much for the PM's promise to lead by example. This costly luxury isn't exactly what Scott would call cutting back. But then, transparency never was a forte of the powerful and wealthy.

Hauling it from the trunk Scott bangs the lid shut. The basket is heavy. Probably the bottle of Moët and jars of caviar. Not to Scott's taste but there will be more palatable food inside, he hopes. One final hearty meal for the condemned, cliche included!

Hazarding a casual glance southward he takes in the van, the woman, the barricade, the police, and William aka Bob. The Scotsman is striding purposefully along the blacktop toward the van, no doubt with news on the reception he received when delivering their demands. For no real reason Scott wonders if William is in the dark about his ultimate fate. A random thought yet not out of present character. The Scotsman is a rebel-rousing freedom fighter, probably more accustomed to smaller jobs which involve getting away! William is a simple man, not the martyr type. Could his agenda differ from the American woman? Could be truly believe the ransom is on the cards? Is the fatalistic outcome solely between the woman and McCann's Italian friend? Have all the disparate parties in this attack different agendas? Scott wants to ask the American. He wants to discover what motivates her. But there will no opportunity. Maybe her daughter can shed a bit of backstory. The young woman doesn't conceal too much!

It takes but a second for all these lurid thoughts to tumble through Scott's brain.

Hunger beckons.

A potential catastrophe is about the occur but hunger represents his nearest danger! Scott has his priorities right, at least!

He is tempted to wait for William to rejoin him.

Scott places the basket upon the roadway and opens it, choosing from the splendiferous selection he pulls out a fresh sandwich, which appears to be nothing but the finest ham and lettuce, from a sealed refrigerated micro-unit. Carefully unwrapping the paper he takes a bite. This is probably the best sandwich he has ever tasted. The bread is soft with a freshly baked taste that is out of this world, while the ham is succulent, off the bone, and the lettuce is as crisp as if it were pulled just prior to use. Certainly this is a worthy last meal for a condemned man, should that outcome be the case.

Scott allows himself a wry smile at the doom'n'gloom.

While the nutrition from the sandwich enlivens his body he next selects a banana, eating it in seconds. Scott now feels one-hundred better. Now all he needs is a Costa, but that's not going to happen just yet! So instead he settles for a can of coffee, which is better than nothing and not an unpleasant flavour, hitting a similar spot to the food. The Champagne beckons with its seductive label.

Placing his litter in the basket Scott closes the lid and lifts it up, aware that William's presence is upon him. He smiles amicably at the Scotsman.

"Care for a bite, my friend?"

"Och no."

"I had a delightful chat with McCann."

"Where ye taking that?"

"I was going to see if I could make a few quid by selling food to the hostages."

"Ye aren't funny, laddie."

"So I've been told, which is why I chose this life instead of becoming a stand-up comedian."

Scott starts strolling northbound, expecting the Scotsman to call him back, but instead William aka Bob follows him, catches him up and keeps apace. Not that Scott gets any impression the man wants a friendly chat. Far from it. It's as though the Scotsman is keeping a close check on him. Never mind, Scott is enjoying his thoughts of escape. Although there is a small measure of guilt in the action which he is contemplating. Not toward William. But for the innocent people he is abandoning. Despite what the Prime Minister has told him, there may very well be far-reaching corruption jeopardising society, but Scott nonetheless is running clear from the present danger.

THIRTY-FOUR

For the second time in twenty-four hours Scott Dalton has the sickening sensation of falling to what is, in his lurid imagination, an excruciatingly painful inevitable death. First time was on a crumbling eyesore with its rusting ladder and a wheels-bin bunker saving his life. This time he has a beautifully woven silk/cotton tartan blanket from Fortnum And Mason's, which he is relying upon to reduce the chances of him plummeting to an ignominious finale, and a better view.

Funny how it was relatively easy for Scott to get into this situation. If he had been trying for an easier escape there would undoubtedly have been numerous complications. Such is life.

When he and a William had reached the northern end of the Humber Bridge they exchanged a few banal words with Ashley and Dee.

"Fancy some caviar?" Scott has asked Dee using his best, suave, sophisticated delivery.

"Naa! It's disgusting. Who'd eat fish eggs?"

"How about some Bratwurst?"

"Mmm, the bigger the better." Was her predictably sensual reply at being offered an impressively sized sausage.

"Cut out the crap, kids." Was Ashley's grumpy old man way of breaking up the ridiculously cliche and not altogether embarrassing flirting.

Scott had wondered at the time, but kept that wonder to himself, how they were possibly going to get such an eye-catching young woman off the bridge without anyone realising she is a part of the Grand Plan. There are too many witnesses, for one thing. Not to mention her unsubtle personality. Or maybe her escape is just a shirt-term situation. Another part of the scheme between her and her mother.

Which once more makes Scott rue the inability for him to discover motivations from the female duo.

And so he had double-backed on himself, only this time it was via the footbridge, with his picnic basket, raising no curiosity from the trio of criminals. Scott located a good enough position as any to chuck himself off the bridge. It still looked like some scary theme park ride. A bungee-jump without the bungee and onto what, from this height, looks like a model woodland. Only the trees are dangerous real, appearing much further away than even the forty-feet the Prime Minister had exaggerated. But he couldn't exactly walk off the bridge. Nobody was going to let him take the easier route. Too many complications, like a bullet in the back of his head, for one thing.

Cracking open a bottle of Fentiman's Cola, deliciously refreshing and wetting his bone dry palate, he removes the blanket as coolly as he can, looking about to see if anyone is observing, and after making one-hundred percent certain the blanket isn't some metre-square one person job, he swiftly hauls himself over the railing.

So far, so easy.

Unbelievably easy, in fact, but who but a suicidal maniac would attempt such a stupid thing?

The lovely sound of the blanket snapping when filled with air above him and the tug from the modicum of drag which it produces is very reassuring, particularly because the falling sensation wrenching at his stomach lasts for barely two seconds. The treetops which seemed so far away moments ago are rushing at him. From a distance their appearance was neat and organised and structured. But not close up. Disorganised nature reaching for the sun. Branches, some with leaves, others striped bare by the weather or birds, stick out like lethal spikes waiting to skewer prey.

Before Scott has the chance to dwell upon his predicament and reflect on his heretofore good fortune, the sweet smell of tree sap is strong in his face.

Dainty, feather light leaves slap in his face as he brushes the tree nearest his falling-off point. A delicate sensation which lasts barely half a second.

The wind whistles in his ears. His legs are forced by gravity to dangle helplessly beneath him. His hands grip the corners of his makeshift parachute.

Scott knows deep down that the chute is working. The pull from the earth would be much more fierce than it is were it not for the help. But the ride is scary.

He tries arching his spine, taking his body away from the tree, but he cannot, he is moving too rapidly and freely. He hits more leaves. Branches snap, splintering against his weight. The chute snags. Jolts.

Scott lets go the blanket just at the correct moment, his elbows scissoring a branch which breaks but the one below it bends, slowing him. And his legs swing inward, toward the trunk. The picnic blanket parachute rips entirely from his grip, blows away in the wind.

When he eventually comes to rest amongst the branches of an evergreen sixty-feet tall oak tree, he is two-thirds of the way down. Just twenty more feet and he would've been a crumpled heap of dead flesh on the ground.

Finally Scott exhales.

The entire fall had lasted maybe five-seconds but it had certainly felt like the longest five-seconds of his entire life, and he cannot help himself but laugh with relief: he is alive! Now all that he has to do is climb down the remainder of the tree and get away before someone arrives to execute him!

THIRTY-FIVE

Scott wonders why something like tree-climbing, which as a child was almost second nature to him, is so much more of a challenge now? Okay, twenty years ago he was smaller, lighter and more agile, but the skill remains the same. Anyway, it's a struggle which results in scrapes and bruises and maximum effort, but eventually Scott's feet are firmly upon Terra-ferma, and it feels good.

Now to get onto the road and hitch a ride.

Or a train.

If he can get onto a freight train escape might be easier. Scott has to remind himself of the possibility that not only will the criminals be after him now but the law too. So a freight train to London, if he is lucky, will be his best option. Then how to locate Giuliano Badalamenti?

All this sounds easy enough in his head but practice is altogether different.

Getting one's bearings in Humber Park is quite easy because the bridge looms forever large, and the trees and foliage aren't too dense because there are footpaths snaking all through. The way forward undulates and traverses streams and pits and roots. There are a few joggers and dog walkers, clearly oblivious to the commotion on the bridge, which is faintly extraordinary considering the average persons need-to-know curiosity. Yet down here, the sounds seem very remote, while visually one is impaired by the sheer scale and height of the concrete and steel structure. So it's possible to be oblivious to the action.

Scott jogs along as best he can, not looking back whence he came. He wonders what William and co. are making of his departure. Are they pursuing him? Does his disappearance really matter that much to them and their timeframe? Nothing can stop them in the detonation of the bomb, as far as they are concerned.

Now ahead and beyond a fenced off hedgerow Scott can hear the traffic. Engines idling, mostly. Held up by the activity on the bridge, of course. So escape by car is going to be out of the question.

Reaching the hedge Scott is able to view the road through a thinned out section of branches. There are people screaming more than their engines. Clearly there is a mixed line of dialogue between what is truly happening and the speculation.

Scott follows the pathway westward, away from the bridge, away from danger. There is no need for worry yet because nobody could possibly guess his route, let alone find him amongst this maze. He can barely find himself!

The ground descends, the hedgerow and embankment rising steadily to his left, the path winds away from it but remains headed in the approximate direction Scott needs to travel. He wishes he were familiar with the layout of the park. No point asking someone because his questions would sound very vague.

He slows the pace. His heart in pounding. Not because he is out of shape, because he is far off being out of shape, but Scott hasn't stopped since dropping from the bridge and climbing down the tree. Ten, fifteen, minutes of maximum exertion might not sound too much, but his cardiovascular system is straining to cope. Slowing helps, like it does with all exercise.

Scott guesses that this area of the park, maybe all of it, in fact, resides in a quarry excavated when the Humber Bridge was under construction. Yet some of the foliage appears to have been in existence for longer. Maybe the ecosystem and Mother Nature can work quickly to repair itself in certain circumstances. In this case, there is clear evidence of repair. The embankment is now well above him, clotted sporadically with moss and tree roots.

Around the next twist in the unmade pathway there is location signage, like those "You Are Here" markers. This one is for direction only. No need for indication of ones whereabouts.

This path is concreted, fenced off with wooden rails, and along with going straight onward or ascending a concrete and wooden footpath into the trees, there is a gaping man-made tunnel under the roadway. According to the signage the tunnel leads to a lawned play-park.

Scott takes this route. There is no rumble of traffic as one might expect. He wonders how far the tailback stretches.

The reinforced concrete tunnel doesn't run far through the earth and its lit naturally during daylight hours. There are few recessed circular fluorescent tubes at the topmost part of the tunnel, not that Scott can imagine too many people wishing to gain access at night.

Emerging the other side, Scott is immediately aware that the land is flatter, but still well above the Humber water level. He wonders if the lush greenery is a consequence of flooding. It is quite unnerving to think that the water level can rise to such a significant degree to reach this high up. Mother-nature going about her business.

Beyond the tree-spotted parkland is a further metal fence which segregates the public area from the train-lines.

Scott follows a gravel footpath in a westerly direction, calculating the height of the fence at approximately seven-feet. It is topped by lacings of gnarled, deadly razor-sharp barbed wire.

Not very promising.

Scott approaches the fence from an angle. There is a further three-hundred yards running parallel with the track before it sharply cuts off at a ninety-degree angle back inland, toward the National Park.

How long until the next train?

If it's another transporter it will undoubtedly be moving sluggishly what with all the weight it will be hauling. Slowly enough for Scott to jump aboard. If it were that simple wouldn't more people just hitch a ride by this means? Like in America. Or the movies, at least.

What are the odds?

A suitable tree with large, sturdy, gnarled branches groping their way all and sundry presents itself. Almost like a challenge. If there's no train forthcoming then at least the walk should be quite direct,

In for a penny, as they say.

Scott hauls himself onto the first, thick, branch. Just like when he was a kid. Only now he is bigger, the branches tighter, the spikes closer. He climbs, grinning stupidly, actually enjoying himself.

A crump of compressed sound fills the air. A shock thumping the eardrums. Rumbling. Booming. Rolling all around.

Scott cannot quite see the explosion atop the bridge owing to his entanglement with the tree, but he can certainly feel the effects shuddering through the branches, billowing the air, loosening leaves.

He stops. The rumbling continues. He hopes the casualties are minimal. He hopes the destruction isn't as bad as it sounds!

Times up.

THIRTY-SIX

Claudinalli Tucamkari wasn't too bothered when the news reached her that the new man called Scott Dalton had somewhat spectacularly thrown himself from the bridge with a makeshift parachute. William, on the other hand, had been bothered. And embarrassed. It was his fault the new guy had been recruited in the first place. The Scotsman had evidently failed to properly vet him. Looking before one leapt had become a metaphor with double meaning. Whether the new man lived or died was soon of little consequence. The man was now very superficial.

Five more minutes was the estimated time of assemblage for the bomb. And then...that will be that.

This formidable woman had received a phone call from her daughter. Dee said that she and Ashley Barber were safely away. The first message from Claudinalli had gone on multiple social media platforms and would soon be a viral sensation. Especially in under six minutes.

Six more minutes of life for Claudinalli Tucamkari. Followed by her second legacy to this world. Her mark along with Dee. The future of the Tucamkari line.

And the death of Prime Minister Alfred McCann. A figure constructed, manipulated and owned by the people responsible for her actions. Or partly responsible. Her actions are her own. Her motives are her own. They just happen to coincide with the intentions of the people holding the British Prime Minister's strings. Claudinalli isn't particularly bothered about what transpired after the man's death, just that she is the person cutting his strings.

The bomb is quite sophisticated in its construction. It utilises the favoured IRA Semtex combined with a healthy dose of Plastique.

All of which covers the fake underside of the long wheelbase truck she was seated in. Plus additional explosives in the central storage truck. All designed for the maximum fury.

Claudinalli smiled to herself. Their placement on the bridge, inside the southern leg, should cause the structure to split in two, toppling one gigantic supporting strut into the central portion of the road with little hope of the length surviving the impact. From there on, the destruction was impossible to predict.

William stood expectantly before her, his eyes showing no signs of his feelings toward the response he is awaiting. He is a man well accustomed to dealing with confrontation. Some people are better equipped to handle criticism than others. William can cope. He is fully aware the Englishman Scott Dalton might now be giving information to the police. Why else would he flee? Alternatively, the man could still be tangled in the tree in which he landed.

"He can't cause us any harm now." Claudinalli tells William with a smile which one might describe as maniacal. It's unnerving to witness it.

The Scotsman 's expression doesn't change. He is neither relieved by her nonchalance nor encouraged. He supposes her plans cannot be altered so why would she be concerned? Scott has fled through cowardice or some other reason but cannot alter their plans. William leaves the woman.

Claudinalli grins with satisfaction. Little does William know how truly inconsequential Scott's departure is. Little does the Scotsman know what will shorty transpire.

"It's ready." The technician announces without glee or fanfare. It's just another job done. He passes an old flip-phone to Claudinalli. Although not that ancient, but any mobile phone device which isn't smart or less then a year old is considered out of date. This one is five years old. Positively ancient. "Turn it on, press to dial out, and one minute to boomtown!"

"Well done."

"No problem, Ma'am. The authorities will quake in their boots."

"Yeah. Literally."

Without any further ado, omitting preamble or the possibility of someone preventing her actions, she does exactly as the technician instructed.

One minute remains.

The technician literally sits staring agog.

Claudinalli drops the now superfluous phone on the ground when she slips out from the rear of the faux-Transit, the suspension not even registering her lack of presence. The woman whose whims cannot be altered surveys her kingdom of imminent destruction with satisfaction. The impotent helicopters hover like bees, media recording, police plotting. Southern end police divert traffic, marshalling the public, quelling the confusion and chaos. The impudent few haughty with their demands. Claudinalli cannot see what happens on the northern end of this gigantic structure, it is too far away and beyond the curvature, out of sight. But she imagines similar events transpiring to its southern counterpart. She pictures Dee, with Ashley Barber, her trusty henchman! They are safe from possibly harm. The devastation is an unknown quantity. Only time, cause and effect shall dictate what occurs.

Ten seconds remain.

How quickly time flies when one is having fun.

Seven seconds remain.

Claudinalli has no regrets. She has succeeded where others have failed.

Four seconds remain.

Her husband was a failure.

Two seconds remain.

Woman power succeeds!

At first nothing happened except silence. An eerie silence all around as if the entire world were holding its breath. Then suddenly a very tiny puffing intake of oxygen, like a balloon expelling air, was followed immediately by an almighty boom cloud of explosive relief gushed out from the base of the faux-Transit van. This was all Claudinalli Tucamkari registered because no sooner was the swept off her feet than she was dead.

Many things occurred all at once.

The van lifted off the ground, glass shattering and plastic melting and metal twisting in its death throes, the technician and driver evaporating, their teeth being the only indication they were ever present.

The surface of the road directly beneath the van was obliterated while the explosive force burst through in a fiery fury. Concrete and steel cowered and splintered, falling into the estuary.

A shockwave pummelled the air, shifting the nearest object, the Prime Minister's car, it's sole occupant, Alfred McCann, watching helplessly from inside, registering with terror the largeness of the bomb, its sheer force incomprehensible particularly when he has just two seconds to take it in. The bullet-proof glass of his car shatters. The metal shrinks back from the stresses. Something cuts into the Prime Minister's head, glass or metal, only a forensics test will confirm which of these it was, but either way, it kills him instantly.

A boom thunders like the most awesome subwoofer which anyone in the county has experienced, heard and felt for miles surrounding, causing rumbling vibrations which are felt by all in the

215

region. The resonance causes the Humber Estuary to ripple - similar to the glass of water in the first Jurassic Park movie, only multiplied a thousand fold.

Like a living being the bridge shudders through its entire expanse, as if knowing its fate, terrified shock reverberating through its body, discarding dust particles into the air. Tiny cracks appear everywhere, some imperceptible to the human eye, deep within the structure. No normal event could cause this level of stress. The Humber Bridge is an amazing feat of human engineering which is perfectly capable to absorbing an enormous amount of pressures upturn upon it. But this human created bomb carries such raw power and strategic direction that nothing can withstand it's power.

THIRTY-SEVEN

Scott Dalton cranes his neck around the tree trunk and through the branches of the great oak which still vibrates from its roots upward, the relentless pummelling of the airwaves continuing. Birds are lifting off in their droves from the woodland to his left. The ground itself seems to quake and shift.

He is now able to see the gigantic southern support as it drops vertically, almost slow-motion, straight and true, losing several feet of height in a few seconds, before it gradually tilts inward, pulling at the thick steel southward restraining ropes.

Scott's heart is in his mouth.

The view across the river Humber is truly electrifying.

Could he have done more to this prevent this from happening? The American woman had wasted no time in detonating the bomb after his departure. He knows she couldn't have been turned off this course, but still, he feels guilty. Responsible. But mostly, Scott feels real anger.

Anger because of his failure to prevent this disaster. Anger because of the ease in which this organisation has been able to carry out this attack. Anger at his manipulation in their hands.

Scott has been right about corruption in the British Government. But wrong about the extent. He was wrong about Alfred McCann. The Prime Minister was merely a puppet on strings. Long, twisted strings manipulated by McCann's own best friend. And whomever he is working for. Giuliano Badalamenti. Italian. The Mafia? No. Too convenient a scapegoat. They couldn't possibly implement such a global scheme. And not terrorism. Whoever this was set this up before England came out of Europe so other EU nations can be discounted as the perpetrators. In fact, this organisation wanted Brexit. Forced it. Created a swift exit from its constraints. They wanted

England to be alone, exposed, at their whim. Now the figurehead has been cut off, killed, murdered. And what happens next? Where is the chain of commands' next link?

A cold sweat breaks out over Scott's every fibre.

The chain of command has been put into place with this terrorist organisations own people in mind.

Alfred McCann was their positive figurehead. He was the English public face, the down-to-earth Middle-class man working for the people. McCann was extremely popular with the average person. And now his martyrdom will promote greater unity within the people. They will be angered that a group of terrorists have cut off the head. The head of snake, but the general public don't know this is a snake. They will see what has happened almost as an act of war. The Government sanctioned media will fuel their fire. The people will call for swift retribution. England will become a country under tighter control. Even more isolated. Even easier to manipulate by the powers who have instigated its downfall.

Where will it all lead?

England hasn't been the powerful country it used to be for many decades now. Controlled by the self-serving bureaucrats. Owned by overseas business. Ruled by a dictating European Union. Financially bowing to Germany, China and the oil rich Arab States. Cowering to the military might of Russia and North Korea. Hanging onto America's apron straps.

Generation You promised more control, more freedom and patriotic unity, and to many degrees they have honoured their promises. They have reintroduced multiple popular policies. On the surface they are working for the common man/woman. And yet by offering freedom what has really transpired is a closer Government control. Suppression of the freedom of speech. A surge in pro-reform groups whose resistance to the word of the Government has been painted as disloyal acts of insurgency, or worse still, acts of terrorism.

But this Government are willing to sacrifice their leader.

Scott Dalton grits his teeth. Fingers beginning to ache. Ears thrumming. The devastation loud and unrelenting.

He climbs the branches, not feeling any of the scratches or pricks he receives to his skin, just sheer will and determination propelling him over the fence, barely millimetres from the deadly razor-wire atop it. Seven feet below is a grassy embankment with a sloping gradient onto unmanaged scrubland.

Take a deep breath. Remember how to fall. Straight legged, knees bending landing, rolling with the gradient, brace body with arms so there are no broken bones, tuck knees into chest and...

Scott crunches into hard dead plants and weeds, coming to a rest on his back. Unhurt, for once. Save for the pounding in his skull. A memento from his concussion. When this is over he is going to take a very long nap. But not right now. Right now he has to snatch a ride to London.

THIRTY-EIGHT

The dust is gradually settling about the Humber Bridge a full twenty minutes after the exploding of the cobbled together high yield explosive device. Concrete and twisted steel protrude in grotesque shapes from their resting place in, and atop, the Estuary. The entire centre span has collapsed but somehow the massive support towers and gigantic steel ropes have snagged tightly, like a warped cats cradle, giving the impression that the expanse of roadway is floating upon the water. Although the southern tower is now pointing forty-five degrees northward, it hasn't toppled completely from its deep-water mooring. This miraculous outcome is just another example of superb engineering, although, in the long-term, salvage is going to be next to impossible because of the sheer mass of concrete.

Scott Dalton looks back the way him came, over the train tracks with their sidings, signals and tall wire fences. Nothing moves. He cannot see any vehicles on the fallen expanse, speculating, correctly, that the faux-Transit has been utterly annihilated and the Prime Minister's car is in the water.

The sight is shocking.

Hard to absorb.

Difficult to believe.

It resembles the carnage of a Hollywood blockbuster. The aftermath of an alien invasion, monsters tussling or comic book heroes fighting their foe. A truly epic disaster has taken place, captured on camera, circulated globally.

What happens afterward? How will the politicians react? What will the public demand?

Strewth. Scott sighs speculatively. This is unquestionably the worst singular attack on the free world since the Twin Towers were destroyed in New York.

Scott saw that attack unfold on the television. On BBC as it transpired. It seemed unreal. A movie unraveling. A devastatingly real movie which even the scriptwriters couldn't possibly conceive.

When Scott looks, beyond the tracks, beyond the trees, across the water, everything is very real.

No trains will be passing through anytime soon, this much is blatantly obvious. And Scott cannot possibly walk the entire track to London! This is a heavy trudge as it is, over hard black gravel, large shifting stones, not fine, making every step slippery and precarious. Scott has to be tentative, aware that with the next step he could slip and twist an ankle. No good using the tracks or rail supports, either. The wooden supports are spaced too far apart, and the track is slick.

How far to the nearest station?

Where was the last station?

Hull?

The next will be a municipal station. A small village. With the local population no doubt enthralled by the ongoing event up the road. The station will be deserted.

And it is just so when Scott reaches it thirty minutes and three miles later. A brisk walk, quite impressive, all things considered. And there is a car park, too, for the long distance travellers, the workers. Some who won't be able to return soon. Later than expected, one will discover his car is no longer parked amidst forty others.

Scott selects a Ford Focus on a new plate. Fast, reliable, anonymous.

Breaking into a car isn't really as easy as it looks on television, or, if you have had yours hot-wired, as simple as one might assume. No. Car theft is not for the opportunistic thief. This kind of crime takes training. Which Scott was fortunate to receive from a reformed professional car-jacker now under the employ of the British Security Service. Who specialised in Ford. Not especially because they are an easy target but because there are more per capita on the roads. If you are driving one, you don't get noticed.

After fifteen anxious minutes, the engine springs into like without much ceremony, the running noise barely perceptible. Scott grins. A full tank of petrol, too. That is a bonus. But he couldn't be a professional car thief, he took too long!

THIRTY-NINE

Lincoln Cathedral spire and the urban sprawl of the congested ring-road eventually yields to the much more pleasant open countryside heading southbound on the A16. If any city in England was overdue a duel-carriageway by-passing it is Lincoln. There really is no other sensible way to navigate the City other than the main A-road, which is beset by numerous round-about's, traffic-light signals and junctions galore. Travelling upward from Norwich along the eastern side of England can often take twice as long anywhere else. And don't get Scott started on Boston. He can recall several summer holiday experiences driving with family from their family home in Hoveton, around Norwich and straight up the A47 to Kings Lynn and more round-about, single lane traffic, off the A17 to Boston which was worse than most Towns because you have to drive directly through it if you want to get to Skegness. A relatively short seventy-five mile journey can three hours if you catch all these places at the wrong time of day.

Yet now Scott is on the open road, heading in the opposite direction, once more, which is unnervingly quieter. Maybe people are staying at home in the suburbs, glued to their television screens, watching the "Terror On The Humber Bridge" unfold with morbid fascination.

Which is fine by him.

Their morbid curiosity means he can drive full speed ahead.

Certainly he has passed every emergency vehicle known to mankind on his more circular route out of Yorkshire and into Lincolnshire, but not much since. The skies are busy too. All heading in the same direction: East Riding of Yorkshire, and the Estuary.

Just before noon, now.

Three hours have gone by since Scott made his leap of faith.

Scott tries not to think of the plight of the ones affected, hoping there were innocent lives saved, not taken. The plotters scheme was to kill the Prime Minister, which was successful. The terrorists alive either side of the well and truly demolished Humber Bridge won't have remained in position for long after the explosion, fleeing, regrouping, being captured.

And there is he himself also fleeing the crime scene. Escaping death. Not so much betraying the terrorists because he had no impact on the outcome, but he can at least effect change to the plans of the real people behind this. Or can he? Realistically? He has to locate Prime Minister Alfred McCann's Italian friend Giuliano Badalamenti. Scott has to get past whatever collection of security and bodyguard detail this man has, which will have increased after today's events, and get McCann's family to safety. Yet how will the deceased leader of England's family be in danger. It's not as if they are being held hostage. Giuliano is probably using the pretext of keeping them safe, protecting them, instead of holding them captive. Why would he? They do not know of his treachery. Where will they be? Oxfordshire? In the Government owned family home amidst some of the best protection conceived, most likely. So that's the place to start. Not with a direct confrontation with this Badalamenti guy, but with Alfred McCann's wife and son. Plant some seeds of doubt. But what if McCann's Italian wife was somehow part of the lure. Part of the grand scheme?

Scott wonders to whom he can impart all his findings. And who will believe him? How can he find the right person? One not only to trust but to act.

Life is similar to a road journey from point A to point B, with challenges and obstacles along the way. Familiar roads with a known destination, unfamiliar roads with quirks.

The A16 is quite familiar to Scott, he is negotiating it without over-focusing. Driving by instinct, radio as background. There are many roads he knows, many safe bets, which instinct navigates. But he doesn't know too many people. At least not those he can have faith through familiarity. Naomi has the talent but not the power to utilise his knowledge, to spread the word. Scott needs someone pro-active. But there is no-one. No man, no woman. No non-gender-specific person.

RAF Waddington airfield is coming up, a familiar sight. The windsock and low-flying aircraft a prerequisite. Left and right. Military buildings and aircraft, no personnel visible.

Scott slows his speed. Although the road is empty he doesn't want to make anyone suspicious. All branches of the military will be on high alert right now. Forces mobilising.

A pair of small jet fighter planes scream in from the east, over trees, landing almost as quickly as Scott saw them approaching.

His heart quickens as his speed slows. A checkpoint has been erected on the roadway ahead of him. He instantly wonders if his photo will have been circulated amongst the military. Will the Security Service extend themselves to this branch, or will they want his fabricated double-cross kept in a tighter loop. Maybe they have reduced the significance of his undercover exploits. They cannot know he has escaped the carnage long ago. They cannot know of his conversation with the late Prime Minister. For all the British Security Service know, Scott Dalton could have been evaporated on the Humber Bridge. Their preoccupation much be with mopping up after the attack. This checkpoint is purely routine. Scott has nothing to worry about.

An MP Sergeant waves him down. A machine gun is strapped casually over his shoulder, like it's nothing, just another piece of uniform. But the weapons presence is enough to make even an innocent man soil his undergarments!

225

Drawing his inconspicuous Ford Focus to a standstill alongside the MP, Scott calmly buzzes his passenger window down, the MP leans in, casual and natural.

"You okay, sir?" The MP asks with practised neutrality.

"Yes, thank you. Better then the people I have been listening to on the radio."

"Yeah."

"Terrible thing. I suppose that's what this is about?

"Something like that, sir."

"Roads are quiet, that's one thing."

"They are at that, sir. Drive carefully."

With this, and after carefully examining the nondescript interior of the car and its lone occupant, the MP steps away and the barrier is raised.

It would seem appropriate to give a polite little wave and pursed grin when passing the Sergeant, which Scott does. They obviously aren't looking for someone fitting his description, which comes as something of a relief, but the outpost has a surveillance camera recording his image. Nothing flagged up to alert the Sergeant right then, but this doesn't mean Big Brother aren't onto him. The people who martyred Prime Minister Alfred McCann for their own nefarious scheme will no doubt want to deal with Scott themselves. But how long does he have before they set a Bulldog on his tail? Has a satellite already locked onto the Ford Focus? This model, though a basic one, undoubtedly has manufacturer standard GPS as part of the purchase package. Stealing a family car is easy but keeping it is difficult!

Finding a replacement car in the next five to ten minutes is going to be tricky. Scott is in the middle of the countryside. The nearest village is probably fifteen minutes away at top speed. He won't have that much of a window of opportunity. If they are onto the car, possibly watching it nowvia satellite, then he needs a built up area so he can lose them, or they lose him, in a crowd.

Scott floors it!

FORTY

Castelingford is the first village Scott Dalton reaches after turning off the A16 and he heads into it via the B1178. The drive from the checkpoint has taken barely twelve minutes. There are no obvious signs of the British Security Services force working for Badalamenti, at least so far. What was he expecting? Helicopters, sirens and an entire task force to swoop down upon him?

This village is a tiny hamlet spread out sparsely across several square miles, with a school, a High Street with one pub, a newsagent, hairdresser, antique store, two charity shops and a takeaway, with houses clusters around the main centre and a few outlying. The village church is half a mile west along a road inventively called Church Road, and it has a gravel car park surrounded by trees and a narrow entrance, concealing the car from a drive-by, which is where Scott parks and leaves the Ford Focus, key in the ignition, engine off. Hopefully this village isn't rife with lawlessness and nobody will steal it.

Scott begins his walk back toward High Street, passing open fields and another small single track lane called Field Road. Despite everything that has happened Scott permits himself a guffaw at the plain simpleness of these road names, which one can find in most counties in England. Unimaginative yet obvious, until the field is developed then the name becomes redundant. Such as an estate called Strawberry Fields where there used to be but no longer are fields of strawberries.

Hedgerows full of blackberries stud the left-side embankment, while on Scott's right until he reaches the junction is an extensively fenced arrangement of paddocks for about a dozen horses, all bound by a knee-high wall and signage declaring surveillance is in operation for the protection of the animals.

Scott veers left into High Street which is eerily deserted. In fact, all the gardens with recessed homes on this stretch, built uniformly in the fifties, are also devoid of life. A lawn mower sits unattended on one unkept grassy patch, which also has a "For Sale" sign curb-side. Washing is strung out on half a dozen lines out front of half a dozen homes, fluttering in the frequent gusts. A pair of kids bicycles lean against a hedge beside someone's open front gate. The pub forecourt is full, a car is parked outside the hairdresser, and a motorbike rests outside one of the charity shop, but there are no humans in sight. It is as if Scott has entered a ghost town abandoned only very recently. At least there are birds in the sky and a couple of cats prowling to reaffirm life.

Saturday.

It is Saturday afternoon, just after noon. Football is on telly or in the pub, or perhaps people are glued to the Humber Bridge coverage. It is also lunchtime. And it is also a quiet hamlet miles from the nearest city.

The reassuring factor about the peace and quiet is that Scott will hear a helicopter or fast approaching car.

And an unattended car is exactly what he needs right now. But he needs to get out of High Street, pass the shops and pub where people might see him. On his journey through the hamlet there had been a collection of twelve homes, six each side, with isolated driveways and at least one car in each. All he needs to do is find one unoccupied and hey presto, new ride.

While walking, Scott wonders if he is being watched by some Eye in the Sky surveillance drone, and absently looks skyward. The only things he can see are clouds, contrails and birds. But it doesn't mean they are aren't up there, watching. Anything is possible in a country where it's capital city has the largest collection of Closed Circuit cameras and facial recognition software than any other city in the world. Probably none in this leafy community where the greatest excitement is Saturday afternoon in the pub watching football!

He finds a deserted property, a car, brand new in fact with just one-hundred miles on the clock, hot-wires it easily and drives away, hoping for the best but as soon as he pulls out the driveway onto the road three black SUV type vehicles approach the hamlet from the direction of the A16. Black SUV's mean Security Service.

Twenty-five minutes to locate his position. Impressive reaction time, really, because resources must be stretched thin right now what with the Humber Bridge attack. Although three cars, six agents minimum, seems a bit extreme to bring in one man!

The trio of BMW SUV's simultaneously start their concealed blue-light's strobing front and rear as they begin their pursuit of Scott Dalton's newly acquired car. His futile attempts to avoid the British Security Service lasted no more than he should have expected. In point of fact, had he not wasted time changing from the Ford Focus in hopes of eluding his inevitable pursuers, he might now be further away from them. Although theoretically they would have been heading directly for him, unless they came from Lincoln. He can only speculate where this particular trio have come from.

Yes, he feels stupid because of his time-wasting exercise.

He knows despite VW's, particularly a Golf like this which is driving, being considered quite nippy, his new acquisition doesn't really have the same top-speed as the three BMW's, but they are all four hindered by the fact this road isn't full of straights, so all he needs do is stay in front of them, in theory.

Scott floors it, spinning the rear wheels in sensational fashion worthy of any boy-racer, bursting forward with a surge of power and drifting the car into the two-lane High Street back the way he came, toward Church Road. The screaming engine, squeal of rubber and puff of dust is sure to attract the attention of the locals but Scott shifts gears in rapid succession, blasting past the shop, pub and homes, so quickly he is onto Church Road in seconds.

A quick glance in his rear-view mirror tells him the trio of BMW's are one-hundred fifty yards back, in precise alignment with each other, like some unrelenting deadly termination force.

Scott flips the car's indicator out of habit, shifts down gears and yanks the wheel round so the car is now pointing down Church Road. Foot to the floor and the wheels spin, the little car shooting forward with a very satisfying lurch of speed.

The church blurs past him and the hedgerows are nothing but smudges of colour, his concentration almost verging on tunnel-vision. He doesn't know where the road leads or when it will merge with something bigger, which it will eventually, but the nippy car negotiates these narrow lanes far better than the bigger cars behind him. Scott cannot see any sign of them. They can track his course via satellite, of course, so they could be driving to a cut-off point somewhere ahead.

Scott activates the cars voice command function.

He says:

"Sat-nav."

"Please repeat command."

"Sat-nav." He repeats with greater emphasis on his enunciation, trying not to sound irritable because what's the point - stupid computer!?

On the small LED screen a mini-map appears with a mini-car symbol jarring its way along a mini-road. Lots of mini-roads wind their way off the road which his vehicle is travelling upon, with mini-symbols telling him what to anticipate en route.

It's a mini-adventure!

At first it is fun. Jinking left and right. Braking. Rapid gear changing. Hearing the power. Feeling the power. Losing his pursuers. But he knows this cannot last forever.

A bold and colourful painted makeshift board on the verge announces an 'Event' writ large next left, two-hundred yards. A quick decision. If the agents are following via sat-nav they might be visually watching at HQ in London, too. But what are they worried about? Do they know his purpose? Did they witness his conversation with the PM? Whichever. They are probably watching him with their Eye in the Sky. So best lose himself in a crowd of people.

Two-hundred yards is really not that far when you are travelling at speed in a fast car. Scott jams on the brakes, skewing into the off-road farm track where a pair of big professionally printed banners announce Harmston Farms Messy Truck Beer Fest. Sounds like fun!

The farm track is pitted with deep ruts and loose clods of earth, making the drive hard, bumpy and noisy as the suspension of Scott's VW is pummelled. So he slows down before the poor vehicle rattles itself to pieces.

Arrows point to car parking, coach parking, and contestants.

Trundling along at ten miles an hour he pulls left and follows a row of ten parked cars which brings him to the edge of a field, and five columns later he is parked up. The event is evidently popular, there much be two-hundred vehicles. Good for the sponsors, and even better for him.

Without any further ado he exits the car, finds the entrance to the event which is evidently free to the public because there are no pay booths, and soon Scott mingles with the crowds of petrol-heads spilling around and inside the concession tents. The people frequenting this event are a varied mixture of age, creed and commitment. Music blares out from turret speakers and bass rumblers on the ground, while the race-track itself is beyond a head-high hedge, where the motor event itself takes place, because Scott can hear cheering, a deep horn and exhaust growl from one of the performing vehicles. He wonders what a "Messy Truck" means, a literal translation would indicate mud covered flat-bed four-wheel-drive vehicles like you see odd-job people or Landscape Gardeners or construction workers driving. Reliable Toyota Hi-Lux, for example. Like he saw in abundance in the car park.

Scott hasn't time to find out for himself.

The smell of hog roast, bacon, burgers, and coffee reminded Scott how hungry he is, so he finds the tent with the shortest queue and purchases a large eco-friendly disposable container of black filter coffee which must've held a pints worth, and a suitably greasy quarter-pound steak burger with cheese and onions in a wholemeal bun.

Standing just inside the right-hand inner flap of the big red gazebo style tent he can watch the pedestrian event entrance through the heads and shoulders and big-hair and hats of the crowd of fans.

The burger is succulent and well worth the hefty pricing. The meat is spectacularly well sourced while the cheese isn't some reformed plastic-type stuff one gets in fast food diners. This is a truly delicious meal. And the hot coffee is amongst the best he has tasted, working wonders to improve his mood, recharging his batteries which he wasn't aware were draining.

The people at this event are a mixture of ages and sexes but Scott must admit there is a general conformity to a certain stereotype. They all possess a certain something which tells you they regularly attend car shows, watch motoring programs on television, or YouTube, and they and their parents take pride in what they drive, cleaning their vehicles religiously and treating them almost like one of the family.

And then Scott sees three men and one woman who couldn't be more out of place if they were meat-free in a steak burger. Four conspicuous British Security Services agents.

FORTY-ONE

Scott Dalton is no taller than anyone around him. Average. His clothing is casual, nothing too bright, nothing attracting attention. Regular. But still, with the side tent flap concealing him as best as it can, he feels like he is exposed for the whole world and the pursuing agents to see. Although he isn't. It's a weird sensation. Through his own eyes he is clearly visible to his watchers, while all the event officials are staring right at him. In reality his nondescript average looks, height and hair are the most perfect camouflage. If Scott looked like Brad Pitt maybe he would attract attention, but he doesn't, so he doesn't!

Two-hundred parked vehicles. Some bicycles. Walkers. Maybe a thousand people. Constant movement. One main exit but a dozen possibilities.

Scott watches the four agents.

Two have been left behind at their vehicles. One in the car park. One waiting outside the farm track, on the road. Speculation on Scott,'s part, but it would make sense. Standard operating procedure.

All six have earpieces. Constant communication.

Scott watches the agents and patrons. Studies them. Seeking an opportunity. His only hope is for some people to depart. He can follow, get in the back of their truck if they have one. Fifty-fifty shot, but worth those odds.

One of the agents waits by the entrance, her eyes alert, professional, full of intent.

The other three split up because why not? They are all in communication. More ground can be covered this way.

Nearest emergency exit is fifty yards to Scott's left, between his tent and the next. He will have to break cover but blending in is no problem. Will the Eye in the Sky be watching? Will they know someone

235

is leaving the group, breaking away? That's a risk Scott is willing to take. He knows he must get away and to Giuliano Badalamenti as quickly as possible. Before his own time runs out. They catch him, it's finished. They shoot at him and he is finished.

Clenching his fists Scott selects his moment when all four are preoccupied, when their eyes are averted from his position.

Weaving through the queue of people getting their burgers and drinks, narrowly avoiding a spillage, Scott smoothly drops his empty container and cup into a recycling bin and slides around the side of the tent. He is brought up short. Almost loses balance. Almost strides straight into the tents guy-ropes.

A quiet curse, a widening of his eyes, Scott ducks under the ropes, passes between the side of the tent and rear of a supply van, weaves through some containers and dives over the waist-high exit rope between the hedges, drops and rolls, landing on his feet and coming to rest on a rough back path. Just five-seconds from the tent to here. Not bad. Very lucky.

The footpath is perhaps forty feet long in either direction. Or appears to be. It might continue in an L-shape, out of sight, to the front of the car park and entry way to where the performing trucks are. And they are loud. Revving engines, horns blaring extra-large! The crowds seem to be lapping it up. No wonder this event is taking place in the middle of nowhere. Neighbours would complain. Distractions which can only help Scott.

Standing upright so he can just see over the top of the bramble hedgerow, Scott surveys the packed area beyond and strolls unhurriedly toward where the pathway eventually breaks at the right-hand edge of the car park.

Next to him is a silvery blue three-berth motorhome replete with chrome wheels and Monster Truck decals. Which is either really cool or really sad. Scott has no feelings about such things, each to their own pleasure, of course.

Through the passenger window and screen of the motorhome Scott can see diagonally along the row to its far end where his car is parked. And the glossy black Service SUV. It is inward facing, the driver wears an earpiece similar to his colleagues, and the whites of his eyes are large because of the constant focused staring.

Scott must keep low to make his escape, then. They are no amateurs.

A family with a bawling child, probably about four, stride through the middle aisle. The eldest child, a couple of years older than his brother, trails behind with reluctant shoulders slumped dejectedly.

"Come on, JJ." The mother says in a soothing voice.

"Don't wanna go." Comes the understandable reply, and he glowers at his brother who is obviously the reason why they are forced to leave.

Dad says nothing.

Scott ducks alongside the motorhome, mentally crossing his fingers these folks have a flatbed truck he can climb in back of, and edges through a trio of parked cars, coming parallel with the family, who are silent apart from the crying. Dad presses the key fob which unlocks the door to a red SUV. Scott is out of luck so must bide his time once more. But how long does he have? If the agents who are after him have satellite surveillance can he realistically hide for much longer?

Movement to his right. Scott ducks out of sight, watches ankle height from the underside of vehicles. A couple. Brown tan boots with bare ankles and black leather boots which are higher up, possibly knee-high. Soiled. Fast of pace. A young couple.

Tracking their progress they pass by before veering inward, towards him, approaching a truck with raised suspension and bigger than average wheels. No electronic key fob this time.

Scott squats on his haunches and thanks his luck. The two twenty-something women are getting into a well used Toyota Hilux circa 1988. A relative antique and collectors item. In a decided fade red with mud spattered chassis and sides, while the drop-tail and number plate are equally adorned. It displays loving dents and scratches which undoubtedly have hundreds of stories behind them.

Scouring the rest of the car park Scott cannot see anyone who might witness his hitchhiking, while the agent in his car is looking away.

Swiftly Scott takes the thirty-yards to the Toyota in ten big strides, pulls himself over the side and into the open flat-bed as the vehicle thumps into life, its Diesel engine puffing, panting and chugging. Scott wonders how many thousand-miles this reliable old warhorse has on its clock, recalling a popular television program putting a similar Toyota through extreme conditions to see how resilient they are.

Once more his luck is with him. Tucked by the drivers cabin is a heavy blue tarpaulin.

The Toyota judders when it's handbrake and clutch are released simultaneously.

Scott skitters across the dust encrusted floor and hauls the tarpaulin over himself as a precautionary measure should the exit be more closely guarded than the car park.

He feels every rut the Toyota hits in the surface of the car park, jarring his teeth and joints. His fingers grip tightly to the blue tarpaulin like it will somehow protect his body from shattering.

The bumping continues, sending him sliding up against the cabin and away. He doesn't want to draw attention to himself, there is only thin metal between himself and the two women, they will hear him. But there is nothing to get a purchase upon. Scott has to anticipate every bump. The suspension doesn't dampen anything. The tarpaulin flaps and shifts. One minute he can see sky, then the inner tailgate, then nothing but blue, then sky again, in an endless unpredictable cycle. A big shift sends him bucking upward. Scott braces his shoulder for the fall a second later, banging onto the surface. But the exhaust pipe rattles and bangs too. It is disguising his presence. And then a sudden brake, stopping, the engine idling.

Scott composes himself, pressing into the corner of the floor and cabin, holding the tarpaulin loosely, like someone it's holding it and hiding beneath it. He wonders if there is a Security Service vehicle parked alongside the verge directly beyond the exit, the occupants watching. Maybe they are spot checking every vehicle with some pretext about the Humber Bridge incident. Not unlikely. A believable precaution.

Then it is with no small measure of relief that the Toyota moves onward, turns onto the smoother road surface, the diesel chugging, the ride becoming moderately more bearable.

FORTY-TWO

Luck has been well and truly on Scott's side, because who knew the two women in the Toyota were heading southbound to Springfield Shopping Outlet on the outskirts of Spalding? They might've been heading any direction. They might've driven to the Humber Bridge to gawp; or Lincoln, or Grantham, or Skegness or anywhere which would've hindered his progress and make him feel stupid. But Scott had journeyed forty miles in exactly the right direction. Uncomfortably, yes, but the right way!

Once settled in a space under a tree in the west end car park and duo had left him, battered and bruised, cold and stiff, Scott shakes free from the dusty tarpaulin and slides out the side of the Toyota.

Scott's legs feel like jelly. He feels dirty from the grit on the floor of the truck and none the better for all the fresh air! He has never ridden a journey that way before and hopes he never has to again.

From Spalding a train journey to London should be no more than an hour. But where is the station located in this town?

It's not too difficult for Scott to find a big board with a map of Spalding upon it, not in a huge space like this. Scott finds the 'You Are Here' arrow, with the train station marked off about two miles to his south-west.

According to a tower clock the time is just after one o'clock.

Looking up at the outlet buildings Scott ruminates over buying himself clean clothes. He hasn't shaved or showered in at least two days, and he could do with freshening up his armpits. So after purchasing some deodorant and hair gel from a pound shop, and a coffee and muffin from a specialist outlet which costs him more than the two ablutions combined, he walks through the streets of Spalding via the A1151, crossing an inlet of the River Welland but onward until the road makes a left turn when he reaches the main Estuary. The road heads on all four points of the compass but he follows the Welland southwards until reaching the next bridge, crossing it, before finding Vine Street leading to The Crescent and finally into Station Road, which is always a good indicator that one is heading the correct way in most any town or city!

The station is as utilitarian as one expects and most facilities except for the convenience store are automated, which is useful, because the fewer people he is forced to interact with the better. Not that needs to worry too much. The station is heaving with football supporters on their way to games hither and thither across England.

A big overhead array of displays lists a variety of departures and arrivals, northbound and southbound, today and the next five days ahead. It's very comprehensive and lists the next First National London bound train as departing platform three in ten minutes. Splendiferous. They appear to flow through the town quite frequently, must be to cater for increased Saturday football fans.

Scott finds an automated ticket machine, discovers it does take cash, and purchases the required ticket which is much cheaper than he remembers, obviously the Generation You governing England has reintegrated the countries rail service from the private sector and dropped its prices accordingly. Very astute.

He boards the train two minutes before departure and it leaves on time.

It is the motion of the carriage, the regular rhythm of the wheels passing over the tracks, the sense of taking a breather, that makes Scott's heavy eyes droop and he drifts off into a splendiferous untroubled sleep. Untroubled and undisturbed until some sixth sense, or the overhead tannoy announcement, signals they had reached their London destination and his departure point: Finsbury Station.

241

Scott's London apartment isn't much more than a thirty minute walk from the station. Despite the risk involved he has decided to head straight there. He needs to change his clothes. Not simply for the purposes of comfort but his description will have been circulated. London has the greatest surveillance camera coverage than anywhere else in the world.

But first Scott must get out of the station undetected.

Walking the length of the train, passengers disembarking around him, bearing him no mind, Scott casually scours the seats he passes. After the third carriage he eventually sees what he wants. The odds were distinctly in his favour, though. More hats and coats are left behind on public transport than any other item. Although it might've been a woman who left a decided feminine hat for him to find, in which case he would've walked from the station slightly more conspicuously than sporting the natty Paisley print wide brimmed Fedora which, if Scott's stereotyping runs true, belonged to someone artistic.

Beneath the hat, head down, eyes up, Scott is focused on the people outside the bustling station, and there are many. Arsenal are playing at home that afternoon. There is a ubiquitous presence of red shirts mixed with blue, presumably the opposing team, on their way to the game. But Scott isn't interested in them. He is looking for anyone who might be watching for him. No reason why they would expect him here. It's too near his apartment, too well watched by cameras, particularly at the moment, and only a fool would come here.

Which is is exactly what Scott is hoping his pursuers figured. Not that it's particularly difficult to hide amidst the hundreds of supporters.

Scott exits at Station Place and continues east, passing the indoor bowling alley, and heading through Finsbury Park at a casual pace, taking a circular route. Nobody is tailing him. But there could be watchers. Although why waste the manpower on him now? Whoever was employing the Security Service agents in Lincolnshire must surely have better things to do, such as protecting the airports and seaports and dignitaries and other parliamentary members who might feel more exposed. The Prime Minister was brutally killed not many hours ago. One of the greatest English constructions has been destroyed. Surely the Security Service need to implement a full lockdown. It's a wonder events such as football games haven't been cancelled to ease pressure on the police force. Yet Scott cannot help but think cynically that big business still rules the world.

Cynical? Or realistic?

Crossing the A503 at his peril Scott ducks down Alexandra Drive, waiting at its apex, looking for any obvious surveillance vehicles parked in anticipation of his arrival, although he still has another two miles of walking to do. Ridiculous how illogical paranoia can make a person.

Smiling to himself, Scott strides along the footpath with various independent retailers either side becoming low-maintenance rental properties, eventually coming upon the higher-end apartments. Cars are parked in the spaces broken by restricted access to the squares behind the visible properties. This is relatively recent real-estate, built not much more than thirty years ago on reclaimed land, so there is a certain modern uniformity and layout in the district. It's not a bad neighbourhood. Inconspicuous. Near to the centre of London and offers easy access to the M25. Which is probably why the Government chose this area for him. He doesn't doubt several other employees live within striking distance.

Scott ducks left, down an alleyway which will bring him to his courtyard apartment from the rear, through a similar fenced alleyway. He meets no one. Sees no suspicious activity. The courtyard is clear. A casual glance and the hundred windows looking upon him give away nothing and no-one. The middle of the courtyard has a beautifully maintained garden with water feature and half a dozen benches facing inward. It is here that Scott sees a young couple, boy about nineteen, girl eighteen, canoodling. Neighbours he doesn't know. Rich students. No threat.

He enters the clean and clear glass entrance double-doors of his building, nods amiably in the direction of the caretaker, who smiles with disinterested recognition, handing him the key to apartment 3D, and Scott ascends the staircase two steps at a time. No sense using an elevator which is easier for someone to be watching.

The wide corridor is clear. The lighting is bright against the sunflower yellow wallpaper, paintings sporadically adorning the walls to add charm to the place. The Government must pay a lot of money for these kinds of embellishments.

And the claret deep-pile carpet which Scott floats upon isn't cheap either.

Two doors down, eyes peeled, he wishes he still has a gun with him when he reaches his own door and swipes the electronic key card, because when he opens the door a familiar face greets him with a familiar gun aimed right at him.

FORTY-THREE

The woman of Polish extract seems to possess no emotional breadth what so ever, exuding a bland facade with a penetrating stare. Her eyes are totally piercing and if not for a twitch from the bottom of her right lid she might be registered dead. But she is no waxwork statue standing in Scott's lounge. She is very real, as is the gun which, if Scott recalls correctly, is the exact same one he was dispossessed of in Scotland by the authorities. Seems like an eternity ago now, but seeing this woman before him brings it back into stark focus, with the realisation it is she who has possibly been manipulating the situation.

Scott's mind works on his strategy. There is only one: keep her talking until he figures out a way to disarm her. She definitely possesses the upper hand.

She waggles the gun as a way of indicating for him to close the door, to which he dutifully complies, stepping casually to the right of it, directly in front of the chest of drawers which has a framed picture of his parents upon it, alongside a small but deadly gold and lead paperweight purchased for him by the couple in the picture for his eighteen birthday.

"Now put your hands on your head."

Scott blinks in confusion . Not from the instruction itself, that's simple enough. The voice. There is no eastern European accent. Not a trace. In fact her English middle class tone is so perfect it's startling. She could be from Herefordshire or Oxfordshire, if not for the slightly olive tone to her skin. But perhaps that's too much of a racist observation for the 21st Century. And now Scott realises her clothing too matches the voice. Khaki skirt, black tights, black shoes, white blouse tight beneath a tailored business jacket that flutes out at her waist. Suddenly his preconceptions dissolve.

What the f...?

"You almost ruined my job, you know?"

Before Scott can reply through his confusion she reminds him about the raising of his hands, to which his complies, slowly, picking up the paperweight as he does so, concealing it in the palm of his hands should be require to apply its usage in a manner for which it wasn't designed.

"You look confused." She states the obvious.

"That's stating the obvious. Who are you? And who do you work for?"

"My name is Molly Smith."

"I'd never have guessed that."

"Don't judge a book, Mister Dalton."

"You're right, of course. And who do you work for, exactly?"

"The same organisation as yourself, Mister Dalton."

"Call me Scott."

"If you insist." Molly actually smiles, wryly, and a twinkle of humour appears in her eyes.

"That wasn't very nice. And neither is that gun. We are on the same side, after all."

"No, Mister...Dalton! Same organisation isn't necessarily indicative of same side. Although it is somewhat old fashioned calling it sides."

"A bit like me assuming you are from Eastern Europe."

"Exactly."

Scott nods, dropping his right arm slightly, unnoticeably. The gun doesn't waver from its target, and her expression doesn't waver from the unreadable.

"So, er, Molly, you weren't really working for William in Scotland, that's clear. Why were you there?"

"I was undercover. Like you."

"But from opposing ends of the same job. Hmm...yes, definitely a few shades of grey in there. How long have you been waiting here for me? Long enough to need food, because I'm a bit hungry, if there's anything my fridge."

"I arrived two hours after the Humber Bridge thing."

"Okay. Do you mind if I make myself a coffee?"

"You took them the last piece of the bomb. Did you know that's what they were making?"

Scott slowly shakes his head. He wonders how long she has been following him, or if he will will ever find out. What does she know about his assignment? Why hasn't she killed him already?

"I guess you think I was working with the terrorists, which is an understandable assumption. But you also know I was working undercover to prevent the act of terrorism from occurring. Which obviously hasn't gone too well. And I didn't exactly have the time to suddenly switch allegiances. But what would you say if I told you it was an inside job? What if I told you that the Government were financing the terrorists?"

"I would say that you haven't watched television since running from the crime scene. The terrorists have posted a video all over the media. A woman called Claudinalli Tucamkari is accepting responsibility for everything."

"I see. That was her name." Scott has another thought. "Was her daughter captured?"

"No. Not yet."

"Interesting. So you were undercover to what...? Prevent the same thing happening at which I failed? Or to stop me from preventing it? Well done, by the way, if that was the case. Which means you couldn't have hired the hitman. So who did, I wonder?

"I don't know about a hitman. But you are right that I was told by our organisation to ensure you succeeded."

"Why don't you just shoot me now, then? You've succeeded. You've done your job. Now for a medal for killing one of the terrorists. Or are you having second thoughts! Perhaps you didn't realise the scope of your bosses actions. Maybe you didn't expect the treachery to run as deeply as this. The Government. Our own people. Themselves criminals. Perish the though. And when you saw me again you realised I too was being played by our people. Because if I were genuinely a terrorist why would I return to this apartment?"

Inscrutable as always she just stares at Scott. She is a good agent. Very good at her work. Scott has discovered this from their two encounters already. She is perfectly adept at hiding her thoughts, that is without question. Being undercover must have been easy. Almost second nature. But her loyalties have obviously been sorely tested by the activities over the past couple of days. She is beginning to have doubts. Similar to the doubts which had festered within Scott for many months, confirmed only today by the Prime Minister himself. How can Scott convince her that she should let him continue on his quest? He needs to act fast. Time is very much of the essence.

She wavers before reaching her decision, slowly lowering the gun.

"Can I get a coffee now please, Molly?"

"Yes. Mines black." The wry grin returns.

"Thank you." He lowers his arms, rubs the circulation back into them and places the paperweight back on the unit behind himself, smiling sheepishly. "Sorry, but I had to be prepared."

FORTY-FOUR

Molly Smith sits on the middle cushion of Scott's brown leather sofa cupping a large mug of coffee in her hands. After establishing that she does not need to report in for at least another half-hour and that she is officially somewhere else, Scott decides he needs to know exactly what happened between Scotland and now, and if there is something which might help their joint causes going forward. Scott needs someone to confide in, tell what he knows, what he suspects, before he goes into the lair of Giuliano Badalamenti. Just to be on the safe side. He doesn't know how much he can trust her but time is if the essence, and there is nobody else.

"When I saw you in Scotland," Molly says, "I knew who you were right away. Naturally I wondered why you were there so I got the lowdown from my contact. She said you were an undercover agent gone rogue and it was fortuitous I should stumble upon you. She told me to keep tracks on your movement, report in, but don't engage."

"Which is exactly what you did."

Scott nods thoughtfully, piecing together other information. Like filling in between the lines, rather than reading between them. She had a quarter of his missing information.

"I followed you quite well," she continues, "until after your gunfight when you seemed to vanish off the grid."

"What happened to the hitman?"

"I don't know."

"You didn't apprehend him?"

"He disappeared."

"Did you tell your contact to check any medic who might have tended his wound, NHS approved or otherwise?"

"Yes. But they never found him."

"Or that's the line they fed you."

"You think our people hired him to take you out?"

"Quite possibly. Maybe he was taking over. After all, I had been attracting some attention from genuine authorities, starting to get my face recognised, so perhaps I was becoming a liability. And when I resurfaced they decided to let me go on."

"Why did you? Go on, I mean? You must've known what you were transporting."

"Yes. That was a mistake. If I had known the outcome would've come so quickly I would've changed my plan. But I didn't and...let's just say it's not my finest moment."

They drink their coffee then, both with their own thoughts, savouring the flavour and reliving the failure. They know they could've both acted differently. If, if, if. Such a small word creates such a huge dilemma. People can beat themselves up for years because of an if. If I had only acted differently can haunt even the most confident person if they dwell upon it.

Molly is the first to break the brief silence.

"So what are you doing now?"

"I am going to pay the person responsible a visit."

"Who is that?"

"Sorry, Molly, but I can't tell you that. I don't know if I can trust you."

"Fair enough."

"Nothing personal."

"No offence taken."

"But I have information which I need someone to act upon should I not be entirely successful."

"Makes sense. What do you need me to do?"

"Not shooting me is a good start. And trusting me is all I need you to do. I've got an old MP3 which my Mum bought for me in that cabinet. It's fully charged. I keep it that way. I'm going to record everything I know onto it and I will send it to you. Just in case. I need to know someone else has the information. Whether you act upon it is up to you but if you do you put yourself at risk."

Molly nods. She doesn't fully understand the implications of receiving his knowledge, and he might still send it elsewhere so she isn't forced into a difficult situation herself. Trust. Scott doesn't know her. Or how career focused she is. What he knows might be best served by a media outlet.

"But I can't tell you were I'm going." Scott says.

"What if I come along? I have a car. And a gun. I could stop you here and now." Molly checks her watch, the latest digital model linked to her phone. "And I need to contact my boss."

"That has also occurred to me." Scott replies. "I suppose I'm in deep enough trouble as it is, how worse can it possibly get? That was rhetorical, by the way."

Scott stands and says:

"I'm making more coffee, showering and changing clothes. Then we leave. Okay?"

And Molly does something which Scott has only seen her do briefly before: she smiles.

FORTY-FIVE

London traffic is almost at a complete standstill which is why Scott doesn't have a car. Public transport might be unpredictable and temperamental but at least when it arrives it moves! The congestion charge didn't help so Generation You abolished it, along with all common sense, it seems. Thankfully Molly, who is driving because it's her car, seems to have inscrutable patience and eyes in both sides and the back of her head.

She is able to manoeuvre the car deftly and expertly when they are able to move but what in theory is a relatively short journey of just twenty miles takes an hour and a half - Scott can do the equivalent distance in fifteen minutes back home in Norfolk on a good day, less on a motorway, just don't tell the police!

The townhouse in Chelsea which Giuliano Badalamenti owns is bound to be under heavy guard, which is certainly no problem with Molly's credentials but more challenging for Scott.

On the journey to break up the boredom Scott has told her everything. Narration, more like. Recording everything on the MP3 player. He has nothing to lose now anyway. He has nowhere to go if she decides one way or the other that he is a good or bad seed. So what is the point keeping quiet? The MP3 recording can still be heard by the media. Maybe he can start his own Blog! That would be interesting. Although the nuts who broadcast any old conspiracy theory are ignored, so why shouldn't he be given the same treatment? At least now he has the sense he is making his own destiny and not being dragged along upon someone else's whim. Although he is trusting Molly. To a degree. She could've handed him over to her boss already. Or is it his boss? Maybe she is seeing where he leads, then she will hand him over. But Scott isn't going to let that happen. Too many people have double-crossed him in the past. Too many women have taken him for a ride. Ironically Molly is literally taking Scott for a ride but this one is by his own request.

Parking adjacent a driveway belonging to a house which sits incongruously out of sync with the rest of the Victorian-era neighbourhood, in fact its meticulous eco-planning, glass frontage and oaken framework, might very well have been one of those grand designs which are featured on popular television programs about elaborate house building projects. This one is on a corner, it's two exposed sides surrounded by well tended hedgerows of high ferns.

Beyond the corner is the gathering of desirable townhouses including the property where Giuliano Badalamenti resides.

This is a very exclusive neighbourhood, and it shows up in the cleanliness, the litter-free footpaths, exquisitely subtle street lighting, the conspicuous surveillance cameras and inconspicuous burglar alarm boxes, the black wrought iron fencing, trimmed and tidy foliage which seems to glow extra proudly in its Autumnal glory. Even the dwindling daylight casts delicate shadow space. No wonder this is a desirable postcode to those who can afford it.

A police van is visible. It is parked curb side adjacent to Molly's car. On the diagonal. A small radar type attachment is central on its curved roof. Constantly rotating. As if detecting sound and motion in its range. Scott would guess it has about a mile wide radius at best. Not too far to confuse sounds but far enough to detect threats.

Still there is no movement anywhere.

"Is this your company car?" Scott asks.

Molly nods.

"Does it have some identifying GPS location tracker?"

"I guess. Probably."

Scott continues watching the crossroads ahead of them. Not even a piece of litter passes through. Only the treetops flutter in the wind, topmost bows bowing.

"Approach the van." Scott tells her. "Show your credentials to whomever you meet. Ask them if these properties are locked down."

"I get the idea. What are you going to do?"

"Wait here for you to come back." He states. "I doubt my ID card will help. They must be on the look out. I'd be rumbled in five seconds. But I do need to know if Alfred McCann's family are in residence with the Badalamenti's."

Molly arches her eyebrows quizzically.

"It isn't them who I am after. It's who they are with."

And it is after this ambiguous declaration from Scott that Molly opens her door and walks towards the van.

Scott watches her as she goes. Surreal, is the thought. When he first clapped eyes on her she was a nondescript and unfriendly Eastern European who he assumed would prefer to see him dead. Now, he watches the casual but sexy sway of her hips as she strides purposefully away from the car. Her coal black hair bounces jauntily, tied tightly at the top, phoney-tail descending half-way down her back. She wears her blouse and skirt loosely, practical for the job, but beneath her generous curves tantalise his eye. Molly has a trained purposeful gait yet feminine and sensual.

Scott apparently possesses a one-track mind!

If Molly gets the information he requires what are his next actions?

Scott definitely doesn't have the luxury of time. Practical issues are pressing. Giuliano will get the wife of McCann out of the country swiftly. Back to Italy. Her home. Is she part of the deception? Could she be complicit in her husbands murder? Doesn't matter, really.

Scott's objective has to be the removal of Giuliano Badalamenti from any power which might be ceded to him. In fact, now Scott ponders the issue, who is in line to take over from Alfred McCann now that the Prime Minister is dead? The deputy Prime Minister is Douglas Atticus. Another Englishman but this one is old school money and silver spoon and Eaton. Traditional through and through. Solid reputation. Not an easy fit with Generation You yet he was still McCann's deputy. So what's the real story here? Atticus is paid for by the Italian's or whoever is in charge?

Is there a Mafia connection?

No. Impossible. Even a second-rate hack reporter would've dragged that detail up long ago. This organisation is larger than the Mafia. This organisation are inside the Mafia and every other powerful collection of minds with money and ambition. This organisation is operating above corporations and industry and terrorism and politics. So who the hell are they?

Molly is returning, her stride brisk, her face the emotionless blank sheet of paper which so many people are these days. She is checking her phone. Scott wonders what her thoughts are upon, his impatience becoming almost unbearable. She opens the drivers door. Slides into the seat. Closes the door. Looks him in the eye. Still nothing.

Scott prompts: "Well?"

"Mrs McCann and her son are in residence."

"Okay."

"But they are travelling down to Kent in thirty minutes."

"Where to?"

"Somewhere called Hawkenbury."

"Never heard of it."

"No reason to. There's nothing much there. I checked on Google Maps."

"So where are they going to?"

"A piece of land with a manor on it owned by McCann's partner, Giuliano Badalamenti."

"That's where we need to be."

Molly stares at him with her blank stare. Scott supposes she is sizing up the situation and prospects. He sure cannot tell. Until finally her decision is apparently reached.

"Okay."

FORTY-SIX

Arriving without a plan is a bit like baking a cake without any flour but the drive through south London was eventful enough to be distracting, and it looks as if no plan is exactly what Scott is going with. If not for Molly's voice of reason he might have continued on such an illogical course. Amidst the road traffic chaos, the news that a curfew is going to be enforced from nine o'clock that night came across the national radio station they were listening to, and all borders are shut down while the authorities chase down remaining terrorist suspects. It took all day for the powers that be to reach this decision, maybe their actions were being governed by the powers of big business aka Premiership Football!

Scott has been slumped in the passenger seat of Molly's car fatalistically. He wonders if he has already reached the end of the line.

When they stop in the gravel parking area of a small public house about three miles after pulling off the motorway, Molly phones in, telling her controller where she is, although the GPS tracker in her car could easily confirm her location. She tells them almost exactly what she has learned and where she is now going to. She also told them she would be stopping for food and drink but didn't mention Scott's presence.

The Harnser Public House is all low dark beams, subtle energy efficient lighting, and a definite homey feeling in a two-storey rectangular building with additions to its Victorian original. Brown wood effect double-glazing, a satellite dish, a new fence surrounding the outdoor seating and children's play area, plus a small conservatory attached to the right side add additional restaurant seating. The bar area is all old oak and brass, worn from years of use. Bottles of various liqueur and glasses of different sizes behind the bar twinkle in the light, and the barman cuts an almost iconic figure in his blue and white checkered shirt and smock with cleaning cloth in hand, bringing a shine to an empty pint glass. He is a grey-haired man in his early fifties, plump ruddy face with a natural smile, about five-eight with a stout body which he might've once been proud of but now the muscle is equalled by fat.

"Evening." The barman says, his eyes and smile affixed on Molly which Scott cannot blame him for because she is by far the more attractive of the duo.

During their brief time together Scott has come to appreciate Molly's attractiveness more and more, accompanied by a mental puzzlement because normally he doesn't find people who are, on the surface, emotionless, appealing. But there is some aura which surrounds Molly that he cannot pinpoint. She is pretty. Without makeup, or the Scottish disguise. Petite but physically very fit, he can see this just from her hands and neck and calves. And her black hair is wonderfully oily, like fine silk.

"Hi." Molly replies. "May we get a table and menu, please?"

The barman's eyebrows register surprise. Scott cannot tell if he is more surprised by the request for food or the perfect diction in Molly's voice accompanying the inscrutable dark eyes.

"Of course. Pick a table."

The barman hands her two menus, barely registering Scott's presence at all.

"Would you like to order drinks straight away?"

Molly looks at Scott, the darks of her eyes turning upward to him, increasing the size of her whites in a yearning manner which momentarily distracts him. She is most definitely in control.

"Umm, yes please. A pint of coke and a large glass of red wine for me, please."

"And a coffee. Decaf, please." Molly finishes their order.

"I'll bring them over to you."

"Thank you."

They choose a seat in the conservatory with Scott sitting in a corner, back to the wall, as is his habit, and Molly opposite, with a clear view of the exit and car park. They don't expect any company but the GPS tracking means anyone from the Service can come spying if they don't trust Molly.

Scott consults the menu, Molly consults her phone - a typical 21st Century date scenario!

"Atticus has taken temporary charge." She says.

"The Deputy PM. Is that good or bad?"

"Temporary. He has no real support. My guess is there will be a snap election."

"Won't that destabilise the Government a little? They were on a bit of a role. How about someone else in Generation You taking charge. Is there a prime candidate?"

"Yes. But it's doubtful. Although...he has lots of support here and abroad. But he isn't English."

"Giuliano Badalamenti. Does he have UK citizenship?"

Molly nods: "His best friend gave it him."

Scott's face drops. This is the ultimate nightmare. Prime Minister Alfred McCann, recently deceased, unwittingly handing power to his murderer.

"But I didn't think Badalamenti was into politics." Scott says. "I thought he was just McCann's business partner from way back."

"I'm afraid not. It's been kept quiet. Out of the usual channels. But not a secret. Plenty of politicians are aware. And those in the business community."

The barman arrives with their drinks. Scott is staring without seeing out the window, unaware of the man's presence until he has gone. The coke and wine are dark in their separate glasses. Thick and mysterious. The smell from the red wine is strong. Deliciously strong. Scott picks up the glass and downs it's contents in swift gulps.

Molly is watching him with the first real expression he has seen from her: bemusement.

"You got a problem?" She asks with what he supposes is wry humour.

"Giuliano Badalamenti is responsible from Alfred McCann's death."

They sit silently looking at each other, the only thing between them is the curl of steam from her black coffee. The barman returns with a pad and pencil to take their order. He notices the empty wine glass.

"Have you folks decided?"

Snapping out of their thoughts, Molly picks up her menu while Scott makes eye contact with the red faced barman for the first time since entering this establishment.

"Can I get your Kentish Burger with fries? And a refill."

Scott hands him the wine glass.

"Certainly, sir. Ma'am?"

"I will have the Caesar Salad and a bowl of fries, please."

The barman takes the menus, informing them the food will be ready in about twenty minutes, which is fine, and he leaves their table once more.

"I don't believe it." Molly says.

"I don't blame you. If someone came up to me and told me something as ridiculous as that I wouldn't believe them too. But it's true. I heard it directly from Alfred McCann himself. Just before I jumped off the Humber Bridge. And who would believe I did that? Sounds ridiculous too, huh? But it happened. McCann was the puppet.

We are all puppets. And Giuliano Badalamenti might not be the topmost ranking person in the organisation but I need to talk with him about his involvement. I will make him tell me who is in charge of him and work my way up the chain."

"I just seems inconceivable."

"Power corrupts."

"But not to this extent. Not in England at least."

"What makes us so special? We are nothing more than an island. We could barely support the influx of immigrants into our country which is the prime reason why a new power like Generation You could step up a notch. Maybe this has been in the planning for years. But whatever, it has happened."

"Okay. It happens in lesser countries. Third world, war torn, countries whose economies are susceptible to corruption. But England is a commerce not easily thrown over."

"So these people have done it the right way, that's all. Greed and money and power are the most corrupting influences the world over."

"I know that."

"So why is it so hard to believe it could happen here?"

They fall silent. The barman returns with a refilled wine glass. Molly picks her drink. Scott just stares into the dark red liquid, it's oily alcohol refracting the overhead light.

"No. Its ludicrous." Molly says, finally, but without much conviction.

"Okay. It's ludicrous." Scott tells her."But I still need to have to have a few words with Badalamenti anyway. Any idea how heavily guarded this manor will be?"

It takes a moment for Molly to compose and reorder her thoughts, although her face has never been anything other than businesslike. She checks her phone once again.

"It's six thirty." She announces. "I am authorised entry at the manor but obviously you aren't."

"I can't hide in the trunk of your car like they do in the movies."

"Of course not. That's stupid. First place to be searched."

"So I wait somewhere on the perimeter. Get into the grounds. And you let me in."

"That's the obvious play. There will be more security that normal, though. Have you got a phone?"

"No. but we passed a store a mile back. I can get a burner from there."

"Okay. That's our first step."

"Second."

The barman cheerily approaches their table with their plates of food, which he sets on the table before them.

"Can I get any sauces.?"

"No, thank you." Molly says.

"I am fine. It looks splendiferous."

"I hope you both enjoy it."

And he wanders back to the bar area once more.

"This," says Scott, "is step one. But first I need to know something. Why do you trust me?"

Molly blanches slightly, and for the first time, she seems embarrassed by her answer.

FORTY-SEVEN

Not too far in the distant past Scott Dalton vowed never to complain again about the cold British weather. This was during his brief visit to Greenland. A name misrepresentation if ever there was one. There is very little green in Greenland. More snow and ice than Iceland. The two countries should officially change names as a matter of honour. Presently they are breaking the trades description act!

But a cold damp night in Kent bites deeply into Scott's very core right now and he reneges on his past promise.

It IS cold!

One might think a person would be used to the weather in his own country because, after all, spending enough years in England Scott should expect this. But being a typical Brit ensures whinging.

Standing outside the flint wall of the northern-most side of Giuliano Badalamenti's Kent manor, Scott only has himself to whinge to.

No cloud, no moon, no street lighting, so absolutely no worries about seeing his dark grey garb and blackened face. Just the whites of his eyes will be visible. Scott's night vision is quite excellent and he soon adjusts to his new surroundings, walking the half-mile along the inner edge of the barren field where Molly has dropped him off, before she continued onward to the manor. A manor no doubt purchased with blood money from Badalamenti's own family. The heritage of this ancient building tainted.

Scott now stands against the trunk of a large oak tree, its branches spindly above his head, after pacing back and forth twenty-yards a dozen times to keep his circulation going. Staying warm as well as alert is imperative. The only sounds he has heard in the past ninety minutes are those of nature. Creatures stirring, snuffling and foraging for food or bedding. Bats with their sonic chirping. An owl calling, souring across the field, it's only sound being the wind in its wings. An airplane ascending distantly, barely a sound yet discernible in the silence.

No traffic. No lights.

The curfew keeping everyone inside. At least those whose conscience is clear. There will be people roaming because there always is. Opportunistic thieves trying their luck. Fearless thrill seekers out for the buzz. Or a prowler awaiting illicit entry into the property owned by the dead Prime Minister's oldest friend.

From within Scott's deep trouser pocket the burner phone vibrates. A startling effect to jerk Scott back to reality. He has received a text message from Molly instructing him to be outside the south western corner of the wall in thirty minutes. Which means almost a complete trek around two entire lengths of the wall. He risks detection by traversing far but must gamble on his luck.

Completely deactivating the phone, Scott dumps it beside the oak tree. There's no sense chancing his luck too much because the Security Service have undoubtedly deployed all manner of surveillance apparatus. It was a risk for Molly to send this message in the first place.

Molly Smith. A bland name for a multifaceted person. An enigma. A fascinating enigma.

With just his instincts and night-vision to guide him, Scott carefully places his strides, making his way along the outside perimeter wall inside the leading edge of the field. The going is soft, about two inches of uncut grass with errant branches and thicker gorse to negotiate. His walking boots barely make a sound. It's quite eerie. The stars are winking above, a thick blanket of dots which must be wonderful for stargazers. It's the right time of year. Not too warm to create a haze, not too cold to put one off.

A white wraith catches Scott off guard, causing him to stumble, and he realises the flying wraith is no ghost but a barn owl soaring across the field not ten yards from him, unaware of the curfew. It's path is parallel to the wall, and to Scott. The air barely breaks from the beat if its wings. The hairs on the back of Scott's neck stand up, and not from the cold, when the owl lets out a mournful hoot.

Scott smiles to himself, settling his nerves. If he were in a horror film the appearance of the owl on the blackest of nights like this one might be a bad omen, a precursor for what Scott might expect to greet him on his adventure. But he knows he isn't in a film. This is definitely real life and he isn't easily spooked. Never has been. He truly thinks it's the imagination of people which powers their beliefs of things otherworldly and supernatural. They become susceptible to suggestion, heightening their fears, and ultimately scare themselves.

Not him.

Twenty minutes later he has successfully circumvented the flint wall and has reached the place where Molly had told him to be. Scott presumes she will somehow find a way to signal him. And hopefully she will find a ladder for him too, he doesn't particularly fancy scaling this wall, it has too many jagged and sharp objects.

Something lands on his shoulder, making him jump, and reminding that maybe he isn't the cool customer he believed himself to be.

Something dangles from the wall in front of his face. A rope. Looped around the tree which overhangs the wall by a distance not easily determined in the darkness. Obviously this is Mollys sign, and the means of his entry.

Taking the robe in his hands, spaced two feet apart, he hauls himself upward and onto the topmost part of the wall with little effort, which was the easy part, because his foot slides on the slippery surface and he grazes his shin painfully. Gritting his is teeth he waits while the pain subsides.

A small voice barely above a whisper asks: "Are you okay?"

"Fine." Scott replies in a voice to match, before hauling up the rope, dropping it down the opposite side and sliding onto the soft ground on the inside of the manor wall.

Instantly Molly is up against him, pressing herself to him hard and at first he is startled, wondering if she has betrayed him. Then her mouth is against his ear. She says nothing. Her breath is hot, panting, urgent. Scott can feel her heart beating fast. She trembles not from the cold but from anticipation. Molly puts her small arms around him, one at his waist, the other over his shoulder, pulling him down slightly so she no longer has to stand on her tiptoes. And kisses him desperately on the lips. Scott reciprocates after a second of confusion, startled by the moment.

FORTY-EIGHT

The unexpected and not to mention surreal experience of making love to Molly on this cold night within the interior of Giuliano Badalamenti's property over, Scott is now comfortably redressed and standing beside Molly on the inner edge of trees bordering the southern rear garden of the manor. He cannot see her face so doesn't know if she has a smile upon it, but the sounds she had made during their coupling were encouraging.

The expanse of lawn between the perimeter trees and manor is a square about two-hundred feet by two-hundred feet, so for him to cross it unseen would be impossible.

Small but bright halogen light bulbs are set into the ornamental knee height wall which partially surrounds the rear of the manor. Facing outward onto the lawn they prevent a clear view of the pathway and house behind it, just a two-storey black rectangular silhouette. There is a light on behind drawn curtains with a feint halo, but apart from this the rear of the manor is in darkness. Presumably the bedrooms are situated here. The front might tell a different story.

No movement means they have ample security out back so don't require a guard. No doubt cameras, motion detectors and audio devices are monitored from a room dedicated to ground surveillance. The lawn is too exposed to offer a successful approach anyway, so Scott writes this possibility off straight away.

"How do I get into the house?" Scott asks, whispering close to Molly's ear, smelling her natural fragrance.

"You don't." She replies. "A helicopter is coming for them tomorrow morning. McCann's wife and son and Badalamenti. They are going to the family chateau in Italy. Apparently it's safer for them there."

Scott nods, then gives an affirmation that he has heard and understood her because in the complete darkness she cannot see him.

"I think I can get you onboard the helicopter."

"Seriously?"

"Yes."

"How?"

"The helicopter lands here. It's pilot will come to the house. Nobody will see you climb aboard."

"That's ludicrously simple. It won't work."

"You can't get into the house. There's no way. I am on perimeter duty right now with a location transponder in my pocket."

"Let's hope it can't detect sound." Scott quips.

"Nobody can get across the lawn right now. There are motion pads under the turf. The side and front are guarded. There are also cameras and motion detectors. Not to mention audio surveillance."

"Why isn't the back here covered?"

"It is usually. I deactivated the audio. They think there's a fault. I told them I would check it out despite them telling me only a fool would try gaining entry over the back wall and through the trees."

"That fool was me!"

"You wouldn't have made it if not for me. No audio. I put a towel over the wall to protect you from the razor wire. And there is only one pathway through the trees which you would never have found in the darkness without tripping some other alarm they have. Trust me. You must stay here until their helicopter arrives. It's a Bell Executive. You can get aboard and conceal yourself without anyone knowing until it's too late."

"As long as the plan goes without a hitch."

"Trust me."

Scott ponders her proposal. He would prefer it if she found a way for him to get into the building undercover of night but she sounds quite adamant that it cannot be done. So he is to hide in the trees until morning, which doesn't sound at all uncomfortable! And if he cannot cross the lawn undetected. If he cannot hide himself in the helicopter. If he is captured or killed. Then what?

"Do you have a gun I can have?"

After a brief amount of rustling on the ground she presents him with something which, to the touch, feels like a rucksack.

"How the hell...?"

"Blanket, food, drink and a gun." Molly tells him without a trace if satisfaction in her voice that she has been able to surprise him yet again.

"You are splendiferously resourceful."

'I know." She says, pulling him toward her and kissing him on the lips. "Thanks for the sex. It was wonderful."

Before Scott can reply she is off and across the lawn, undeterred by the motion pads because whoever is manning the security station knows it is her anyway. He smiles to himself, mentally agreeing with her remark about their brief by wholly satisfying physical encounter. She is obviously a woman of surprises. Scott hopes that after this is over they can couple up again. But tomorrow is an unknown entity. What will happen? What will the outcome be? Will he get the opportunity to meet Molly again? Will he in fact survive the night under a blanket in the damp cold woodland of this Kent manor?

As quietly as possible he opens the bag which Molly left him with, extracting the blanket. He checks the gun, 500ml plastic drink bottle which probably holds water, and three small oblong packets which might be nutrition bars or chocolate bars, Scott cannot tell.

Folding the blanket around himself Scott feels no benefit whatsoever. But it's the thought that counts. He closes his eyes. His vision flickers from all the imagery of his day, the lack of rest, while even the rustling of the trees create bursts of imaginary light.

Scott sighs. Opens his eyes to fight off the overwhelming sense of mental vertigo spiralling through his subconscious. The lawn yawns at him while the bedroom light winks off. He grins back facetiously, taking one last swift surveillance of the ground as best as he can. The starry sky is spectacular. Pity the situation negates appreciation. Blinking, twinkling, soft sighing treetops.

Too alert to sleep, too uncomfortable to rest.

The blueness lightens. Birds begin their dawn chorus.

Scott wipes the fog of sleep from his eyes. He presumes he slept. Restlessly, yet sleep is sleep, he supposes, so be thankful for small mercies.

The lights at the rear of the old Manor House still blaze, more dazzling now than during the pitch darkness. The bedroom light halo is there once more.

Nothing stirs, except for the birds in the trees whose crescendo rises along with the sun. Nothing stirs except for his stomach. Cramps through the position he kept. Or pain through tension. Scott shifts his legs around so he is laying flat. Can't exactly stand up. The discomfort persists. If there was something wrong with the food last night he would've surely found out by now. He doesn't need this. His stomach is churning, like he's going to be sick or faced with some messy bowel issue. Drink.

Sitting upright once again, Scott pulls the drink bottle from the bag which Molly provided for him. He wonders what she has been doing throughout the night. Has she slept? Has she been worrying about the morning? Wondering if Scott's scheme will work? Which is really her scheme. She seemed convinced of its viability. Scott, not so much.

The water feels wonderfully refreshing. Scott detects a hint of citrus flavouring. The liquid seems to be magical in the curing of his pain. Scott considers maybe it is stress causing it. He devours one of the multigrain breakfast bars, feeling seventy-five percent better within minutes. Talk about relief. The first success of the day?

As the dawn breaks into daylight the lawn seems to stretch out before Scott, while the trees gain stature and the Manor House itself recedes further backward. All an illusion. Tricks of the light. And maybe impending trepidation on Scott's part.

Scott sits there, concealed in the woodland, watching as minutes unfold into an hour with eventual movement in the windows as curtains and blinds are parted; a security guard prowls the manor's perimeter as part of his morning routine, displaying no knowledge of Scott's presence; Molly appears around the northern edge cupping a steaming mug of coffee in both hands, ever the professional, acting as causally as she possibly can with no sign of stress, although she must be feeling similarly to Scott. She glances his way.

The calm before the storm.

Scott can only wonder what the rest the country are waking up to. The realisation that yesterday's death of their beloved Prime Minister wasn't fiction. Last nights curfew was real, what does that signify going forward? The media will be all over this, discussing what might have been done differently, the world implications and trying to predict what's next.

At seven thirty a familiar clatter breaks the otherwise silent air. A distant sound, gaining, but it's direction of approach is impossible to pinpoint. The helicopter.

Scott lays flat on the earth and woodland debris using minute movements, trying to get as hidden in the foliage as possible.

The helicopter is a twin-engined white and blue Bell 430 Executive with retractable wheeled undercarriage, not the skids. This particular model has been custom designed for the deceased Prime Minister, possessing six passenger seats with a storage space where two additional seats were. This is a a longer and more powerful helicopter whose forerunner was the old 222 model familiar from the eighties television series Airwolf.

Scott feels it's arrival as the ground beneath him reverberates and leaves tumble upon him from above. Witnessing the beautiful sleek aircraft settle delicately onto the lawn is quite something. And better still from Scott's point of view is the fact that it couldn't be better positioned, side-on with the starboard passenger door directly in front of him. All he needs is to sprint thirty feet without being seen and he is home and dry.

The engine powers down, the rota blades swirl under their own momentum for a few moments afterward, and there is activity from the rear of the Manor House as two men, presumably Security Service agents, walk toward the craft. Within the cockpit the pilot and co-pilot converse briefly before disembarking, removing their helmets. The pilot is a thirty-something woman with blonde hair, the co-pilot a younger man with jet black hair. They converse with one of the agents, nod at something he says, and follow him through an open back door into the manor.

The second Security Service agent admires the helicopter, nodding absentmindedly to herself like she is reminiscing over a past event in her life which involved a helicopter. She walks around the craft, eyes briefly flicking to her right, the woodland, directly at where Scott is hiding. He could swear she makes eye contact with him. Her stride slows imperceptibly. But in less than two-seconds Scott's worry passes because she continues her admiration of the helicopter, which is indeed a thing of beauty.

Before Scott gets time to wonder when the opportunity for him to move will arrive that opportunity is created for him by Molly.

From the side of the house the young agent whom Scott enjoyed a moment of intimacy with not many hours ago catches the agents attention. Her back his to him. Molly faces the woodland. The two exchange words.

And Scott reacts.

Mustering the courage he sits, stands and runs, completely ignoring any lethargy which might dare rear its ugly head, telling himself he's thirty not eighty, adding a very politically incorrect rebuttal about being a man not a mouse! In less time than it takes to check a pointless social media post he is inside the pristine Bell 430, opens the designer cargo hold, squeezes inside and closes the hatch.

Scott's first miracle has been accomplished, now for the next: not being discovered before the bird flies.

FORTY-NINE

Scott tests the door to the small storage holding area between the twin rear seats on the Bell 430 before concealing himself within. He tested it in as much as he ensured he could open it easily enough while inside. Only a complete fool would lock themselves into a helicopter with no means of getting out. The only light entering into his cubbyhole is a thin line through the top of the hatch. He can hear the mechanical ticking of the engine cooling above him.

Scott doesn't have his passport for entry into Italy, but never mind!

Soon he can hear the pulse in his neck and whoosh of blood pumping past his ears. Everything around him is muffled, like he is underwater. Birds are crying but it's a vague sound. He thinks he hears a voice. It could be the helicopter's radio, someone calling, but he doubts it.

The tension is soon overridden by tedium.

Seconds drag into minutes turn into an hour before Scott hears a definite voice. Two, in fact. The pilot and her co-pilot, close, circling their helicopter, voices muffled but it doesn't take a knowledgeable person to realise they are carrying out their preflight check.

Ten minutes pass and the duo board the aircraft.

Scott wonders if all six passenger seats shall be occupied, and if so, by whom? Three people he knows of.

Will there be Security with guns?

Probably, but nobody will shoot anyone at close range because that would just be stupid. Which gives Scott a definite advantage. They won't know if he is stupid! At first they might believe him to be a terrorist. Which makes his ease of entry to his present location that much more far fetched. Or is it? He had insider help. Without it, he nor anybody else could've done it.

Will they perform a search of this area, however small?

Will there be luggage going in here?

Scott grins at the cleverness of his stupidity. If luggage is placed in here he will be discovered, no doubt about it. Then what? A gunfight?

More muffled voices. Several of them. Getting louder. Arguing? No. They are protesting about something. Needing to stick to the flight plan? The voices getting lower and words indistinct until Scott feels movement and people boarding the helicopter. He cannot tell exactly how many but he pretty soon realises there is no luggage which might indicate the passenger manifest has altered. Scott wishes Molly were able to let him know what's going on.

After about sixty seconds the engine powers into life, followed by the gradually increasing whine of the rota-blades turning, beating the air until full-power is reached. Scott feels the perceptible jerk of their lift-off and ascent and the motion of veering to the starboard, circling the property before departing.

And silent passengers.

Scott feels frustration. What if Giuliano Badalamenti isn't onboard after all?

Only one way to find out because Scott has had enough waiting. He pulls the gun from out of where he had secured it under his stomach and pushes the hatch open. Light floods into the tiny compartment, stinging Scott's eyes which soon adjust. So far nobody onboard has seen the movement.

The two rear seats are unoccupied. There are three men in the remaining four seats. McCann's wife and son clearly aren't aboard, which must have been the subject of discussion.

Scott slithers out from the hold.

Scott takes his time. Nobody has seen him yet. He stretches out his limbs and loosens his muscles. Checks the gun. Safety off. Not anticipating using it but a gun is always a good threat.

The three men are evidently very occupied. There is no talking amongst them. One checks information on an expensive top of the line tablet, another is consulting his smart phone for who knows what. Scott doesn't know either of these two although they less resemble Security Service agents, more likely they are Government consultants of some type. If there were security they wouldn't have their heads down because a sixth sense would've detected Scott already. The third man Scott recognises. He is Giuliano Badalamenti. And he is reading through some good old-fashioned real paperwork neatly bound together in a crimson folder.

The trio are understandably startled when Scott appears amongst them, acting casual, flaunting the gun, smiling demurely at them. He sits on the empty seat in the central area.

"What is this?" The man with tablet predictably asks.

"Who are you?" The man with phone is equally obvious in his line of question.

Badalamenti on the other hand recognises Scott: "This is Scott Dalton." He says. "He works for the Security Service. He was undercover then our great leader, and my friend, was assassinated. Mister Dalton ran from the scene and has been missing ever since. Until now, of course."

"Very good." Scott acknowledges. "It's sometimes nice being well-known, saves on wasted introductions and explanations."

"What are you doing here?" The tablet guy is predictable once more.

Scott rests the gun in his leg, not relaxing his poise but trying to keep its presence as a casual threat. Two out of three of these men are clearly intimidated by it because they are looking nervous, they eyes furtive, postures stiff. Badalamenti isn't. The Italian with the unscrupulous history is obviously not a newcomer to such signs of power and aggression. Giuliano's eyes are youthfully bright, his Mediterranean complexion healthy, his physique toned from exercise. Yes, Scott thinks, this man is very good at hiding his terrorist activities behind the suave Italian bravado. He was able to fool his best friend for countless years. He was able to manipulate the most powerful man in the country. And Scott can see why.

"I am here to set a few facts straight." Scott says cryptically, addressing his next question to tablet- and phone- guy. "Do you know who assassinated your Prime Minister?"

"Terrorists." Smart phone guy says condescendingly. "Claudinalli Tucamkari has claimed responsibility and even though I don't agree with internet fame she has gathered quite a following because of her admission and strong words."

"But who financed her?"

"Some Middle Eastern fanatic most likely."

"Or the Russian's." Tablet guy chips in. "This woman disappeared for several years, her husband was a known quantity, killed by us, in fact, and she was seeking revenge. Russia could've harboured her and paid for her."

Giuliano Badalamenti nods and smiles at their plausible answers, shifting in his seat, sliding his hand inside his jacket which to the untrained casual observer is nothing to be concerned about, but to Scott it presents a potential danger. He raises his gun, pointing it at the Italian's stomach.

277

"Good thinking, Secret Agent Dalton!" Giuliano mocks. "You never seen an action movie? Shoot me in here and we all die."

Removing his hand, Giuliano pulls out a cigarette case which he places on his lap.

"I suppose you will tell me smoking is harmful to my health?" The Italian says.

"What's this all about?" Smart phone guy asks. "Are you going to tell us how and why you are here, Mister Dalton? We have an important meeting to attend and I demand to know what's going on."

"I concur." Agrees tablet guy with self-importance.

"I am here," Scott says, "to tell you who is responsible for assassinating the Prime Minister and why it was done. The woman, Claudinalli Tucamkari, is just a very convenient patsy...as the Americans might say. Her aims were entirely different from her more local team members. They did not know a bomb was going to be exploded. They believed they were going to ransom the Prime Minister as a statement of how this country has become run more like a dictatorship since Generation You came to power. A fact which only the blind sheep cannot see." Scott address smart phone and tablet guy directly. "I don't know who you two are. I don't know if you are aware of the real facts. But I very much doubt it. The organisation responsible for the assassination of Alfred McCann keep things close to their chest. So close, in fact, that nobody really knows who is in charge, except their aims are identical."

"And what are those aims?" Asks tablet guy.

"The usual thing, really." Scott says like it's obvious. "But the usual thing normally takes place in the Gulf or Africa or East. To destabilise Government. To ruin economy. To incite civil unrest. This time it's happening here, isn't it?"

This last question is directed at Giuliano and causes the other two men to look with greater curiosity at Badalamenti. Scott realises there and then that they know nothing of the bigger picture, they aren't a part of the grand scheme. These two are as expendable as the Prime Minister. Or Scott. Who shouldn't really have been too surprised.

Giuliano imperceptibly moves his right hand down to the cigarette case resting upon his lap. Casually he takes it in his hand, arousing no suspicion, except from Scott.

Scott points the gun at the chest of the Italian.

"Hands up." Scott says.

"Really!?"

Giuliano looks Scott in the eye, his Italian twinkle catching the sun through the window. He slides the case open, not at the top, but from it's side, and tosses it across the cabin to land between tablet- and phone-guy. A thin white gas puffs into the cabin and several things happen at once-

Tablet-guy stands and bangs his head-

Phone-guy shifts sideways in his seat-

Scott puts his hand over nose and mouth-

And Giuliano leaps like a cat from his seat, knocking the gun in Scott's grip twenty-degrees left. The gas, the movement, knock and general surprise factor causes Scott to loose off one round and all occupants of the cabin are treated to the same lurching sensation. They all lose control of their individual actions-

Tablet-guy bangs against the back of the co-pilots chair-

Phone-guy slips off his seat and also loses his breakfast-

Scott is pushed into Giuliano and both go sprawling across the cabin, the gun skittering out of reach and out of sight.

The helicopter jerks violently, spinning and spiralling. The air around it screams and whistles. Metal struggles and strains and protests at the stresses upon them. The co-pilot acts as calmly as he can to regain control but it's too late. The engine stalls. And only disaster remains.

Scott is held in place by the g-forces pummelling his every fibre. He feels no pain, no real discomfort, in fact, but he is pinned helplessly to the floor while his stomach lurches and equilibrium takes a pounding. His final thoughts are of Molly. In the early hours. And the hopefulness that she will be able to act upon his suspicions, prove his theories, bring some modicum of justice to the events of the past two days, instigate some kind of Government reshuffle, point the country in the right direction before there truly is no going back, before this terrorist organisation leads England into a dictatorship after years of freedom and subjugation. Scott can hope. He can dream. He can imagine. But he won't be a part of this new world because the beautiful Bell helicopter becomes a crumpled wreckage of twisted burning metal on the English countryside.

EPILOGUE

Brian Oakes tries his utmost to be patient at the delay but it's been five minutes since the two-lanes of traffic edged forward seemingly as one and then barely by a single car length. It's hard to see how far ahead of them the plume of rising black smoke is, exactly, but clearly this is the cause of their delay. The Stop/Start engine on his new car rests silently, conserving their fuel, which is at least one positive thing salvaged from this absolute tedium. And the view is a consolation. The young woman in the car which rests alongside his on the duel-carriageway is a pretty blond with a cracking smile, a generous flash of shoulder flesh on show, and who didn't automatically avoid his eyes when he smiled back at her. Result!

Charlene winds down the passenger side window, introducing the cool Autumn breeze into the family saloon and negates using the air-conditioning, much to the protests of their two kids in back.

Brian reluctantly diverts his eyes from the blond toward his wife instead, an older blond than the one in the car alongside them and despite raising two kids and holding down a demanding job she retains everything of what attracted her to him physically. It's okay to window shop, Brian tells himself.

"Why don't we sing a holiday song while we wait?" Brian jokingly suggests before he begins his own rendition of Cliff Richard's seasonal favourite Summer Holiday.

"Dad." His two kids in back groan simultaneously.

"It's because it's Autumn," Brian says, "not summer, that's why you want me stop, right?"

Turning in his seat, Brian grins at his kids.

"When are we going to be there?" Lucy, the youngest of the two girls, at nine, asks with the impatience of one her age.

"Sorry, Sugar Plum, I don't know." He tells her truthfully.

They have been travelling for three hours already, since six o'clock's curfew lifted, skirting around London via the M25 from their home in Cambridge. The sleepy girls had dozed on and off for the first couple of hours while Charlene had slept like a log in the passenger seat beside him, until about an hour ago when they got snagged in this unexpected tailback. Although why should it be unexpected? Everyone is running later today.

Brian is hungry and could do with a coffee but the way southbound had been free-flowing and the thought of their holiday destination outweighed his necessity to stop. And the view in the car to his right had been more than tolerable for a while. But now, despite his outwardly cheery disposition, he is definitely regretting the decision not to stop earlier for coffee. Frustratingly a Rest Stop is signposted three tantalising miles ahead.

"How about the SatNav?" Charlene asks. "Is there another route we can take?"

"Probably not." Brian says, seeing no signposts or junctions in the near distance. "We don't even know what the hold up is." He sighs heavily. "Except that smoke!"

To conserve battery power the car automatically cuts the radio off about five minutes after engine inactivity, so they cannot even check local radio.

Ever resourceful Charlene switches on her phone and tries connecting but her network is down, probably backed-up and busy from everyone else attempting the same thing. Technology is wonderful when it functions but when it fails the human-race flounders!

Brian sighs. Car's in front and back are in the same proverbial boat. How many car's are there here exactly? A hundred? Two-hundred? Where is his family in the queue? Where was the pre-warning? Where are the emergency vehicles if there's been an accident? They had set off nice and early to reach their holiday destination on the south coast in good time, making the most of the meagre time the family has together. Sitting here is a frustrating waste of that precious time.

Yesterday Brian had been at work, his mood had been upbeat with four days of chillaxing to look forward to. Not that running a bank of checkouts in a supermarket is rocket science but there are unique challenges inherent when dealing with the public on a daily basis. Physically the work isn't too strenuous, either, but when combined with the wavering emotions of humankind a triple threat can produce enough stress to tax the calmest mind. He had been in holiday mode so yesterday had been a good day. The calm before the calmer. Or at least that's what is should've been but the opposite is now occurring.

Brian grins at Charlene.

His wife packed their suitcases for their six day break, all organised and secure in the rear luggage space.

The kids should be at school tomorrow, Monday, but who knows what will be happening after yesterday and Brian will be damned if he is paying the rip-off prices which holiday firms charge in-season. Charlene will phone the school's to say the kids are both sick. Where's the harm? Why should he be penalised when the scourge of society gets away with social freebies while he works his backside off to provide for his family unit? Because the rich and privileged take care of themselves, the skivers get handouts, and the workers toil for them both! Some things really don't change with each successive Government despite the promises. Although Brian concedes to his blinkered optimistic half that life has improved slightly since Generation You took power, there has been good done, but how much is really voter-bating propaganda? And what's going to happen now, with the country in turmoil? Brian mentally shrugs, assuming things shall plod along as they always have, as they always will, with more learned folk than the common man knowing what's best for everyone else.

This morning for Brian and his family these are distant worries, minor issues to be discussed on another occasion. Neither he or Charlene are politically savvy. They tow the line. They abide by the laws. Pragmatic while observing what goes on. Realistic regarding those changes which affect their lives.

This morning is for the long awaited and much needed family holiday, not for the events transpiring elsewhere which they cannot influence. Maybe the rest of these people caught in this snarl up suffer similar issues. Who knows? Who cares?.

"And we're off." His wife announces from beside him, putting a halt to Brian's daydreaming.

Up on the road ahead as it rises against the hillock, the traffic is definitely moving forward, bunching up as they veer onto the left-hand hard-shoulder where a big overhead sign begins flashing it's warning diversion.

The girls cheer from back.

"We're not there yet!" Brian states, wondering how far a deviation from the route this diversion will take them, and where will the nearest rest stop be once they are on the move? He berates himself again, shifting in his seat but not saying a word, knowing that an admission of thirst, hunger or requiring the toilet would set off an instant chain reaction in the vehicle. Brian has been tempted to run up the verge and relieve himself before the movement of traffic reached them, as he had seen other men do, but this action too would fatally remind his children of how long they had been between toilet stops. Never mind. Grin a bear it. They are on holiday. A delay is a minor setback really and inevitable on these British roads. They cannot actually gain access to their accommodation until three o'clock this afternoon, so what's the rush? There are worse things that can happen. And judging by the smoke, worse things have happened to someone else. Brian is with his wife and two beautiful daughters, they are on holiday, he has no work for seven days, his life is sweet.

MORE

SCOTT DALTON

ADVENTURES

Living on the Edge

Danger on the Edge

Over the Edge of the Abyss

By

Paul R Starling

All available from

AMAZON

37460653R00161

Printed in Poland
by Amazon Fulfillment
Poland Sp. z o.o., Wrocław